D1084858

THINGS UNDONE

THINGS UNDONE

Max Childers

WYRICK & COMPANY

Published by Wyrick & Company
Post Office Box 89
Charleston, South Carolina 29402

Library of Congress Cataloging-In-Publication Data

Childers, Max,
   Things undone / Max Childers
        p.   cm.
   ISBN 0-941711-10-2   : $16.95
   I. Title.
PS3553.H4855T4   1989   89-9173
813'.54—dc20   CIP

I

Tinka's family always picked the hottest day of the year for the reunion. There were fifteen or twenty of them gathered at a muddy boat landing beside the red-brown river. They stayed most of the day, eating heavy, thick-smelling food, riding in cousin Larry's boat, and wading in the water. As they left at dusk they always told each other that they could not wait until next year to do it all again.

Charles hated Tinka's family, but he never missed a reunion. It gave him a chance to watch the monkeys.

A small store stood by the boat landing. The store sold soft drinks, live bait, vienna sausages, pickled eggs, beer, and *The Weekly World News*. Behind the store, surrounded by busted refrigerators and rusted-out cars, was the monkey cage. While Tinka's family ate, Charles sat in an ancient lawn glider facing the cage and drank vodka from a pint bottle, his crutches propped next to him.

The cage emitted a powerful smell, but Charles did not mind. The monkeys were enough. There were three of them, two males and a small female. Most of the time, the animals sat stupefied in the heat, flies and feces. Then, without warning, they would begin to leap and chatter, bounding from the bars to the floor to the trapeze.

He waited and watched for signs. He halfway heard the boat's engine. Tinka and her family were somewhere down the beach. He drained the bottle and tossed it into the high grass near one of the cars. The monkeys remained motionless.

"Stinking things, ain't they?"

The man who ran the store stood beside the glider. The sun was bright behind the tree line on the far side of the river.

"You sure watch them monkeys a lot," the man said.

Charles did not answer. He wanted the man to go away.

The larger male monkey dug at his crotch.

"I like them. I like to sit here with them," Charles said.

The man squatted next to the glider.

"Watch the big'un frig hisself. There was a couple drunks down here last week, and one of them grabbed at him while he was doing it. Monkey bit the hell outa him."

The smaller male jumped from the floor to the bars, chattering and showing his teeth. The larger male swung on the trapeze and made deep noises in his throat. The female cowered in a corner, then began to race in circles. It was the moment that Charles had waited for.

"They get excited. Can't tell what makes them do it. They do it by themselves. But maybe not," Charles said.

The man stood and yawned. His presence had ruined everything.

"Hell, I don't know. Never paid it much attention.

Used to have a bear. Traded it to a man in Mount Holly for them monkeys."

The monkeys reached a climax of sound and movement. Quickly, they turned listless again, picking at fleas, grunting. The heat hit him, and Charles felt the sweat run down his back. The day was hazy with gasoline fumes and the smoky, dead air from up the river toward the dye plant.

"I wish I knew why they do it," Charles said.

"Do what? I ain't ever seen them monkeys do anything. Man I traded with said they was trick monkeys, that they would perform and ride bicycles and do stunts. I got lied to."

"That ain't what I meant," Charles said.

The purple '67 Pontiac hit a long straight-away. Tinka drove, Charles propped against the door on the passenger side. Half-asleep, he pressed his face into the Pontiac's window. He often dreamed, either asleep or awake. Much of the time the difference did not matter. Tinka never dreamed. She talked. About her family. About the neighbors. About food and the weather, and about what Reverend Cumby at the Power House Church of the Second Coming said last Sunday.

When her words interfered too much with his dreams, Charles beat her. After they married it had taken him a while to figure out how it could be done. The crutches turned out to be the best way. He had to catch her from behind and trip her. After she went down the rest was easy. He pounded with one crutch, and then the other, until she shut up. It did not matter that she was taller and heavier. She never fought back. Instead, she screamed and cried, and when it was over, she prayed for him, prayed that he would be delivered from the Devil, from drink.

Charles slipped closer to a dream. He heard the

monkeys, but he could not see them. Then he was on television, and somehow the television show came from the boat landing. A black-hulled submarine surfaced in the river. Crewmen, their faces covered by black masks, ran forward to man the deck gun. They fired round after round into the family reunion, into cousin Larry's boat, into the store. The monkeys cheered as each shell exploded. Tinka fled across a field, clutching a bowl of potato salad, chewing a chicken leg, trying to speak. A shell landed near her, but she kept on running. His lips parted and his breathing grew deep and regular. The moon passed behind hot, pink clouds.

The Pontiac coasted to a stop sign. The intersection was clear, and Tinka slowly edged the car forward. She did not see the lights until they were huge in the rear-view mirror, and she did not feel the impact until she flew through the open door. It was as if the wind had grabbed her and would drop her in a place so far from home that she could never return.

Charles jerked awake when the eighteen-wheeler rear-ended the Pontiac and hurled it across the intersection. The disintegrating car strained toward the moon, shook, fell and rolled. Charles began to spin. He heard faint music and felt a hard thump race up his spine before the sweaty darkness covered him.

He lay pressed into the Pontiac's roof. His chest and arms were heavy. He heard someone speak, but could not tell what was said, nor the direction from which the words came. His field of vision had narrowed to a small slit in the roof. He heard more words, and a woman weeping. An acetylene torch flared and he passed out.

It took over an hour to free Charles from the wreck. The rescue squad worked and cursed. The highway patrolman yawned and sucked a cigarette as he took the truck driver's statement. The truck's load, thousands of packages of frozen hamburger patties, lay scattered across the intersection.

An ambulance hauled Tinka away, but Charles did not know this. He would not remember the hands that lifted him from the wreck, or when he was lowered onto the stretcher. But he knew the voice when it spoke to him. It was bright, assured and well-modulated like that of a T.V. man urging Charles to try a new product. The voice told him that he would be fine, that there was nothing to worry about.

The ambulance got underway, its blue light flashing, its siren wild in the night. Charles sat up. He was unaware of the siren, the rush of the ambulance, or the needle the startled attendant quickly jammed into his arm. The cooing of the voice was all there was.

Charles came to hours later. His head and arms ached, and his mouth was sour. Dimly he understood that he was in the hospital, and that Tinka stood by his bed. Her right arm was in a sling, and a couple of dozen tiny cuts covered her face.

"Oh, Charles. This is the most awfullest thing that ever happened to me."

"What happened?" he asked.

She sat heaving on the edge of the bed, tilting it a little.

"We was in a *wreck*, Charles. A big truck. . ."

She began to cry.

"It's more than I can stand. My face. It's ruined. Hurts so bad. My arm, too. The doctor give me pills, but it hurts anyhow. I tried to call Momma, then I remembered that she was staying at Verleen's house, and when I called there her little boy just laughed and hung up the phone. So I called back. . ."

"That's enough."

". . . and Momma started screaming when she heard. And I didn't get *no* sleep last night. Tossed and turned. There was this mean old woman in the room with me. She cussed at me all night. Thought I was her daughter-in-law. And I cried and cried. . ."

5

"I SAID THAT'S ENOUGH!"

"I'll stop, Charles. I'll be quiet," she said quickly.

"I got something to tell you. It's all gonna be all right."

"How do you know?"

"I been told. A voice told me."

"A voice? Whose voice?"

"I'm gonna find out."

Tinka stopped crying.

"It was the Lord's voice," she said. "How did He sound? Like thunder? Did you shiver? When the Lord spoke to me the first time, it made me shake all over. I shook and shook. . ."

"I done told you. You gonna have to shut up."

"But it had to be the Lord. Who else could it be? And to think that I nearly give up on you getting saved. But I kept right on praying for you. And sure enough. . ."

"SHUT YOUR GODDAMN MOUTH! I HEARD IT! IT COME TO ME, NOT YOU!"

"Yes, Charles. I know you want to feel the love. . ."

"Get out."

She paused at the door.

"It has to be the Lord, though. I'm getting out of here this morning, and I'm going right to Reverend Cumby and tell him. He'll be so pleased."

"Don't come back until I call you."

That night the voice returned. It was loud and so strong that at times he thought the whole hospital could hear it. A nurse came in to give him a shot, and he was sure that the voice would be silent. Instead, it came out of her mouth and out of the television, the walls and the air itself. At first it sounded like Dan Rather. Then it was a woman's voice, like the women's voices on T.V. that spoke of laxatives and sanitary napkins. Later it was a child's voice, like T.V. children who loved cereal, pudding and fruit drinks. Toward midnight, as he became sleepy again, the voice was all the voices that he had ever heard. Later, as he awoke near dawn, it was something new, his own special voice. It whispered and murmured and told him that things would be as they had never been before.

II

The sun hit Bunch between the eyes, the glare bouncing from the asphalt to the Confederate monument to the facade of the courthouse. Bunch slipped his sunglasses on and picked his way down the courthouse steps and through the squatting crowd of defendants and plaintiffs, fugitives, and those who longed to be fugitives.

"Another crappy day."

Bunch spoke these words to the soldier atop the monument. The soldier's back was straight, his uniform in good order, his gaze resolute and noble—as if there were no situation so desperate, no turn of fate so preposterous that it could not be overcome. Bunch often spoke to the soldier, consoled by the granite gaze that could see beyond the mob on the steps. The mob had been there a long time, as long as Bunch could remember. When times were bad, the mob grew larger; but even during prosperity, of whatever kind, it was present.

Bunch crossed Broad Street, loosening his tie. He was

a big man, over six feet, balding, running to fat. He moved slowly. Gravity exerted more force upon him than upon other men, welding him to the earth, holding him down. He had not always been this way. For a few years after law school he believed in the ponderous words that had been jammed into his head. Eventually, he had discovered that the words were not the law. The law was the ravaged people waiting for him in his office. The law was the mass of papers growing babel-like upon his desk. He began to drink. He roamed the night, living like his clients. His wife, a proper southern girl from a Presbyterian lady's college, left with the children before he turned thirty. He barely noticed.

Bunch entered the One O'Clock Diner. The place was nearly empty. An hour earlier, it would have been filled with lawyers babbling about their morning cases or about how much money they made. Bunch did not enjoy the company of other lawyers. They all wore the same suit, smiled the same smile. And they kept their eye out for the big score.

He did not want to think of the case he had tried that morning. His client, a three-time loser, had lost for a fourth. Breaking and entering, and Judge Righter was sure to give the three-time loser a few years in Raleigh. When the verdict came, the three-time loser, whose name was Virgil, but who liked to be called Deuce, had told Bunch that he, Roy A. Bunch, was an ignorant cocksucker. Bunch, fighting a bad hangover and a little jerk of a D.A., had loudly asked Virgil—or Deuce—where the rest of his fee was. The D.A., a young, smooth boy recently out of law school, had laughed at Bunch. In a pleasant voice, Bunch had called the smooth boy an ass-hole. It had cost Bunch three hundred dollars to say that word. And Virgil, the four-time loser, had only paid him one-fifty. Judge Righter, who like most judges found Bunch basically unsound, had berated him a good fifteen minutes before leveling the fine.

Bunch lowered himself onto a stool and picked up a menu.

"Hello, Roy. Used the couch in the backroom lately?"

A skinny, young man in a Richard Petty T-shirt sat down one stool away from Bunch. Bunch shrugged and turned away. The waitress, a pear-shaped girl with the name Betty inscribed on the left breast of her uniform, came down the counter to take Bunch's order.

"O.K. Gimme chicken livers, mashed potatoes, gravy, okra, and cornbread. And iced tea."

Bunch picked up a newspaper that had been left on the counter. As he slowly flipped through the pages, he felt the young man's narrow eyes. Ignore, he thought. Ignore it. It might go away. A large headline announced: WIDOWS FAIL IN SUIT AGAINST FAITH OF OUR FATHERS.

Betty shoved a steaming plate in front of him.

Bunch, still reading, began to shovel down the food.

". . . the jury deliberated only twelve minutes before deciding that the deceased textile workers, Harold Chapley and Buddy Brady, had not died as a result of unsafe machinery in use at the Paradise Textile Plant Number Eight. Both men were decapitated in the plant's cardroom in what was termed a freak accident. Noble 'Trip' Gant, counsel for the Faith of Our Father's Insurance Company, Paradise's insurer, stated that his client was pleased with the verdict. . . "

Bunch took a large swallow of iced tea. Bunch had had a few cases with Gant, and had lost all of them. No matter how good the case seemed to Bunch when he took it, it turned bad once Gant opened his mouth. Bunch hated him, hated his success, his expensive suits, hated him for all the big scores he had ever made.

Bunch enjoyed his hatred so much that, at first, he barely felt the dampness and the heat. He forgot his hatred completely when his crotch began to burn. He fell backwards from the stool, grabbing the air for balance. The plate spiraled behind him, raining chicken livers, gravy, potatoes. The thin young man stood over him, holding the coffee cup he had emptied into Bunch's lap. As he spoke, his voice began to break into a whine, like a machine driven to the limits of its capabilities.

"You. . . you Goddamned lawyer! What you done to Charlene in that dirty old office of yours. I oughta cut your fucking throat."

Bunch struggled to rise from the slick floor. He *had* done something to Charlene. She did not have the fee on a dope case, so he took her in the back room. It was cold that day. He remembered that he had wanted to cover her with a blanket. Instead, they shivered on the couch and she covered her face with her hands.

The thin young man grabbed a fork. Bunch managed to get to his feet. He backed away from the fork, and found a heavy, glass sugar dispenser on the counter. The skinny young man paused for a moment, the fork held out in front of him.

"Don't do it," said Bunch.

The skinny young man charged.

"I don't even know your name!" shouted Bunch. Then he drove the dispenser into the young man's howling face. The fork clattered on the floor on the third or fourth blow. Bunch felt something give, and stopped pounding. The thin young man folded to the floor.

Bunch grabbed his briefcase, halfway running for the door. The thin young man sat up, and blood began to run down his shirt, over the face of Richard Petty. The door to the One O'Clock Diner slammed. Betty yelled after Bunch.

"Hey! You owe two ninety-six!"

Bunch stared out the window. He had told Alda, his secretary, to cancel the rest of his appointments. She had gasped when he came through the office door, but she knew better than to ask him what had happened. Too often Bunch told her the truth.

He tried to wipe away the coffee and gravy with paper towels from the bathroom, but he was irrevocably stained. He watched the street below and the thunderheads rolling in from the river. A phrase festered in his mind: "The unalterable law." He could not remember when he first heard it, but it seemed appropriate. Suitable for all occasions, he thought.

The rain began. In a moment it would cover the city, washing over the shopping malls, the housing tracts, the cotton mills, the Confederate soldier. The rain would scatter the mob on the courthouse steps. Thunder sounded from across the river, and lightning flashed on the horizon. Bunch pulled a bottle from a drawer, took a long pull of bourbon, and settled back with his feet on the desk.

"The unalterable law," he whispered.

The rain came in blue-gray sheets, obscuring the city below. It was just as well to Bunch. Even from five floors up he found Helmsville a depressing sight. There was a knock on the door. Alda peeked in as if she were afraid of what she might see.

"There's a Mr. Fite to see you."

Bunch dropped the bottle into a drawer and slammed it shut.

"I told you—no appointments. Goddamnit, I need a little peace, a little quiet. . . "

". . . but Mr. Bunch, he's come twice to see you. And besides, he's crippled. . . and he waited all morning."

Bunch gave up.

"Yes, of course. The unalterable law. It has me by the balls."

"What's that, Mr. Bunch?" said Alda.

"Nothing. O.K., send him in." Bunch straightened his tie and pulled his chair close to his desk to hide his stains.

Roy Bunch heard Charles Fite before he saw him. The scraping of the crutches preceded Charles into the office. A small, swarthy man, his huge head topped by a massive, glittering pompadour, his arms large and powerful, he sat down and propped his crutches next to his chair. Behind him, at a respectful distance, came one of the largest women Bunch had ever seen.

Bunch introduced himself and wrote down their names and address.

"What can I do for you?" he asked.

The woman smiled brightly. The man, his eyes large, said nothing. Bunch waited, his pen poised over the legal pad. A minute passed. Two minutes. No one spoke. Bunch cleared his throat.

"I said, can I help you with something?"

Charles spoke, the words tumbling over each other, his voice rich and deep. Bunch jotted down a few notes as Charles described a wreck. As he listened, he remembered a small dog his mother had owned when he was a boy. It was a mongrel, pampered and vicious, but possessed of an enormous penis.

". . . then there was this ambulance. That's when I heard it the first time."

Charles paused. Bunch realized that the little man expected a response of some kind. Bunch glanced up from the pad.

This, too, was part of the unalterable law, he thought; that I will be forced, forever, to guess what men like this one might be thinking.

"I give up, Mr. Fite. What did you hear?"

Charles drew himself up in the chair.

"THE VOICE!"

Charles smiled, showing large mahogany teeth. Bunch leaned back from the desk. He could see that it would matter little to them whether or not his pants were stained.

"The voice? Whose voice?"

"It wasn't no *human* voice! It was THE VOICE!" Charles bellowed.

"It's a miracle!" Tinka said. "The Lord has chosen Charles. Oh, when I read the scripture, I think of Charles out there at the Bessemer City Road and I remember St. Paul. It's the same. The very same. . . "

Charles gave Tinka a quick glance and she stopped speaking.

"I talk to it now. I hear it all the time. Yesterday it came to me while I was watching wrestling on T.V. It came from everywhere at once. From the wrestling men's mouths. From the ceiling. . . "

Bunch lit a cigarette and returned to his note-taking. At the top of the page he wrote *Personal Injury*. He took down the rest of Charles' story; how the voice had directed him to Bunch's office so that he might receive the rewards that were meant for him; how the voice wanted Charles to have a million dollars.

Later, after the authorizations and the contract were signed, and after Charles and Tinka had left, Bunch took another pull of bourbon. The storm had passed. Bunch looked out over the city and thought that there must be many other Charles Fites out there.

"Now, Ed. According to the reports from our doctors, there's not a thing wrong with her. That's an old back injury. Four years at least. I know she was cut, but what are those scars going to come to? Three thousand? I *did* read the medical report. I'm trying to be fair, but you know what it's going to come down to. Wait a minute. Listen to me. Is a jury going to believe the staff of the Manners Clinic, or is it going to believe that Chinese doctor you dug up over in Shelby? Think about how it will look. . ."

Trip Gant rolled his eyes toward the ceiling and drummed his fingers on the edge of the large oak desk.

"Have I ever been anything but fair with you? I'm waiting, Ed. What do you have to say about that?"

Gant owned an athlete's face, a scholar's face, framed by a helmet of perfect blond hair.

"Listen, Ed, and get this right. Faith of Our Fathers is prepared to offer three thousand, plus the medical. Just like I said in the letter. You *did* get the letter? Good. I thought that maybe you hadn't. Are you still listening? If you don't like what I've said, and if your client doesn't like it, we can go in front of Judge Righter next month and neither one of you will get a Goddamned cent."

He pictured Ed Snavely in his shabby office, worried about making payments on his daughter's treatment in the expensive asylum in Asheville.

"Why sure, Ed. I'll give you a day or so to think about it. I'm sure we can work it out. Call me tomorrow. By the way, Martha and I would love to see you and Dixie Anne at the banquet. Take care, old buddy."

He slid the receiver into the cradle and picked up the pocket recorder.

"You can prepare a settlement in *Witherspoon vs. Ballard Trucking Company*, 87 CVD 1214. Three thousand to Mrs. Archie O. Witherspoon, plus any medical expenses. Get a copy to Ed Snavely's office. It will be confirmed tomorrow."

The office walls were lined with photographs, diplomas, degrees, and certificates. During the rare intervals when Gant was not dictating letter, complaints, or speaking on the telephone, he studied the photographs. There he was in his football uniform—All-Southern, star of the Blue-Gray game. There was his boyish smile on the day he passed the bar exam, and his mature smile on the day he became a full partner at the age of thirty. There he was in the state legislature. And there he was shaking hands with two presidents, six governors, and twelve justices of the North Carolina Supreme Court.

"In response to the defendant's motion, the court will enter a summary judgment. The plaintiff has failed to present a case that is justiciable in nature. . ."

Judge Righter, white-haired and red-faced, sipped water and continued.

". . . and judgment shall hereby be entered on behalf of the defendant."

The plaintiff's lawyer, a soft boy with a face like a pillow, jumped to his feet, knocking to the floor a pile of notes, pleadings and memorandums. The papers scattered and drifted across the worn carpet.

"Your. . . ah. . . Honor. Plaintiff would like to serve notice of appeal. And. . ."

His voice trailed off. Judge Righter shook his white mane and tucked a couple of chins into the collar of his robe.

"What did you say, boy? You got to speak up if you want the court to hear you. Talk like a man. You aren't a sissy, are you? I got lawyers coming in here everyday that look like sissies and talk like Yankees. And all of you got a bunch a *papers*. You don't need papers. You need a case. I mean a *good* case. And ain't nobody gonna hear you if you just WHIMPER!"

The judge demonstrated.

"NOW SAY IT LIKE I DO. YOUR HONOR. . ."

The soft boy tried to speak. Judge Righter banged his gavel.

"I SAID SAY IT! WHAT DO THEY TEACH YOU IN LAW SCHOOL THESE DAYS? HOW TO BE RELEVANT? A LAWYER'S GOT TO BELLOW!"

"Your Honor. . ." The soft boy's voice trailed off again. The two bailiffs nudged each other and chortled.

"NO!" said Righter. "THAT AIN'T GOOD ENOUGH. NOW TRY IT AGAIN. YOUR HONOR. . ."

"YOUR HONOR," the boy shouted.

"PLAINTIFF WOULD LIKE. . ."

"PLAINTIFF WOULD LIKE. . ."

"TO SERVE NOTICE. . ."

"TO SERVE NOTICE. . ."

"OF APPEAL. . ."

"OF APPEAL. . ."

Judge Righter grudgingly nodded approval.

"Well, son. . . whatever your name is. . . that's a little better. Someday you might even make a lawyer. I doubt it, but stranger things have come to pass. This court, by the way, takes notice of your appeal. And I suggest you get those papers off the floor. I don't want the court-rooms of Darden County turned into a hog wallow. There's enough hoggishness in this courthouse any-how. . ."

The bailiffs laughed and slapped their thighs. Trip Gant smiled. The judge gave him an almost impercept-ible wink. A signal between buddies.

"Now suppose, son," said Judge Righter, "I let every lawyer dump his trash in the courtroom. That wouldn't be right. I'd be knee-deep before long. You'd put your cigarettes out on the table. You'd spit on the floor. You *must've* heard of precedents, and throwing papers on the floor is a bad precedent to follow. Not as bad as some acts I've seen. You must remember the prisoner from the county jail urinating in the trash can in the corridor. Assuredly, that's a worse offense against the letter and spirit of the judicial system. And yet, we must judge the essence, as well as, the quality of the act. . ."

Gant had never lost a case or a motion in front of Righter. And he was mildly amused by the judge's rant-ings. All Righter really wanted was to be colorful, he thought.

When Righter finished his speech, the soft boy dropped to his knees and began to toss papers on to the table. He sweated heavily. His client, an old woman in a red polyester pants suit who had lost an eye to an ex-ploding soft drink bottle, was finally aware of the fact that she would not get any of the money her lawyer had talked about for months. She sighed, accepting. The glass eye fit pretty well, even if her cousin had used it until he died. The proceedings of the court bored and confused her anyway. And when she had seen that Trip Gant was the other attorney, she had figured that she would lose. He was too handsome to be on her side. Gant extended his hand to the soft young lawyer.

"I want you to know that it was nothing personal," said Gant.

The soft lawyer nodded absently.

"Thank you, Mr. Gant," he said. "I appreciate that."

"Call me Trip. When I started out, old Runt Hareum up in Lincolnton did the same thing to me. Thought I'd never live it down."

Gant enjoyed kindly little lies. The one-eyed woman nodded to him, coy and girlish.

"The next time I need a lawyer, I'm getting me a handsome man," she said. "Like you. And you're smart, too. I swear. You're the smartest man I've ever seen."

Gant patted her shoulder. The soft lawyer stuffed the papers into his briefcase and bolted from the courtroom.

Gant worked through the lunch hour. After he turned eighteen he could never eat a large meal. There were many days when he could not eat at all. By the time he was twenty-one, he discovered that his lower tract was turned the wrong way. He dosed himself with laxatives and fed on prunes and raisins. Enemas were often necessary. When he played football, the aging black trainer pumped him full of mineral oil and soothed him when the team doctor said that he was too clogged to play in the Duke game. That was during his senior year. Law school made it worse; the retention, the absorption. Everything he heard, read, and wrote turned into solid matter.

He never discussed his condition with anyone, except for a few doctors. Martha, his wife, did not know. He could never reveal to a woman who had majored in art history at Agnes Scott that he had not had a decent bowel movement since high school. Part of his life was built around creams, lubricants, oils, softening agents, and regular secret visits to medical specialists. None of them could help him. And there was the necessity of a private bathroom, connected to his office by a short corridor. He installed it at his own expense after he became the chief partner in the firm.

He dictated a letter and reviewed pending cases. Around three o'clock, his insides rose and flopped upon themselves. His mouth tasted of acid. Deep within him there was a heavy, churning sound. Today, he thought, there will be some small measure of relief. He studied the photograph of himself and John F. Kennedy. It occurred to him that it would have been a better thing to have been wounded in battle than to have his affliction. A wound was an admirable thing.

At four, he changed into his jogging suit. He had been a runner all of his life. He moved with a halfback's stride; deceptive, ground-devouring, as if he were putting forth no effort.

His route covered the tree-lined streets near his office. He had grown up in the neighborhood; when he was a boy it had been the best part of town, where the nice people made their homes. The houses were Victorian mansions erected by hard-headed men who had discovered that they could make themselves rich by turning their neighbors into mill hands. Now the mansions served as offices for doctors, lawyers, and insurance agents. The new money men took the old homes as their prizes. None of them lived in town. They preferred the suburbs, with streets named after English counties and the city just a smudge beyond the newly-planted trees.

Running made Gant forget his bowels, and remember that his body was still good. He felt a satisfying contempt as he passed the other law offices. His opponents moldered there, stranded in the air-conditioning, pumping nicotine into their lungs. He lengthened his stride, visualizing their pale faces by the windows. They could see that he was still young and strong, while fat pocketed their bodies and gray death hovered by their hearts.

The sweat ran evenly; good, pure, without salt. He glided by Hodges Boulevard, a four lane street that bisected the city. Across the traffic islands lay the jail, the courthouse, the rotted-out heart of town where the twenty dollar whores tried to climb into passing cars, where boys and girls drank wine and shot dope and made it in abandoned stores and sad alleys.

Ed Snavely's office was down there. A knot of lawyers, mostly bad ones, practiced in the city's oldest skyscraper. It was six stories tall, and had been built when it seemed that the city might be bigger than it turned out to be. His father's office had been there. Now it belonged to Ed and those like him. Gant had watched them for years as they scuffled along, and whined, and pissed everything away. The building was an appropriate place for them; dingy, crummy, with bad lighting and drafty corridors.

Gant turned a corner and started down Beaumont Street, back toward the office. He had made four miles, and he felt like he could make three more. His stomach was calm, for the moment. It was usually docile when he ran, or tried an important case, or whipped someone's ass in one way or another. He passed a pretty girl. She caught his eye, but he ran on. There had been a time when he would have stopped to talk, making plans. He had once pursued women with the same thoroughness and energy with which he defended insurance companies and public utilities. Now women mattered little. He could not remember when he began to distance himself from that particular kind of triumph. He now found it trivial, and this knowledge made him happy.

He took the long slope of Beaumont Street at a slower pace. His old home stood at the top of the hill; built by his grandfather, who owned the mills and the land where the interstate converged and the shopping malls clustered. Gant's father had lost it all. His father did not drink or gamble or chase women. He did not practice any sort of reckless extravagance. As a boy, Gant understood that his father lost everything because he was weak and afraid. From time to time, Gant returned to a single, vivid memory. He used to spy on his father in his study. At times he seemed to work, reading important-looking papers, jotting notes and adding columns of figures. Most of the time, however, his father stared at some invisible, fixed object that Gant could never see or imagine. At those times, his father's lips twitched as if he were about to speak—or scream.

Once Gant saw him cry, his shoulders shaking with quick, orgasmic jerks, tears splashing down his good-natured, patrician face. The tears were endless, pouring out a lifetime of good intentions and good manners. Other men used him with smiles, promises, and hand shakes until there was nothing left. One fall morning when Gant was sixteen, his father left for the office and was never seen again. His creditors searched for him, but he hid his tracks well. The house was sold. The land and mills were already gone.

When Gant won his first big case, he purchased the house and donated it to the city. The donation turned out to be a nice tax break, and Gant got his name in the local newspaper. The city turned the house into a rarely visited museum of local history. Tourists seldom stopped in the city, and the inhabitants never thought about history. Gant enjoyed the tax break and the publicity, but these were not as important as the brass plaque beside the museum door:

THE NOBLE ROBERT GANT III
MUSEUM OF HISTORY
FOUNDED THROUGH THE GENEROUS GOODWILL
OF A DISTINGUISHED CITIZEN
OF THE COMMUNITY

He slowed down to read the plaque each time he ran by the museum. Once a week he sent a secretary to shine the brass.

The desk had been cleared of work before he went jogging. But there, soiling the order and accomplishment, was another complaint, thick and brimming with arguments and assertions. As he showered and changed, he had felt more rumblings in his lower tract. That told him something would happen that day. It had been nearly two weeks. He wanted to concentrate on his lower tract, to will it to do as it should. And now there was another complaint to be read.

"Charles Junior Fite and Tinka Arndt Fite, Plaintiffs *vs.* Loomis Trucking and Freight Company and Leon Nestor Smyre, Defendants." Gant recognized it as a penny-ante personal injury case that should have been handled by an insurance adjuster. He could not figure out why there was so much of it. It seemed unimportant enough to pass on to Woodside, the new associate. Gant flipped to the last page.

"Damn," he said aloud. "They're asking for a million bucks on a rear-end collision." He noticed the name at the bottom of the page: "Roy A. Bunch, Attorney for the Plaintiffs." Gant tried to place him. Then he remembered. Bunch was shabby and a little wild-eyed. He was also sullen, as if he wanted to spit on everyone. Bunch lurched through the courthouse in a J. C. Penney suit; a two-bit lawyer with two-bit clients, his round country-man's face white and smirking. Bunch's office was in the skyscraper, like Ed Snavely's and those other lost men. A dangerous man, thought Gant. Dangerous to himself.

Gant composed a short note to Woodside recommending settlement at around fifteen hundred. If Bunch did not like that, there was always delay, discovery, and probably a dismissal in the end. Gant knew, however, that Bunch would take the money. Fifteen hundred split between Bunch and his type of clients would seem like plenty, he thought. Gant wondered where Bunch came up with a million buck damage figure. Bunch could have been drunk when he drew up the complaint. He appeared drunk most of the times Gant had ever seen him. Gant opened the complaint again.

". . . and the Plaintiff, Charles Junior Fite, as a result

of the collision of August 25, 1987, and through the negligence of the Defendant's agent and driver Leon Nester Smyre, has suffered recurrent mental delusions of an auditory nature; that as a result of the accident of August 25, 1987, the Plaintiff's home life has been disrupted; that he is subject to fits and trances and that he suffers from insomnia and dementia. . ."

Gant closed the complaint and hefted it. Only a desperate man could write such words.

Twilight. The secretaries were gone. The lawyers were leaving for their first drink of the weekend. Noble "Trip" Gant, placed his hands firmly on the bathroom wall and pushed. The muzak from the outer office shimmered, faint and celestial: "Raindrops Keep Fallin' on My Head," by the Norman Luboff Choir. Gant grunted.

He waited a moment before he pushed again. The dull, hot ache within him shifted, sending shock waves through his belly, throat, and eyes. Points of light danced about him, and he breathed in harsh, deep, gurgles. He pushed again. The muzak grew louder, then soft, as if a madman had his hands on the volume control. He pushed harder, feeling as if his hands would break through and hang suspended below the photographs on his office wall. The bathroom flashed black, then ground-zero white. Above the muzak and his strained breath, he heard something hard and metallic strike the porcelain below.

IV

In the Conquistador Room of the Ramada Inn Interstate Hotel and Convention Center the remains of the banquet meal congealed on dozens of plates. The room, dominated by a twenty-foot polymer painting of DeSoto or Cortez or perhaps Fernando Lamas, bulged with lawyers and their mates. The after-dinner speeches progressed from anecdote to stately phrase. The listeners half-dozed. First they heard Carver and Watkins, the two district court judges, who mumbled and squeaked into the microphone. Both stated that they were grateful and happy and that everyone else should be too. Judge Righter followed with a long, mostly incoherent address which centered around a story about a man finding his wife in bed with an undertaker. Ashley Woodside, President of the Young Lawyers Associations, spoke of coming social events: pig-pickings, oyster roasts, and the softball game with the county sheriff's office. He reminded the association members of their dues and urged non-members to join.

He told the listeners that they "should do yourselves a favor—have a little fun."

Gant paid little attention to the other speakers. He watched the crowd. There was not a single first-rate man among them; a few good technicians perhaps. Several of the younger ones lacked skill, but possessed enthusiasm. The enthusiasm would fade in a couple of years. All of them, he thought, live for safety—good and bad, young and old. The bar association treasurer began Gant's introduction.

". . . our most distinguished member. The man responsible for establishing the state-wide continuing education legal workshops. . . former state senator. . . former head of the governor's council on crime prevention. . . president of the board of trustees of Darden Community College. . ."

The treasurer went on with the list of honors and achievements. Gant thought of adding a couple that the bar association would not understand: tolerator of the weak, the precision tool of his own will.

"I give you our president: Noble 'Trip' Gant."

The applause was undercut by a metallic screeching in the darkened rear of the Conquistador Room. From the podium, Gant searched for the source of the noise. A man stumbled amid folding chairs as a woman attempted to guide him to a table. Heads turned. The man half shouted in a choked voice. The words were garbled, but Gant thought he heard the man call his name. Gant's bowels locked down tightly. He began his speech.

"I am a man more sinned against than sinning. So says William Shakespeare in *King Lear*. . ."

Gant had fished the words out of his father's old copy of Bartlett's *Familiar Quotations*. While still in high school he had learned that it was a good idea to give the crowd a little culture.

"When I reflect upon these words, I am reminded of

the position of the attorney in our society. To be sure, we have our sinners. . ."

Uneasy laughter bounced around the Conquistador Room. From the direction of the stumbling man, Gant heard another shout.

". . . but we also fulfill our special role in society. That small number of sinners among us has been the source of broad attacks that unfairly include all members of the profession. We deserve our critics. However, many of the attacks upon us originate with those either unwilling or unable to appreciate the American legal system."

Gant paused amid the applause. The stumbling man gestured with the loose, expansive movements of a drunk.

"It may be true that some members of the profession, through lack of character or moral blindness, side-step the strictures of the code of ethics. We hear much of these transgressions. I dare say that attorneys are more shocked and disheartened than the average citizen over the discovery of these acts. For example, we all remember the Watergate Scandal. To think that most of the men involved in that awful affair were lawyers filled me with concern. Should we condemn an entire profession? Do we condemn all pilots because there is an aircraft disaster? Do we blame all doctors when a complex operation fails? I think not. This brings us to the question of safeguarding the standards of the legal calling. This we must do, and this we have done. We must let the public know that we will not tolerate the unprincipled, the incompetent, or the careless."

Gant paused again. The applause was fainter, as if the audience was not quite sure it agreed. The man in the back of the room laid his head on the table.

"I return to our special role in society. I'm sure that I do not need to remind you of our duty. . ."

Gant spoke for ten more minutes. He spoke of tradition, responsibility, and honesty. He praised the bar and the courts of Darden County. The crowd liked these sentiments and the applause grew more frequent. The man at the table in the back attempted to stand. The woman pulled him back into his chair.

"In conclusion, I would remind you that in our day-to-day actions, both in public and among ourselves, we maintain the standards of the law. Behind us lie centuries of people like ourselves. We must obey the dictates of tradition and use its power and force for the good of the future. Thank you."

The listeners applauded enthusiastically, then began to move toward the door. Above the noise of the departing lawyers came more clapping, unsynchronized and derisive.

For Bunch, there had been much bourbon that day, starting with a shot on the way to work from the bottle he kept under the car seat. The coming excess was palpable, settling heavily in his head and chest. He had held back until two, after he had finished a couple of divorces. By four, he was having a hard time. A man named Snipes had described a complicated transaction involving himself, his ex-wife, and a religious foundation in Ohio that had claimed his family home. Bunch nodded a great deal and gave grunts of understanding. Snipes had grown alarmed when Bunch put out a cigarette on a stack of files. Snipes asked if he was O.K. Bunch could not make out the man's face very well. There was an impression of a blob atop a long neck.

"Focus," said Bunch to himself. He wanted to speak calmly, but the excess was about to bubble over and fill the office. He closed his eyes.

"Focus, focus, focus, focus. . ."

When he opened his eyes, Snipes was gone. Later, Alda came in and said she was going home for the day. He told Alda to focus. It was dark outside when he remembered he was supposed to take Faye to the banquet. Faye thought the Bar Association banquet would be very high class. Slowly, he drove to her apartment, sliding under red lights and jumping the curb a couple of times.

She lived with her seven year old son, Billy Junior, in an apartment complex near the city's largest mall. She ran a beauty salon. To Bunch, her energy seemed limitless. I could settle down with her, he sometimes thought. Give up the law. Learn to cook and clean.

Faye was packed tightly into a silver dress, cut low so that half of her breasts bounced about like airborne vanilla pudding. She was an agreeable woman. She had a plain face and the body of a topless dancer. She believed in hard work, strong men, and heavy make-up. She smiled nervously when she saw Bunch.

"Roy, honey, I think we're going to be late," she said.

Bunch brushed past her into the living room.

"We won't miss anything," he said. "In fact, we got time for a drink. What you got?"

"I might have a beer. Are you sure. . ."

Bunch sagged into a chair.

"Sure of what? Yeah. I need one. A hard day. A hard, hard day."

Billy Junior, clad in jeans and a Darth Vadar T-shirt, handed Bunch a beer.

"Uncle Roy, you don't smell so good," said Billy Junior.

Bunch wiped the foam from his mouth.

"That's the way a man smells when he's been working hard," Bunch said. "That's the smell of work. Some day you'll smell that way too."

Billy Junior climbed into Bunch's lap and sipped from the beer can. They liked each other.

"You smell that way when you haven't been working," said Billy Junior. "Like the time you took me to the baseball game and we got lost coming home."

Bunch finished the beer.

"O.K. *That* smell. It's the headache medicine. Years ago, a doctor told me that I had to drink a lot of headache medicine."

Bunch felt good. Billy Junior usually put him in a good mood.

"Billy Junior, the important word is focus. Focus and you won't go wrong."

Billy Junior laughed. Faye came in from the bedroom carrying a golden hand bag.

"Let's go, Roy, honey."

Bunch sighed and reluctantly stood. His good mood would not last long. Such moods were meant to be short.

"You remember that, Billy Junior. Focus. We're concerned with focus. Think about it."

Faye took Bunch's arm.

"He'll remember, Roy."

"Focus, Billy Junior."

He bent low and hugged the boy.

"That headache medicine sure is strong," said Billy Junior.

"The stronger the better," said Bunch.

Bunch insisted on driving. As he wheeled out onto the interstate, he pulled the bottle from under the seat.

"Please, Roy," said Faye.

He thrust the bottle toward her.

"Have one. Go on. There's plenty."

She decided to change the subject.

"I hope this dress is all right."

Bunch held the bottle between his knees. The wheel of his old Ford seemed enormous. He felt as if he were the helmsman of a large ship. Faye tried again.

"Do I look acceptable, Roy, honey?"

Bunch squeezed a silver thigh.

"Just like Disneyland."

"Oh, Roy!"

Bunch's good mood left him in the Ramada Inn parking lot. Grimly, he pulled Faye through the lobby. As they entered the darkened rear of the Conquistador Room, he banged a knee against a chair, cursed loudly, and stumbled to a table. Gant, elevated above the crowd, was a distant gesturing figure. Now and then a couple of words filtered through to Bunch. Excess began to flood.

"YOU TELL 'EM TRIP. THAT'S THE GODDAMNED TRUTH!"

Faye shoved her chair to the far side of the table.

"What's the matter, sugar?" said Bunch.

Faye whispered that he must be quiet. Bunch reached for her, running his hand down her leg.

"Roy! Somebody might see you."

"See? Can you imagine what's going on beneath these tables? A veritable jungle of moving hands. Possibly even tongues."

"FOCUS, TRIP. FOCUS!" he shouted.

Faye spoke to someone off to her left. A man, Bunch guessed. Bunch lunged from his seat and the man backed off.

"Don't creep up on me that way," said Bunch.

The man wanted Bunch to sit down. Faye tugged at his arm.

"Roy, he says that you're making it difficult to hear the speech. People are complaining."

Bunch pulled her close to him and squinted at the man.

"Who the hell are you?" said Bunch.

The man said a name, but Bunch did not understand it.

"I don't know that name," said Bunch.

The man said something else. "Disturbance" was one word.

"What the fuck do you know about a disturbance," said Bunch.

The man did not answer.

"That's what I thought. You don't know disturbance from shit."

The man walked away. He shouted toward where the man once stood.

"I'm sorry if I caused a fucking disturbance. No. Wait a minute. I'm not sorry. I'm not glad, but I'm not sorry either."

His legs dissolved beneath him and he fell into a chair. There did not seem to be much left to say.

He had trouble making one hand hit the other, but he felt he must try. Modest achievements, he thought. Begin with modest achievements. Faye asked if the banquet was over. Bunch did not pay any attention. He involved himself in the process of applause. He worked on his applause until the hall emptied, the lights dimmed, and a busboy asked Bunch and Faye to leave so that he could finish cleaning up.

Neither spoke until Bunch guided the car off the interstate and turned into the subdivision where he lived.

"I want to go home," said Faye. "Not to your place. I'm sorry to say this, but it's so nasty. It's been nasty since I've known you."

Bunch guided the car up to the curb and tried to pull her to him, but she planted herself firmly against the door on the passenger side. A bad sign, he thought. Must make it up to her. He drove on.

"Dear, my home is your home. My car is your car. You get the idea. When it comes to material possessions, and of course spiritual affinities, we are one. United."

"That don't make sense. I want to go home."

Bunch eased the car into the driveway.

"You are home, my dear. Here we are at the castle of our collective heart: Bunchwood, my ancestral estate since 1967."

The deep grass, alive with insects, brushed high above their knees. Bunch held tightly to Faye's hand.

"My neighbors have two religions: grass-cutting and children. I am no longer of either faith."

Bunch had signed the mortgage after his first child was born. Dreams of young marrieds: three bedrooms, a carport, breakfast nook. Bunch opened the front door and coaxed Faye into the living room. The room was empty except for a twenty year old couch, a portable television, and a beanbag chair. Newspapers covered the floor. A beer can lay on the couch. Balls of dust floated gently in the corners. Every time Bunch came through the door, he was reminded of his wife and her ceaseless decorating - hunting prints, pictures of their son and daughter, the furniture shopping which he did not pretend to take an interest in. Then, too, there had been the parties for the other lawyers and their wives. Everyone drank a little more than was good for them, and laughed a little too loudly at small jokes. He thought, too, of how his wife had cleaned the house. She hated housework, but went at it with an evangelical fervor. The walls were bright, the floor shone. He kidded her that the place looked and smelled like a hospital, and she smiled the tight, dry smile of a woman who had learned too late that she had decided on the wrong man.

The house was supposed to be a stepping-stone. Next, would be a neo-colonial, quasi-mansion on the rich side of town. Bunch never contemplated the next step. His wife left him the house, and not much else. The couch and beanbag chair came from a second hand store, the T.V. from a client who owed him fifty dollars. There was also a bed, a box of textbooks from law school, and a crude painting of the scales of justice done in prison by one of Bunch's clients.

Bunch led Faye to the couch.

"And can I get you a drink? I might not have the most,

shall we say, deluxe accommodations, but I sure as hell got a drink."

She shook her head. In the kitchen he found a clean jelly glass and filled it with bourbon. When he returned to the living room, she was gone, the front door left open. Bunch went into the yard. He saw her under the street light, heading toward the interstate, her dress shimmering. He called to her.

"I'll drive you home if you want."

She hobbled on into the darkness, the bright silver of her dress pulling against her legs. Soon she passed behind the glow of the light and into the darkness. She was a simple woman, Bunch thought. He liked that about her. The world was fixed a certain way and you lived and worked and got ahead.

Back inside, he stripped to his underwear, brought the bottle from the kitchen, warmed up the television, and settled into the beanbag chair. The late show: Brian Donleavy was a submarine captain. He loved Virginia Mayo. But she loved Lloyd Nolan. Brian and Lloyd sailed the Pacific sinking Japanese aircraft carriers and dueling for Virginia's affection. Bunch realized he had been sleeping when he awakened to see John Wayne strangling a Comanche brave. He leaned backwards once more into sleep, his torso spread across the softness of the chair, his legs wide apart, his head thrown straight back, his arms folded across his belly. He would stay that way all night, his snores competing with the Duke's commands and the whir and pop of the television.

V

The day was cool for October, with a light wind and low clouds. From the front porch, Charles could hear the songs gushing from the Powerhouse Church of the Second Coming. The church sat at the bottom of the hill, a low cinderblock building amid white frame houses, across the street from the mill. The Fites lived in a four room white frame house, erected by the mill fifty years earlier, which had been passed from Charles' parents to him. A narrow street ran up the hill and ended at his front yard, just outside the chain link fence.

The singing rose high and long, a sad, wild noise. After a while, the singing stopped and Charles made out Reverend Cumby's voice above the wails and exhortations of the congregation. He took another sip from the pint bottle of vodka. Cumby was louder than the others, he thought. Maybe if he gets loud enough no one will see that he's a liar. Tinka had brought Cumby to see him the day Charles got out of the hospital. Cumby had tried to offer a prayer of Thanksgiving, but Charles had told him that praying was for dumb asses. Cumby gave up on the prayer and tried to question Charles about the "miracle'. Charles had refused to answer. Cumby offered to improve on the miracle by healing Charles' legs. Charles had told him to get out. The preacher went back to his cinderblock church. Tinka, however, had no place to go. Charles managed to get his hands on his crutches and beat her until he could no longer lift his arms.

There had been other preachers; the ones his parents took him to on Sundays and at special healing revivals. His parents believed in them, and they believed too that one day Charles would be touched in the right way. The touch would come and Charles would shake off the crutches. He once envied those preachers. They made mothers throw their babies into the air. They made old men leap over pews. They made young girls lift their dresses and moan. Cumby tried to make people do these things, but there were not many preachers left like him, shouting in forgotten, nearly-deserted places. Most of the ones like Cumby had died away. The big ones were on television. Charles watched them in their day-glo suits and expensive hair-dos. Their voices were rich, but not like *the* voice. They talked to themselves, ordering what they wanted from the world. They did not scare him like the voice did when it came to him from places he did not expect, when it swirled around him and pressed tightly against his ear and heart.

The song was louder, slamming against the walls of the church and climbing the hill. There were no more than a dozen members in the Powerhouse Church of the Second Coming, but their worship echoed through the silent Sunday neighborhood. Cumby had started them at nine and it was close to eleven; they would be at it for a least another hour. Tinka was there, lost in the noise. When she returned she would tell Charles of how God's face was seen shimmering near the ceiling, fading in and out of view.

He drank deeply and lit a cigarette. When Cumby finished with them, the congregation would rush sweating from the church. Tinka would come home and eat, then rub against him, cooing, her heavy, red-splotched, white arms engulfing him. He would feel sick and shove her away, wishing for the voice, waiting.

He had waited most of his life, endless blank hours relieved by the television, and vodka, and those times, now, when the voice came to him. The waiting could go forever. Every time he called Bunch, he felt the endless waiting. Bunch made a speech which said: "It takes time. I'm working on it." And now Bunch wanted him to see a head doctor. He guessed a head doctor would be much like a preacher or a lawyer. All of them babbled endless words.

Still, he had been told that a lawyer was needed. When the voice told him to find a lawyer, he had opened his telephone book and his eyes had gone right to Bunch's name. It did not matter what Bunch was like, as long as the voice approved of him. The main thing was to get the money. When the money was his, he would go on television. This much was clear.

Once on television, he would not ask for contributions. He would not give away prizes. He would tell people what they needed to hear, not about the Holy Ghost or redemption, or Sermons on the Mount. Once he got on television, everybody would start to act like they had sense.

To the east, the clouds darkened and dropped closer to the town. Charles took another drink and studied the sky. When he was a boy, his parents propped him on the porch and left for work. He remembered staring into the empty blue void, not expecting anything. That has changed, he thought. I couldn't see then. I couldn't hear. The clouds dipped closer, black and rolling.

Two boys, about seventeen, came up the hill. They stopped outside the chain link fence. The parts of their faces were mis-matched, like composite photographs: the eyes did not belong with the noses; the chins and foreheads were all wrong; their cheeks were pits, as if they had been boiled and compressed, or were suffering from a draining disease. One wore a T-shirt which bore the words, "Get Your Shit Together." The other was shirtless, his concave chest hairless and pale.

"Hey! Down here," yelled the boy in the T-shirt. His name was Darren; his buddy was Troy. Charles turned from the sky.

"What you see up there?" Darren said. Charles did not answer.

"I ask you what you seen up there. You been watching for a long time."

When Charles was young there had been such boys. They had mocked him. They had hid his crutches. They had laughed at him.

"Maybe he can't talk. Can't walk. Can't talk," Troy laughed.

Darren leaned heavily on the fence.

"Naw. He can talk. I heard him yelling the other day. Seen Preacher Cumby come outa the house. Lotsa yelling."

Charles lit another cigarette. He saw a gigantic hand thrust from the earth and squeeze the boys into paste.

"We heard about you," Darren said.

Charles blew a cloud of smoke toward them. It drifted and disappeared in the wind, which was stronger now, coming straight in on him.

"What'd you hear?" Charles said.

"That you're fucking crazy," Troy said.

Charles had seen the boys many times. They lived on his street, and he sensed that they did all the things that he had missed as a child and as a young man.

Darren scooped up a handful of gravel from the roadside and began to toss the tiny rocks toward the porch. When the gravel landed, it made a slight clicking noise around Charles' feet.

"Up there. What do you see?" Darren said.

Charles did not answer.

The boys came through the gate and climbed onto the porch. The sound from the church was subdued, low, wistful, as if the people there were united in a great, endless longing. Charles finished the vodka. Blackbirds flew before the cloud mass, their cries lost in the sky. Darren grabbed the bottle from Charles' hand.

"How come you didn't give us none?" Troy said.

The clouds picked up speed, tumbling like an avalanche.

"What do you see? What do you hear?" demanded Darren.

Charles did not know, but he wanted the voice to come to him and give him a way. He searched for the voice like a man in a darkened room fumbling at a door.

Darren threw the bottle. It shattered on the road. The clouds churned and twisted. The air turned colder. The blackbirds settled on power lines, watching, pecking, calling. Cumby's voice rose again in the church, shouting about the brightness of the devil, of Satan's false beauty. Darren squatted, his face close to Charles'.

"You gonna tell me," Darren said, his voice flat and somehow old. The wind shook the blackbirds in their rows. Lights flickered across the city. Rain fell.

Charles felt it. He turned his eyes back to the sky.

Troy rubbed his arms back and forth across his chest. "I'm cold, Darren. Let's go."

Darren did not move.

"I'm talking here. I'm gonna find out something," said Darren in his flat, old man's voice.

He stood again, picking up the crutches. With a windup, he threw them over the fence. He squatted down once more.

"You like that? I can do other things. Lotsa things. Whatever I want."

Charles did not hear him. A single cloud had detached itself from the mass. When it began its journey, it was

gray, but it turned white, then golden. It began to glow
as it landed in the yard and traveled up the porch steps,
wrapping itself around Charles.

Darren slapped Charles.

"Goddamn it. You answer me!"

Charles laughed. The cloud was in him. It filled his
heart, his lungs. It coursed through his veins, and raced
the length of his spine. It tickled his genitals and he felt
a power. He was the cloud, but he suddenly changed
once more, into the voice.

When Charles laughed, Darren backed away. The
boys stumbled from the porch when Charles climbed out
of his chair. Troy hit the yard at a run, the hard rain
beating on his shoulders. Darren fell backwards, slith-
ering toward the gate. Charles took the first step. He
walked awkwardly, like a child trying out a first pair of
stilts. He reached the street and started down the hill.
The cold rain ran down his face, but he was not aware of
it. He went slowly, measuring each step. He began to
sing his favorite song.

"You deserve a break today—at McDonalds. They do
it all for you. . ."

Tinka knew something was wrong when she found
the crutches in the street. She had climbed the hill, still
panting from church, and she began to call for Charles
when she saw that he was not on the porch and that
the front door was open. She quickly and skittishly
searched the four rooms of the house, remembering the
tricks Charles had played on her; hiding and scaring
her when she found him. Once he hid all day in a closet,
grabbing her legs when she opened the door to hang
some clothes. After her search, she sat at the kitchen
table and tried to figure out where Charles had gone. It
came to her finally. The rapture had come. Charles was
one of the chosen. She could not understand why she
had not been allowed to go, why Preacher Cumby had
not been taken. She decided that it must have been the

voice. Charles knew the time had come, but would tell no one. She shivered. Soon giant scorpions and seven-headed beasts would run through the streets. A star called Wormwood would dip close to the earth. The rain slackened. She wondered how Charles was making out in heaven, and if he had met Jesus yet.

It took Charles a long time to reach the river. His legs, despite their ability to function, had not been used since he was a child. They were thin, and his powerful torso looked as if it were stuck upon a pair of tooth picks. He was not aware of the city as he passed through it. Finally, he saw the river in the distance. It was blood, flooding the banks, running thigh-deep. Again he remembered the preachers, the ones that said they could fix his legs. They shouted about being washed in the blood. But they never spoke of swimming in it. Whose blood? thought Charles. Was it the blood that came out of the television wrestlers' heads when they beat each other? Was it the blood of the television men who got shot? It was not the blood of Jesus. That blood had dried up a long time before he was born. Jesus' blood had never done any good. Somebody forgot what the blood of Jesus was supposed to do. It was like crutches. It did not fix anything.

The land dropped down to the river. Charles found himself on a dirt road that ran past the chemical plants and the junkyard where the burning tires always smoldered; past the abandoned cars where the hair tonic drinkers lived in the summer, through the kudzu to the greasy, coarse grass of the river banks. He reached the cage.

The monkeys lay on the cage floor, their yellow teeth chattering. Charles began to pull at the padlock.

"Hey! What're you doing?" someone yelled.

Charles did not respond. He yanked harder, and the lock began to give way.

The man was tall and emaciated. He had the crumbling, disjointed look of a drunk. He went on talking, his voice filtered through a wall of phlegm.

"Buddy's gone to Florida. Went there with a nineteen year old girl. I'm watching the place." He sounded as if he had not spoken to anyone in a long time.

Charles continued to dig at the padlock. The monkeys walked in a slow circle, picking up speed as Charles grunted and yanked. The strength of the voice pumped through him. His hands turned red, as if the blood would spurt out of them and run into the river. The man watched Charles for a while; then ambled off through the tall grass. The monkeys hopped and chattered. Charles twisted the rusty metal. The cage rocked. The man returned with a bottle and resumed watching Charles.

"Say," the man gurgled through the up-turned bottle. "You're right strong ain't you? Specially for a little guy."

The earth vibrated around the cage. The monkeys skidded from the floor to the bars to the trapeze. The wind pushed through Charles again, battering against the cage, the river, the sky. The lock dropped away, the door opened. Charles rushed into the cage. The monkeys clustered around him, climbed to his shoulders, hung from his back. The animals gamboled, danced, and raced; and they followed him.

As they moved up the road from the river, Charles realized that this hands were wet. He raised them to his face. They were bruised and bloody, but there was no pain. He laughed as he had laughed when the cloud entered him.

The skinny man watched Charles and the monkeys until they were halfway up the hill. On the highway, he caught up to Charles.

"My name's Luther Stamey. I'm fifty-one years old, and I ain't ever seen nothing like what you done."

There was a pleasant, electric sensation within Charles.

"Yeah. See what ain't been seen around here," Charles said.

Bunch felt energetic. Uncharacteristic, he thought. He tried to think of a reason why he should feel good. There were bills to pay, and his kid's tuition, and Alda's salary. He was getting older and more of his hair fell out every day. Maybe, he though, I've found inner peace. Like those pilgrims who discover the meaning of life; who sell plans to make you a warm, loving, creative individual.

It was nearly four, and Bunch had been working since noon, trying to find ammunition for the Fite case. He picked up the legal pad and read his notes.

Brayboy vs. Carolina Coal Company, 49 S.E. 251 (1922). Plaintiff's son was a professor at the University of North Carolina. He was a little eccentric. Took naps in the coal cellar. Defendant's employee dumped a ton down the chute. When plaintiff's son was uncovered, he was found to have a broken arm and to have become more eccentric. Lived in his father's birddog kennel for awhile. Gave up teaching. Said God had a mission for him: to preach to the Negro citizens of America. Declared incompetent. Institutionalized. Escaped and went to Kingstree, South Carolina. Set up a church. Held revivals. Plaintiff, his family, sued as guardians in his name after he was recaptured. The court held that defendant's acts had considerably agitated an already existing mental condition and that plaintiff was entitled to damages for emotional distress.

Bunch tried to imagine Professor Brayboy. The professor probably taught classics.

He read the rest of his notes, underlining a point here and there. *Winesap vs. Annie's Touchdown Lounge*, 196 S.E. 2d 235 (1969). A topless dancer gets hit in the head with a pool cue by a bouncer. She claimed it turned her into a nymphomaniac. Held: the plaintiff's pre-existing social activities are indicative of, but not conclusive, in establishing a pre-existing condition. Defendant's agent induced nymphomania. She got away with it. Bunch underlined these last words three times. She was easier to imagine than Professor Brayboy.

Pre-existing conditions. Yes, he thought. Charles Fite is subject to pre-existing conditions of a peculiar kind. He opened the file and scanned the report from the Department of Social Services, written, thought Bunch, by a well-intentioned soul, a Ms. Williams. Ms. Williams noted that Mr. Fite was uncommunicative and sullen and seemed to have no outside interests. "When asked about his sex life, he did not respond verbally, but instead smiled at the interviewer. When asked about his relationship with his wife, Tinka, he responded by raising his crutches and rapidly banging them together. At this point, the interview was terminated."

The Social Services yearly report was completed six months before the wreck; the other reports, stretching back to where Charles' mother died when he was seventeen, all reached the same conclusion: Mr. Fite had attitudinal problems. He needed help. Bunch did not have to imagine how Gant's boy Woodside would make these reports sound. There had not been a word from Woodside since an answer to the complaint, not even an offer to settle. Bunch lit a cigarette. Gant wouldn't even bother to handle it himself, at least up front.

Bunch leaned back in his chair and surveyed the litter of books and papers that covered his desk. He could guess what most lawyers would think of the case. But most lawyers he knew operated on what they imagined to be solid ground.

He yawned, and felt the last of the energy melt away. He though of the assault charge and the long-haired young man. His name was Goforth. Mean white trash. When such people hold a grudge, they keep it for life. Grudges and revenge. Life in a revenge culture is difficult, he thought. He remembered a client he had represented when he was just starting his practice. Rudisill was a middle-aged textile worker whose wife had been unfaithful. She left him and fled to Atlanta. The other man booted her out after a few weeks. She wandered around Atlanta for a couple of years, then returned to Rudisill. Rudisill welcomed her home, got her drunk, tied her to the bed, and beat her to death. Bunch could still recall Rudisill's face; it was long and sad with deep eyes and a craggy nose. A little like Lincoln's. Before he was given his life sentence, Rudisill told Bunch that he had done another thing to the woman before he killed her. He had poured a bottle of Tabasco sauce into her vagina. "Why," asked Bunch, "did you do that?" Rudisill did not hesitate. "Because, Mr. Bunch, it was the right thing to do." Yes. The right thing to do.

The streets were shiny and wet under a blue sky. The air was cool and the wind felt good in Bunch's face. He went over the case again. Get Charles to the shrink for an examination. Get more background on Charles. Write a letter to Gant's office. His footsteps echoed in the empty streets. Memory returned. Bunch liked to keep the memory switch turned off most of the time. How did I end up here? he thought. I must've believed I was going to a better place. At least, when I was young. No. Probably not even then. You're supposed to think that when you're young. Before that, there were those Sundays when I was a kid and the whole family sweated and sang at the First Methodist Church. When I was thirteen, I got caught feeling up Denise Albright in the back pew and the minister expelled me from the youth fellowship. Denise's father came over when he heard about it. He looked a lot like Rudisill. And he had this long belt and I hid out in the woods behind the house while my old man calmed him down and promised I would be punished. And I got one of those weak whippings the old man gave out and I yelled in gratitude that it was not Mr. Albright working on me. The old man didn't have much to say after that. He was proud when I became a lawyer, I guess. But he still didn't have much to say.

Then there were those Sundays with the wife and kids and I stared out the Goddamned picture window with a bad hangover and Jane went on about the furniture and I would leave—I'm always running—and drive out of this city on a dirt road and drink. Hair of the dog. I usually stayed until the stars came out and I was drunk enough not to care whether she talked about the furniture, or my irresponsibility, or the new house she wanted, or whether or not the kids needed piano lessons. And she would ask where I'd been, and I would say that I was out becoming one with the cosmos. And she would say that was nonsense and I would tell her Whitman did it, and if a queer could do it, I could too. And she would rush from the room because she hated words like "queer" or "shit" or any of the words I have to use to keep from stuttering. Her favorite word was nice. This was nice. The party was nice. The sofa. The draperies. As long as it had nothing to do with me, it was nice.

From above the low buildings the Confederate soldier watched. Sunday in this place, thought Bunch. It's worse than when the streets are filled with people. He remembered a bad movie he had seen in college. It was about the end of the world, and many of the scenes were of empty, abandoned city streets. I might not mind that, he thought. I could catch up on my sleep. Take walks without worrying about some bastard jumping me. That's no good either. It would take me the rest of my life to get used to it.

Ah yes. Sunday. The old man serving up the fried chicken and big bowls of butter beans and a thing called congealed salad that had the consistency of cold flesh. The house was on the edge of town. Swallowed up. There is a Seven-Eleven there now and boys that look and act like a younger version of Goforth play Pac-Man and read *Penthouse* and what will they be able to remember? The one thing that can make them bend to some inexplicable action. There were three like Goforth in the office a few months back. They had been riding around in a Camaro sniffing paint thinner. One of them lit a cigarette. The vapors ignited. The car was blown off the road, the doors blown off, burned big clumps of hair from their heads and shredded their clothing, threw them into a ditch. I'm not sure what they wanted. They sat before me, picking at their bald spots and the scabs on their arms, their faces luminous with burn cream. Like Fite. They just naturally came to me. Like Charlene too.

And there was the Sunday a few weeks back. Friday and Saturday I was drunk, and I thought it was Monday and I rushed to shower and shave and dress, and shagged ass to the courthouse, my mouth tasting awful and my hands shaking. And I roared into the parking lot, hitting all the speed bumps, and I yanked and cursed and pulled at the locked door until I realized it was Sunday and that even the mob on the steps had gone home, wherever that may be.

Bunch had walked a half block past his car. It was then that he saw them as they came down a side street. The monkeys led the way, swinging from awnings and parking meters as they went. He squinted towards them, into the sun. He could not make them fit into time or place. Stupidly, he thought: I've seen all sorts of things around here. Charles came next. And another man. They passed from view, behind the buildings a block down, going in the opposite direction. Three blocks later he caught up to them. He called to Charles, who turned and waited, moving a little, shifting his weight from foot to foot as if he could not bear standing still. Bunch did not know what to say. He looks like Charles Fite, he thought. Only there's more of him. It's the super deluxe version of Charles Fite.

"I came from the river," said Charles. "I been to the river. I know all about it now."

"About what?" asked Bunch.

"Everything."

The other man stuck out his hand.

"I'm Luther Stamey. I come up from the river, too. I seen what he done. Boy, I'm telling you. . ."

Bunch left Luther's hand dangling in mid air.

"What'd you do, Charles?"

"Freed the precious spirits. Freed the blood."

Bunch glanced up and down the street. No one has seen this but me, he thought.

"When did you start walking?"

"This morning, when the voice came. I understand now. Before, I didn't know enough. Now I do. And I'm gonna keep walking. And there's something else. I want the money. That's what we said we'd get. I got good reasons."

Charles turned and bobbed away from Bunch. Bunch watched Charles, Luther, and the monkeys disappear around a corner. He started back toward his car. The town was still gray. The sky was still blue. The soldier stood before the courthouse. It was still Sunday.

Tinka watched television all afternoon, waiting for some word of the rapture. But television was the same as usual; football games and pretty people. She was not as frightened as she had been when she discovered Charles was gone. The Lord's ways were not to be understood. Several times noises from outside the house startled her. She rushed to a window, expecting to, wanting to, see a monstrous spider or a lizard with the face of a man. But it was only a car or children at play. Disappointed, she returned to television, switching channels, hoping for an announcement that would signify that the Lord's will was being done. At twilight she heard something on the porch.

Charles walked past her into the kitchen, the monkeys and Luther Stamey close behind. The monkeys began to eat from a pot of beans that sat on the stove. Charles took a bottle of vodka from a cabinet. Tinka's heart was so loud she thought it would explode. She did not know if her nerves could take it. In one moment she had learned that Charles could walk and that the rapture had not come. The Lord tried to surprise her too much sometimes.

Charles tilted the bottle up and handed it to Luther. He wiped his mouth with the back of his hand and stroked the monkeys. As his hand ran over the animals, he stared at Tinka. The stare went deep inside her and burned.

"Don't say nothing," Charles commanded.

She nodded. He went into the bedroom and she knew that she was meant to follow.

The wind blew all through the night. The television yelled about wars, floods, and epidemics. The monkeys frolicked about the house, pulling the Jesus pictures from the wall, overturning furniture, hanging from curtains. Luther slept, folded over the kitchen table. Charles drove down hard on Tinka. It had gone on for hours. For a while she begged him to stop, but he pounded at her like a steam drill turned against a soft, clay bank. That which was in him was inexhaustible. He could taste it. It flowed and washed over all, pouring down mountain sides, flooding creation. He drove against her on into the night.

VI

Charles left the house a little past sunrise. Tinka stayed in bed, swollen and exhausted. Luther still slept, and the precious spirits were quiet. At the bottom of the hill, Charles saw the two boys from the day before, crouched next to the back wall of the Power House Church of the Second Coming. Silently, they watched as he passed by.

He took a road that led out of the city. The boys followed. At intervals, he stopped and turned. The boys stopped too. They faced each other for a few minutes, squinting down the highway. Charles moved on, his walk stronger, faster.

He liked knowing that they were behind him. He knew that they wanted him to give them a word. There would be a moment when they would hear it. He had waited for years without even knowing the voice existed. The two boys could wait a little longer.

An hour, two hours passed. The sun was high in the clear, mid-morning sky. The two-lane blacktop narrowed and curved around a wooded hill and straightened as it crossed a small creek. Charles stopped in the middle of the splintered wooden bridge, and looked into the thick, oily water. Things moved beneath the surface. Further down, beneath the creek bed, were layers of mud and vines, bits of metal and busted radiators, entwined and matted into the substance of the earth.

Troy and Darren waited at the end of the bridge. Gradually, a step at a time, they edged their way toward him. Finally, they stood beside him. Charles began to walk again. They flanked him, moving into the morning sun.

They paused a couple of times while Charles gazed into the sky or at the earth. Troy and Darren froze each time, like mimes awaiting a cue.

They came to a rusted, corrugated sign that read: PREPARE TO MEET THY GOD. Charles had first seen such signs when he was young, posted on every highway. He turned to Troy.

"Can you read that?"

Troy moved his lips and shook his head. Darren shouted it out.

"PRE. . . PRE. . . PRE-PARE TO MEET THIGH GOD!"

"What do you think that means?" Charles asked.

Darren wrinkled his brow and scratched his head.

"Uh. . . I ain't sure. I don't know. Does it have something to do with you?"

"Ain't nothing that's even been seen or heard that's about me. That sign don't mean nothing. That's all. You see something like this and you know it don't mean nothing."

He looked from boy to boy, making sure that each understood. They gaped back at him, as if the idea of meaning was new.

Charles halted them in front of a deserted store. The paint had long since peeled. The signs advertising Mail

Pouch Chewing Tobacco, Nehi sodas, and Cities Service gasoline were rusted through. Kudzu vines entwined the building and snaked through the holes where the doors and windows once were.

His father, Verlen, had died in front of such a store. Verlen was arguing with another man. Charles could not remember what they were arguing about. Verlen held strong opinions on many subjects: what car ran best; how far it was from Charlotte to Greensboro; whether or not it was possible for a nigger to water ski; where Russia was; and whether Jesus was really a Jew. Charles, aged nine, sat in the car and listened to Verlen and the other man as they argued. Charles' mother, Pauline, begged his father to leave so they could make the revival in Belmont. His father said that the other man might not be as smart as he thought he was, and that "when they start to jump, there ain't nothing that can stop them." Charles had tried to figure out what these words meant. If he had known why his father and the other man argued, it might have made sense.

After yelling these words, Verlen went through a series of sudden transformations. His head sagged, his eyes bulged, and his color passed from red to white to green to blue. He performed an elaborate, stumbling, arm-waving dance around the gas pump, and was, at the dance's conclusion, drawn to the gravel and dirt. Charles leaned out of the car to get a better look. All he saw before his mother pulled him close to her was his father's rolling eyes and twitching leg. He was disappointed that he did not see the rest of the dance. He did not have to be told that his father was dead. The only thing left for him after that moment was to die.

Now, instead of country stores, there were shopping malls, K-Marts, and A&Ps. Each time Charles had been in these places he had watched and waited, wishing for the dance and its end, the same kind of conclusion his father had reached. He imagined the streets of the city filled with dancers, of people in other cities watching it on television and rushing from homes, churches, offices, and bars to take up the dance themselves.

And there was another sign. Beside the store lay a dead dog. It had been there for a long time. It had been a big dog, part German Shepherd and part Collie. Its legs were stiff with rigor mortis. Its eyes were gone. Charles squatted beside it.

"Get me a stick," he said.

The piece of pine tapered like a spear. Charles bent over the dog.

"Look at it," said Charles. "Look at me. Watch."

Charles pried at the viscera over the dog's middle. The dried flesh came up in a leathery sheet. The internal organs were jumbled from quick, hard death, but the heart, liver, and intestines could be seen. Charles thrust a hand into the body cavity. The dog's interior was soft and cold. He moved his hand around carefully, tapping, squeezing. When he withdrew his hand, it glistened in the sun. He motioned to Darren.

"You do it."

Darren did not move.

"I. . . I can't touch that thing," said Darren.

Charles spread his fingers and held his hand before Darren's face.

"I done it," Charles said. "You afraid of it? You can't be afraid no more. You'll be sick if you are. It once moved like a precious spirit without knowing why or where. We got to learn to be like it was."

Charles and Darren knelt beside the dog. Troy hung back, waiting. Charles slowly guided Darren's hand into the body cavity. Darren breathed slowly, but he did not try to withdraw his hand. When Charles released his wrist, Darren's hand stayed inside. Troy knelt with them.

Later, the boys scooped out a grave in the hard ground and buried the dog. Charles was satisfied. Things were off to a good start.

"We've started to learn today," began Charles in a

voice like a serious T.V. man talking about the goodness of America. "Me and these poor, dumb boys. We all part of the same thing now. We can all touch now."

As he spoke, he wrapped an arm around the waist of each boy.

"This dog died on the road. Killed by a car. I was given the voice on a road, in a wrecked car. There is a dance this precious spirit did right up until it was smushed. In fact, it never danced no better than when it was hit. I never danced at all until the cloud came and went into me."

He began to shuffle to imaginary music. The boys followed along until the three of them moved as one. They danced on the grave until the earth was packed hard.

They followed the road through the yellow and green fields until they came to a trailer park that had been hacked out of a small grove of pines. The single street was mud and trash. One of the trailers was fire-gutted. Its sides had buckled from the heat. Papers and smashed furniture surrounded it. A doll's head rested beside a ruined hair dryer. Two doors down, a man sporting a three-inch high flattop loaded cardboard boxes and black garbage bags into a pick-up truck. Two children huddled in the truck's cab. The man worked quickly, making trip after trip into the silver trailer. A woman, young and blonde, stood beside the door, her arms folded across her chest. The man spoke as he moved. Charles stopped to listen.

". . . and Momma needs me. And she needs Shane and Misty Marie. *You* don't care about them. All you care about is whining and bitching."

He hoisted a garbage bag into the truck. Sheets and shoes, towels and underwear, spilled into the truck bed. The man did not seem to notice. He kept moving, talking, brushing past the woman in the trailer. He returned with a T.V. set. Gently, he lowered it into the truck.

". . . when I met you, I thought you was a good woman. I was wrong. I come home from work and you ain't got supper ready. . ."

The man brought out a five-foot plastic reproduction of the Venus Di Milo and leaned it against the truck cab.

". . . just sit around reading them astrology magazines and telling me what Phil Donahue said today. . ."

He returned with a shotgun and a painted bust of Elvis Presley. He place the shotgun in the cab between the children and cushioned the bust against a pile of garbage bags.

". . . and you told your nasty-ass girlfriend how good-looking Tom Selleck is. You ain't even *once* told me that I'm good-looking. . ."

The man climbed into the truck and rolled down the window.

". . . don't come around and don't call."

The truck skidded in the muddy street and turned back toward the city. The woman slowly slumped down in the doorway.

"You don't feel right, do you?" said Charles.

She raised her head. There were tears in her eyes. Normally, she was blank and pretty, like a talented child's drawing of feminine beauty. Now, her face was taut, as if it had been pulled into permanent rigidity.

"I can look at you and tell," Charles said.

She stood and stared at where the truck had been.

"Who are you?" she said.

"It don't matter. I know you though. I seen you a million times. You can't remember feeling good."

She nodded, hearing Charles' words for the first time.

"You wanta feel good. You used to dance."

She tried to remember.

"Yes," she said. She rose and went into the trailer. Charles, Troy, and Darren followed.

Most of the furniture had been hauled away by Cecil, Wanda's husband. She fixed coffee and talked of Cecil and the children.

Wanda said that she was married at sixteen. Cecil was twenty-nine. He made her pregnant in the same pick-up he left in. She spoke in a slow monotone, as if she were not used to talking.

"After little Misty Marie was born, I thought he would be happy. Cecil had a good job. But it. . . it was like he didn't care about nothing. He went off by himself a lot. Hunting, he said. The car races. Left me alone with Misty Marie and Shane, and all I did was take care of them. I love them. I ain't saying I don't. But it was them kids day in and day out and the only thing I enjoyed was singing along with the radio. He caught a. . . bad disease. . . and gave it to me. . ."

There were only two cups left in the trailer, so they were passed around. They drank the coffee slowly as Wanda passed the cup. Each time Wanda handed a cup to Charles, she brushed against him; a breast, an arm, leg against leg. When the coffee was finished, Charles asked if there were any liquor in the trailer. Wanda found half a fifth of bourbon in a kitchen cabinet.

Wanda stopped speaking. She was out of words. She turned to Charles. The sunlight through the back window shown around his head and made it difficult to see much of his face, except for the eyes and teeth. His eyes locked on her and she began to undress. Her breasts swung free from the bra. By the time she began to undo her jeans, Darren and Troy were helping her. They yanked and pulled and she winced a little.

When they finished, it was late afternoon. Charles' energy had bourne them all. After Wanda was stripped, he had joined them, directing and leading. They could have gone on for days, but he felt the need to move again. They rested and dressed. Charles took his seat in the Lazy Boy.

"You ready to come with us?" he asked Wanda.

She was taut again, but with expectation instead of dread.

"Where you going?" she said.

"We walking. We gonna walk and see. And dance."

She left the room. When she returned, she was clutching a small overnight bag. Charles stood back and took her arm.

"Would you like to do anything else before you go?" he said.

It did not take long for her to create a mound of astrology magazines, *People*, *The National Enquirer*, and *T.V. Guide*. Onto the mound she tossed aerosol cans of oven cleaner, deodorant, insecticide, and furniture wax. She poured cleaning fluid over all, and it soaked through to the carpet.

They followed the road to the top of a hill. The flames danced above the pines. The aerosol cans exploded. The roof of the trailer began to give way. The shouts of neighbors could be heard in the cool stillness of the early autumn twilight. They moved into the darkness. Soon the only light came from passing cars.

They walked for three more days. Rituals were refined, repeated. They did not eat very often. Twice Darren stole lunch meat, bread, and cigarettes. Troy rolled an old man at a gas station for liquor money. They slept, when they slept at all, knotted together in woods, abandoned houses, and, once, in a trash dumpster. The touching was continuous, as if they were, for a time, welded together. On the morning of the fourth day, they awoke in a bathroom at a rest stop on the interstate that led back to the city. They finished the last of the liquor at a picnic table as the sun broke over the interstate.

Charles thought of the city and how much was to be done there. He remembered Tinka, Luther, and the precious spirits. I've started, he told himself. Someday, I'll be more important than Johnny Carson. I'll be watched more than the six o'clock news. He bounded from the picnic table. His legs were strong now; the power of the voice flowed and leaped through them.

"We going home," he said.

As they walked toward the interstate, an ancient Ford smoked into the rest area parking lot. The engine idled, then sputtered out. The driver, an old man, remained behind the wheel. Charles approached the car to get a better look.

The old man had probably been handsome at one time. Now his face sagged. His skin was withered like a turtle's neck. He had the eyes of a child. Charles tapped on the window.

"Can't go no more, can you?" said Charles.

The old man opened the window a bit.

"Ah. . . pardon me?"

"You stopped because you couldn't go no more. Maybe you been moving in the wrong direction."

The man spoke quickly in a cultured, feathery voice.

"Well. . . actually I was trying to get to Helmsville. I think I know some people there. They were friends. I haven't seen them in a good many years. I only thought of them last night. And I drove and drove. The road is long, and. . . I got so tired. I get tired easily. . . I. . ."

"Have you ever cried much?" asked Charles.

"I. . . yes. I've cried many times. On crowded streets. In empty rooms. While running in the night. Why do you ask?"

"You look like you have," said Charles. "Things ain't gone right in a long time, have they?"

The old man rolled the window up and locked the door. He stared at the dash. Charles yelled through the glass.

"You ain't got no friends in Helmsville. You like we used to be. . ."

Charles pointed toward Darren, Troy, and Wanda.

". . . only you trying to pretend you ain't."

Slowly, the window came down.

"I hardly exist. I have been a vapor for years. I have only a few wants. Last night, in Augusta, Georgia, I wanted this automobile. I came to this place. . ."

Charles enjoyed the old man's speech. It reminded him of noble, sad actors he had seen on the late show. They had been brought down. They sounded as if they were educated and rich, but they were usually down and out in some foreign country; lots of times in hot places where even the cops were Mexicans and niggers.

". . . once in New Orleans, a lovely town, I lived for a month in Jackson Square. I was tired, as I am now. I counted pigeons, homosexuals, prostitutes and tourists. I slept beside the general's horse. It was there that I became a vapor. People could literally see through me. The tourists took photographs of the French Market, the cathedral, whatever, through my body. They passed through me to buy souvenir ashtrays, hot dogs, and Dixie Beer. Once I stood on a stage, on Bourbon Street, in front of a performing stripper. She did not ask me to move. Neither did any of the drunks in the audience. I was not there."

The old man stopped speaking. Charles remained by the window, studying his aristocratic profile. The voice was at work again, but this time Charles did not even have to speak. The old man got out of the car.

"You can call me Smith. That will be good enough for now."

Wanda drove. Smith sat between Wanda and Charles. Darren and Troy rode in the back. The Ford wheezed onto the interstate. Smith's voice was querulous.

"Oh. Where are we going now?"

Charles slid an arm across Smith's shoulders.

"To the right place. The place of the precious spirits and the blood."

Smith's eyes grew wider.

"Will there be good things there?" he asked.

"Better than *Life Styles of the Rich and Famous*," answered Charles.

Smith closed his eyes and was soon asleep.

They drew closer to the city. Troy discovered a book. He handed it to Charles. It was *The Book of Common Prayer*, a tattered copy with a broken binding. Charles thumbed through it. Many of the pages were covered with a minute, spidery scrawl. He made out a phrase: Moloch in Arcadia. He shook Smith awake.

"Is this yours?" Charles asked. Smith nodded.

"You ain't gonna need it no more," Charles said.

Smith's voice was amiable, but remote, as if the words were being channeled through him from a far distant transmission station.

"If you say so. I am completely in your hands. I've owned that book for years. Carried it with me into Honduras, Mexico, Morocco, Spain. God knows where else. I read it in jails, hotels, and on those many occasions when I was lost beside the road. I think it was a good book at one time. Now I have no idea what it means. Not even the words I wrote."

"Good. I'm glad it ain't nothin important," said Charles.

Charles tossed the book into the slipstream of the car. It disintegrated as it hit the asphalt and the pages were scattered in the high, dirty wind of the eighteen wheelers.

At the Power House Church of the Second Coming, a revival was in progress. A hand-painted wooden sign propped against the front cinder-block wall of the church announced that the Reverend Leon Cumby would preach on the End of Time. Inside the church, the Reverend Cumby lead the singing of a hymn entitled: "I AM A BIBLE-BELIEVING APOSTOLIC CHRISTIAN

AND A MEMBER OF THE CHURCH OF THE FIRST BORN." His voice was hoarse and deep, like a football coach. His chest was like a coach's too—thick and broad. There was no tapering between chest and stomach; his torso was a meat-block. His head was perfectly round, completely bald, and very small.

He carried the singing. There were few there to join in. Henry and Thad; twin brothers who seldom spoke. They were in their forties and unemployed. They wore dark blue plastic jackets and yellow plaid pants. Even in church they wore baseball caps advertising Lummy's Country Sausage. There was one way to tell them apart. Thad wore an artificial leg. Across the aisle from Thad and Henry sat Thelma and Marcelline. They were soft, enormous women who came to the Power House Church of the Second Coming in the hope that Henry and Thad would ask them to marry. They had never spoken to the twins, and except for the leg, they could not be sure which was which. But they believed each week that the proposal would come and that they would be happy forever.

Aside from the Reverend Cumby, Henry, Thad, Marcelline, and Thelma, the church was empty. Tinka Fite had not even shown up; she seldom missed a Sunday, much less a mid-week revival. The rest of Revered Cumby's flock, a half dozen or so, was at home watching a television mini-series based on the life of Johnny Unitas.

The Reverend Cumby began his sermon. He spoke of sin and death. He thought of sin and death from the time he awoke, while eating, praying, while on the job as a cook at the Steak'N'Egg Kitchen. As he fried eggs, or grilled hamburgers, or lifted baskets of french fries from the deep fat fryer, he thought of the immodest dress of women, the worthlessness of youth, and with satisfaction and a grin of finality, of the restless grave which was to come for the wicked, the depraved, and the mistaken.

"This morning, there was a terrible earthquake in I-Ran. A thousand or more died. There was another earthquake last week in Jay-Pan. Can you see it? Can you see the earth opening up and swallowing a *city*? Can you see them Japanese people in them little cars driving into big cracks in the ground? Screaming all the way to the center of the earth? Well, I can. I can see them. I-Ranians, all dressed up in sheets and masks, trying to run. Trying to jump over them big cracks. Only they can't make it. And they kick and howl all the way to the bottom, landing on them Japanese in their cars. All of them, I say all of them, are stewing and bubbling in HELL!"

He paused to let the congregation think. He loved to shout about Hell. When he did not think about sin and death, he thought about Hell. He thought of all the people that had ever gone there, and how crowded Hell must be. He scanned the congregation. Their eyes would not meet his. This was a sign of their uncleanliness. But they were not as unclean as those who refused to listen.

"Do you think them earthquakes was an accident? No. God don't allow for no accidents. Them earthquakes came because the world is *flush* with sin. With waste. With corruption. Jay-Pan and I-Ran is two countries that don't believe in Jesus Christ. But do we have to look overseas for sin? IT'S RIGHT HERE!"

He pounded the dented kitchen table that held his Bible and paint-by-numbers portrait of the Last Supper that he had purchased at a flea market.

"You can see it everywhere. Women carrying on half-nekked. People going down to the beach and getting out there on that sand and wiggling and squirming in the sun like *LIZARDS*! Then we got foul language. Dirty-minded men and women that is corrupt. I SAY COR-RUPT! And what will God do about this sin? He tells us."

The Reverend Cumby flipped open the Bible as neatly as he turned a pancake at the Steak'N'Egg Kitchen.

"I'm reading now from the word of the Lord. The Book of Revelation. Chapter nine, Verse two.

"And he opened the bottomless *PIT*; and there arose a smoke out of the *PIT*. As the smoke of a great furnace; and the sun and the air were darkened by reason of the smoke of the *PIT*; and there came out of the smoke locusts upon the earth and unto them was given power, as the scorpions of the earth have power. And it was commanded them that they should not hurt the grass of the earth, neither any green thing, neither any tree; but only those men which have not the seal of *GOD* on their *FOREHEADS!*"

The reading concluded. Henry and Thad rubbed their hands rapidly on their plaid, polyester pants. They knew that the locusts would be like those they saw on the late show that attacked the Mexican Army and wiped it out. Marcelline and Thelma tried to figure out what the words meant. It was clear, however, that the preacher spoke of bad times. The preacher always spoke of bad times. They watched as Henry and Thad increased the speed with which they rubbed their legs, both natural and artificial. This made them long for the twins. Marcelline whispered to Thelma: "They can rub *so fast.*"

Cumby rumbled again, working himself up for the shouts and howls he loved so well.

"Think about it, brothers and sisters. This is what God is telling us is gonna happen. And if God says it's gonna happen, you better believe it. How many, I say, HOW MANY OF YOU WILL HAVE THE *LORD* ON YOUR SIDE? HOW MANY WILL EX-CAPE THE TERRIBLE TIME OF TRIBULATION? HOW MANY OF YOU WILL HAVE THE MARK OF THE BEAST ON YOUR FOREHEAD AND BE CONDEMNED TO THE STINKING FIRES OF HELL?"

Cumby threw back his head and closed his eyes. He wanted them to think about the fires of hell. He could see the flames, waving, dancing in the darkness. And he could see himself, peering out of a little window in heaven, gloating with Jesus over the well-deserved suffering below. He and Jesus were clothed in white robes, shining and clean in heaven's air conditioning. Heaven was an endless, beautiful Ramada Inn lobby. He had been to the Ramada Inn once: to see it, to smell it. He told the congregation that it was a sinful, Sodom-like place. But he knew heaven could have nothing more beautiful than the deep carpeting, the soft couches, and the angelic women passing back and forth.

He opened his eyes. The heads of the congregation were turned toward the aisle, where Charles Fite stood. Four other people waited stiffly by the church door, as if they were at attention.

"Praise God!" shouted the Reverend. "It is a miracle from on high. The lame have been made to walk, the lost sheep has returned to the fold of Christ the Shepherd. The one has joined the ninety and nine! The foulest sinner I've ever seen has accepted the redemption of Jesus! I forgive you Brother Fite! I forgive you for running me out of your house, for the drunkness and blasphemy of your past! I forgive and Jesus has forgiven. . ."

Cumby raised his hands in praise of this miracle. He began to sing "The Joy of My Heart is Pumping Forth in Jesus." Tears of gratitude formed in his eyes.

"Jesus called me today.
Said that I must go away!
The joy of my heart is pumping forth in Jesus!"

Charles listened to Cumby's song. He was going to let him finish before he got down to business.

In the end, Cumby was left alone on the altar, preaching at the backs of Charles and the others. He called Charles a devil, the anti-Christ, Abbadon. No amount of scripture or threats of damnation could make them return. When the song ended, Charles motioned to them and they followed. They left quietly, without shouts or hosannas, as if beginning a long-feared, yet long-hoped-for pilgrimage. Cumby, hoarse and sweating, shrieked at them from the door of the church.

"He is the angel from the bottomless pit, the Son of the Morning. He's gonna lead you into the MAW OF DAMNATION!"

Cumby squinted into the night. They were gone. It was as if they had been swallowed. He listened for steps and voices, but he only heard a dog's bark and a faraway train whistle. He watched the lights as they came on in Charles' house, and heard shouts and garbled voices. He thought of climbing the hill, to continue the Lord's battle, but he could not bring himself to do it.

VII

Judge Oral S. Carver, of the District Court of Darden County, rolled up the left sleeve of his robe and scratched a mole nestled just above the elbow. The court reporter stopped typing. The bailiffs yawned. The crowd in the court room—whores, drunk drivers, divorcees, child neglecters, lawyers, cops, and probation officers—shifted restlessly on the hard benches. A tattooed blond boy, up on shoplifting charges, hummed tunelessly until a cop told him to shut up.

Bunch, the defendant in the *State vs. Roy A. Bunch,* 87 CD 1103, raised his eyes and studied the ceiling of the courtroom. He found it difficult to look at Oral S. Carver for very long. Maybe, Bunch thought, he's covered with invisible ants. Or ticks. He can't keep still; scratching, squeezing, digging.

The judge was a thin man with a leathery, two dimensional face who spoke in a high-pitched drawl. Bunch turned his eyes from the ceiling.

". . . and Mr. Bunch, there seems to be a question of propriety here. Legal ethics. While there is no *solid*

66

proof of. . . uh. . . your relationship, shall we say, with a female client, there is a *scintilla* of evidence that. . . your actions. . . may constitute a breach of the attorney's code of conduct. However, we cannot act upon a mere scintilla. Your former client decided to leave for Florida and is unavailable as a witness. . ."

And thank God for that, Bunch thought.

". . . although I don't doubt that the county bar association would be interested in hearing more about this. . . uh. . . alleged incident."

Carver expertly wiggled a finger into his left nostril.

". . . but in returning to the case before the bench. . ."

Carver regarded his finger with satisfaction and continued.

"Yes. The case before the bench. The law is clear on the point upon which this case turns. That is: self-defense. A man has a right to use non-deadly force to protect himself from a non-deadly attack. In this situation, Mr. Bunch used a sugar dispenser to repel an attack where hot coffee and a dining fork were the principal weapons. . ."

Someone snickered in the back of the courtroom. Judge Carver stared absently toward the sound, cracked his knuckles, and scratched his head.

"Who laughed back there?" Carver said, searching the crowd. A bailiff jerked the blond tattooed boy to his feet.

"Here he is Your Honor." The boy grinned shyly.

Carver yanked several hairs out of his large ears.

"Son," he said to the tattooed boy. "Where are you from?"

"West Pelzer, South Carolina, Your Honor."

"That's good," Carver said. "You know to call me 'Your Honor.' How long have you been in Darden County?"

"Sixty-two days," the boy answered.

"How long have you been in the county jail?" said Carver.

"Sixty-one days," said the boy. The crowd laughed. Except for Goforth. The scar on his forehead was purple and brown. He did not let his gaze leave Bunch's profile.

Judge Carver shook his head and wiggled a paper clip in his ear.

"You can add another thirty to that. I don't like that kind of snickering. It gets on my nerves. You can sit down now."

The boy did as he was told. His grin was gone.

"At any rate, let's get back to business. The law favors the defendant here in that he was set upon by the prosecuting witness. However, I must admonish both parties to refrain in the future from violent actions. I find the defendant, Roy Bunch, not guilty. Next case."

Bunch bolted from the courtroom and lunged into the hall. He heard his name called, and turned to see Goforth in pursuit.

"It ain't over, Bunch," Goforth shouted. "It ain't ever gonna end."

Bunch lost Goforth in the crowd that spilled out of the District Courtrooms, and made for the back stairs. Dignity, he said to himself. A little fucking dignity is not too much to ask. The sound of the courtroom and hallways ceased as he slammed the heavy metal door of the stairwell behind him. He paused on the landing. Try to forget it, he thought. Goforth. He won't forget. He has a cause now. Bunch caught his breath and started down the stairs. But, he thought, I can forget Charlene and those embarrassing questions that judges like to ask. Once the world's Charlenes go to Florida, they never come back. She's probably got a shack job down there. Besides, if the ethics committee went after every lawyer who took it out in trade, there wouldn't be anybody left to do traffic cases. A bad precedent.

Bunch took the steps slowly. Footsteps sounded in the opposite direction. Bunch tensed, half expecting to meet Goforth. Instead, on the second floor landing, he met

Noble "Trip" Gant. They moved around each other without speaking. When Gant was a few steps above Bunch, he turned, smiling down.

"It's Bunch, isn't it? Roy Bunch?"

"That's right."

Gant stepped back down to the landing and extended his hand. Bunch paused for a moment, then shook.

"I understand you had a little problem today," said Gant. "Wasn't it up in front of Oral Carver?"

You know it was, Bunch thought. You know everything that goes on around here.

"Yeah. But it worked out."

"Not guilty?"

"That's right."

"Well, I know you're relieved." Gant checked his watch. "I need to be in courtroom A. Going for summary judgment in the Ramsey case. An associate of mine is working on Fite. That's one of yours, isn't it?"

"Yeah," answered Bunch. "Your boy Woodside."

"A fine young man," said Gant. "We're very pleased with him over at the firm. Most promising."

Bunch turned his back and clumped heavily toward the first floor. Gant called to his back.

"Say, did you tell me the name of the kid who brought those assault charges against you?" Gant waited a moment for an answer, but all he heard was the closing of the door at the bottom of the stairwell.

Before Gant got his summary judgment, there was an unpleasant duty to attend to. Righter's secretary showed Gant into the judge's chambers. Righter, in his robe, faced the window. When he turned, Gant could tell that he had been drinking: his eyes were puffy and red, his once healthy fat sagged in pouches. I can smell him, Gant thought.

"Things aren't good, Trip. They're not good at all." Righter lit a cigarette. His hand shook.

"I'm not going to tell you everything is O.K.," Gant said.

"I'm sorry, Trip. I'm sorry for what I did."

"Well, Claude. Being sorry might not be enough this time. Taking pay-offs is serious. Especially when certain persons find out."

Righter inhaled deeply.

"All I ever wanted to be was a judge. I love being a judge. I like sitting at the bench and wearing black robes and instructing juries and having people call me judge. And it's not fair. Just because some reporter finds out about a little money. . ."

Gant was weary of him. He had been weary for a long time. Being an imaginary buddy had its price.

"You're going to resign, Claude. You have no other choice. It's that or it's all going to be in the Sunday papers. You fucked up once too often. Five thousand doesn't sound like much when it's in the bank, but when the idiots around here read that you took it in exchange for a decision, there's going to be a real shit-storm. Think about it. The attorney general will send down a prosecutor. You'll be censured, at least. The worst thing that can happen is prison. Think about that, too. How long do you think an ex-superior court judge could make it in prison."

Righter did not answer. Gant went on.

"Have you thought about what's going to happen to you if you fight this? It isn't going to be just your ass. What about Evelyn? What about your sons? Are they going to be able to live with this?"

Righter lit another cigarette. A cloud of blue smoke surrounded his head. When he spoke again, his voice was a whisper.

"Can. . . can you help me, Trip? I'll give the money back. I swear to God, if that's what it takes. I don't mind that."

Gant started for the door.

"Where're you going, Trip? Don't leave me. I'm knee-deep."

Righter emitted a tinny laugh.

"Remember when we used to say 'knee-deep' all the time? Lord, we said it for everything. If we had a load of work to do, it was knee-deep. If some defendant was telling lies, the shit was knee-deep. . ."

Righter chuckled, the smoke whirling around him. Gant stopped and walked back across the room. Righter's smell, the odor of rot, was strong in his nostrils.

"I've known you for twenty years, Claude. . ."

Righter laughed again.

"That's right! I remember. . ."

Gant slammed a hand flat on the desk. The judge blinked rapidly and began to stutter.

"We. . . we. . . go back. Long way. . ."

Gant slammed the hand once more.

"Shut up, Claude. Now. No more words. You're not doing well with words today."

The judge nodded. He still smiled, but a single tear rolled down each cheek.

"You're ignorant, Claude, and reckless. But I feel some responsibility toward you. Don't ask me why. Civic duty I suppose. Now, I've made arrangements to help you. I've taken care of things at the newspaper. If you resign today, this minute, there will be no story. If you do not resign, I will not only not help you, but I will see to it that your ass is permanently hung in a sling. You're a liability to me and everyone else who has ever dealt with you. This morning, I've been on the phone to the attorney general's office and I've even fixed it so you can get partial benefits for early retirement. No questions asked. No headlines. No committees. The public will never hear of any of this, as long as you keep your dumb fucking mouth shut. Agreed?"

Righter no longer smiled. The cigarette burned down to the filter and went out.

"Are you O.K., Claude?" asked Gant. "You're not going mental, are you?"

"I'm fine," Righter peeped.

Gant opened his briefcase and spread five copies of a letter across Righter's desk.

"You're to sign each of these. One copy is for you. The other is mine. A third is for the House Judiciary Committee. A fourth goes to the attorney general's office. The last one goes to the newspaper."

Righter signed each copy and Gant placed four of the letters in his briefcase. Righter did not read his copy. Gant started for the door once more.

"Can I keep my robes?" asked Righter.

"I guess so. I don't know what harm it would do."

"Trip?" Gant looked at his watch.

"I'm due in courtroom A in five minutes."

"Trip? Did I ever take a bribe from you?"

Gant smiled.

"Yes. But you never knew it."

Gant closed the door softly behind him. He felt a twitch in his bowels, but it passed quickly.

"I saw him walking down Broad Street. I called him the next morning, but couldn't get an answer. So I called for three days. I finally got through to him last night and I couldn't understand a Goddamned word he said."

Roland T. Pffippert, clinical psychologist, poured bird seed into the cockateel feeder.

"And when you met him, he couldn't walk? Quite interesting."

Bunch watched as Pffippert stroked the cockateel through the bars of the cage. Quite interesting, Bunch repeated to himself. I wonder what would surprise Pffippert. Levitation?

"Yeah. I found it at least interesting. Considering he's been a cripple most of his life."

Pffippert watered his plants. There were a couple of dozen in his plush, newly-decorated office.

"Such incidents are rare, but hardly unheard of. Spontaneous healing. There is a good bit of new research on it. In fact, I've done some reading lately on the subject—*How to Heal Yourself Holistically*. Fascinating. The author claims to have healed himself of cancer. I understand private sessions with him are a thousand an hour."

Bunch shifted in the wicker chair. Roland T. Pffippert. Bunch pondered Pffippert's style. He can get away with an office full of bushes and funny-looking birds. And chairs that were never meant to hold the human body. What would the perfect, well-adjusted Pffippert person be like? I wouldn't be able to tell what sex, he, or she, was. No bad habits. Tanned. Eats brown rice and yogurt. Hasn't had a cheeseburger since high school. Jogs every three hours.

Pffippert began to do sit-ups.

"Tell me, Roy. How do you propose to show that your client has been changed for the worse by the accident? Since he's gotten his legs back, it sounds like his self-concept is stronger."

Bunch noticed a painting above the stereo system. It consisted of purple and black blocks arranged randomly on a gray background.

"I've never heard of a traffic accident that was good for anybody. . ."

"Except lawyers?" Pffippert did one-handed push-ups.

"Yeah," Bunch said. "Except for lawyers. Look, are you gonna be my expert or aren't you? I need some help on this thing. I don't need you to tell me that the accident was good for him, or that he's able to work miracles on himself, or any similar varieties of bullshit. I want you to examine him and run all the test. Then I want you to get up in court and say that he's nuts. You've done this before. . ."

Pffippert ceased his exercises. He pulled a bottle of Perrier water from the office refrigerator, and turned on the stereo. The office filled with vibrating, electronic music. He sat cross-legged on the thick, deep brown carpet. He was a tall man, lithe and healthy, with a well-trimmed beard and neatly-cropped hair. He wore jogging shorts and shoes and a gray U.C.L.A. T-shirt. His expression was amused, quizzical; like a professor in conference with a promising, but lazy student.

"To begin with, you must disabuse yourself of the notion that people are nuts. Or crazy. Or any such layman's terms. I treat personality disorders."

Bunch gave up trying to make himself comfortable in the wicker chair. Only Pffippert's people could find ease there, he thought. He stood and the circulation returned to his legs.

"Roland, are you gonna tell me that Arnold Phelps wasn't crazy?"

Pffippert finished the Perrier, abandoned the floor and sat on the edge of his shining, designer desk.

"No, Roy. The state decided that Phelps was unable to understand the nature and quality of his act. What I said on the stand was that he presented a case of severe maladjustment. Phelps wasn't responsible."

"I'd say that Phelps wasn't responsible," Bunch said. "He beats out his wife's brains with a claw hammer, puts on her clothes, and visits his mother-in-law."

Pffippert began to manipulate a Rubik's cube.

"Phelps had a history. . . of adjustment problems. And besides, he might have been sent to Death Row, which would not have done him, or the state, the least bit of good."

"Your social consciousness is admirable, Roland," said Bunch.

Pffippert quickly and properly aligned the colors of the cube. Bunch glanced up at the painting. The blocks of color had shifted positions. The cockateels pranced in their cage. The music tickled the bottoms of Bunch's feet.

"So," Bunch said, "it's not good for society, or Charles Fite, to collect money from an insurance company."

Pffippert tossed the cube onto the desk. "Now, Roy, money is not an accurate measure of either psychological damage or of justice. I'm sure *you* understand that. Besides, I must spend some time with your client. It's going to take a good bit of my energy to work up his profile. . ."

I should have known, thought Bunch. He wants more money than last time.

". . . and there are some new tests I want to run on him. They're quite interesting."

"And what are these new, interesting tests going to cost?" Bunch said. Pffippert ignored the question.

"The concept was developed by Von Bey at the Leipzig Institute in the 1920's. Only it's seldom been applied. Until today. Von Bey dealt specifically with patients laboring under religious delusions. Does that intrigue you, Roy? Does it arouse your interest?"

"Go on," Bunch said.

"Now the reason that Von Bey's work has become important is because of the marked increase in what the venerable Doctor James termed Religious Dementia. There is more of it today than when Von Bey was investigating the problem."

"I can buy that," said Bunch. "Only it looks normal when you see it on the street, or on television."

"Exactly!" trilled Pffippert. "I can see that we'll work well together on this one. But to return to Von Bey. People want the mystery and terror of God, or else they want to turn God into a larger version of themselves. And no matter how they see God, they want to act out their vision. The new God is a public figure manifested in a billion faces and an incalculable number of gestures. The people that want this God reject the kind of world envisioned by social planners, scientists, technocrats, and so on. They want to perform, to get in on God's act."

Bunch sat down again. Pffippert continued to pace. ". . . Von Bey, and hardly anyone else who thought about it at the time, would ever have imagined that religious mania would sweep the west again, at least with such power and frenzy. We were supposed to be too advanced for that. So Von Bey faded into obscurity, although he did do some interesting work on the treatment of Rostokovich's syndrome. Have you ever heard of that particular disorder? The patient believes himself to be an inanimate object. It is prevalent in a consumer society. I see a man twice a month who fears that he is turning into a bottle-green, air-brushed, Dodge van. Quite interesting. But to return to your client; these tests are going to take time. Which is not without value."

The pay-off, thought Bunch. He builds me up with Religious Dementia, the decline of the west, and Rostokovich's syndrome. I've got to hand it to Pffippert though; at least he's entertaining.

"That's what you were getting at," said Bunch. "All right. I can pay fifty an hour, plus three hundred as an expert."

Pffippert cleared his throat and opened an appointment book.

"Perhaps we need to discuss the rates again. Renegotiate, as those of you in the legal profession say."

"Wait a minute. I gave you that rate on Phelps."

"That was last year. Besides, Phelps was easy. His personality disorder spilled out all over the place."

"All right. How much do you want? You're the only shrink around here who will have anything to do with me. I have no choice."

Pffippert began to write in the appointment book. "It's seventy-five an hour and twelve hundred as a witness. And you must remember, that because we have worked together in the past, I'm giving you a lower rate."

"Lower. You got balls, Pffippert. You came into this city and nobody knew your name. Then I help you get your name in the paper as an expert witness and all of a sudden you have a refrigerator full of French water, two birds, and music and pictures that don't make a bit of sense. If you hadn't met me, you'd still be working for the county."

Pffippert's handsome face was pained, sincere.

"Roy, I am unjustly accused. I no longer work exclusively for the county. I have many clients from out in Buckingham Hills. Rich, bored, women and their children. Teenage dopers and nymphomaniacs. Then there are the homosexuals who think they're artistic. And don't forget the guilty businessmen, professors, lawyers. Imagine, if you can, what lawyers tell me. And I minister to the less affluent, like that poor fellow suffering from Rostokovich's syndrome. . ."

"And I bet vocational rehab pays for that," said Bunch.

Pffippert ignored the interruption. "They all think that I'm wonderful. They all pay well, never less than a hundred an hour, and they all pay on time. And Roy, I don't owe you a dime for any of them. In fact, what would you say to a few sessions? For yourself, I mean. I'll give you the same rate as your client. You may as well get into the swing of things. Why, Helmsville and Darden County have gotten to be like California when I was in graduate school. Everyone has to have a shrink. I'm the most fashionable shrink in town. The others around here come off as authority figures. I make the clients believe that I'm their friend, and it's good for them. As for you, Roy, I think you would have to admit that therapy would do you some good. I could work you into my schedule every other Friday. What do you say?"

Bunch laughed. "No thanks, Pffippert. I'll stick to liquor and an occasional piece of pussy. The Bunch treatment I call it." Pffippert shook his head.

"What can I do for those who won't help themselves? It is seventy-five and twelve hundred? Right?"

"Yeah, Goddamnit. Right. How did you get into this business? Start out with Amway?"

"I'm shocked, Roy, that you would even think such a thing. No, my friend, it is a calling; like any other among the helping arts. And I'm surprised to hear an attorney make such a statement about an allied profession."

"Ask me about attorneys some time," said Bunch. Pffippert scribbled on a small note pad and handed the sheet to Bunch.

"Have your client here at nine Monday. Tell him to be ready to stay all day, if necessary."

"You're in a good mood today, aren't you?" asked Bunch.

Pffippert switched the music to a fast, heavy rock and roll beat. He danced gracefully around the room.

"Roy, I'm always in a good mood." The cockateels whistled as Bunch left.

It was late in the afternoon when Bunch returned to his office. The waiting room was empty. Alda pounded away at the typewriter. She did not notice that Bunch was there until he leaned over her desk. He startled her and she hit the "p" key nine times.

"Oh, Mr. Bunch. I wish you wouldn't sneak up on me like that. You know how my nerves are."

"Yeah. They're bad. What're you typing?"

"The letters you dictated yesterday on the Fite case. I've done the requests for medical records and insurance information."

Bunch picked up a stack of mail from Alda's desk.

"Charles and Tinka. Our star clients. Have there been any phone calls?"

Alda frowned. "Just some smart aleck boy. I think he's the same one that brought those charges against you. He kept saying, 'It's not over! It's not over!' He must have called five times. I don't understand some people."

Bunch tossed letters into the trash can. There was one from his ex-wife. Another was a circular announcing the publication of a treatise on Alaskan ecological law as applied to the tundra. He saved a letter from the law firm of Gant, Whitlock, Morrison, Bright and Testerman.

"Alda, I understand them. All of them, not just Bobby Goforth. They suffer from personality disorders. Von Bey's complaint. Rostokovich's syndrome. It's simple." Alda looked up from the typewriter. She was about Bunch's age and had the face of a small bird.

"What did you say, Mr. Bunch?"

"It isn't important. Believe me." Bunch was halfway through the door of his office when Alda called to him. She sounded more tentative than usual.

"Mr. Bunch, the afternoon paper has a story in it about your trial."

She rose from her desk and handed the paper to Bunch. It was folded to a headline that read:

LOCAL ATTORNEY ACQUITTED ON ASSAULT CHARGES

"Roy Alfred Bunch was found not guilty of charges stemming from an affray which took place August 31st at the One O'Clock Diner, 211 Broad Street in the city. The charges were preferred by Bobby Odel Goforth of Monte Vista Lane. According to witnesses. . ."

Bunch tossed the newspaper into the trash can.

"I should feel honored. The world's coming to an end. Everywhere you go, somebody is trying to kill somebody else. Powerful men have atomic weapons, and want to use them. Whole countries are starving to death. And it's decided to put the story of my trial out for all to see."

"But you were found not guilty. That's the main thing. Try to look on the bright side."

As Bunch closed the office door, he gave Alda a long look.

"The bright side. Yes. Fuck the bright side."

Alda resumed typing.

Bunch pulled a bottle of bourbon from his desk. He poured a coffee cup half full and fingered the letter from Gant's office. The envelope even looked high-class. A message from the land of the big scores. He drank most of the bourbon down, filled the cup to the brim, and opened the envelope.

Dear Roy:

In regards to *Fite vs. Loomis Trucking and Freight Company*, 87 CVD 1241: It has been decided to file a motion for summary judgment on the issue of mental suffering. You will receive notice from the clerk's office within the week. However, in light of your client's disability and financial state, Loomis Trucking has authorized us to offer your clients the sum of one thousand dollars ($1,000) in settlement of the above-numbered case. We feel that this sum is more than adequate compensation for the medical expenses of your clients, as well as damages to their 1967 Pontiac automobile. I would appreciate hearing from you as soon as possible as we are anxious to get this matter out of the way.

> Yours,
> Ashley T. Woodside,
> Associate
> Gant, Whitlock, Morrison,
> Bright, and Testerman

Bunch folded the letter and slid it back into the envelope. The bourbon's heat crept up to his head. I could get three hundred of it, he thought. I wouldn't have to pay Pffippert to tell the world about his theories. I wouldn't have to spend the next six months messing with the Fites. There might even be a little peace. I'm a tired man. But still. . .

He shrugged and tore the letter into tiny pieces. He took his time, each white shred drifting slowly to the floor.

VIII

Bunch peered through the windshield, searching for the interstate exit ramp. Trucks ripped by, throwing sheets of gray water over his car. He drove slowly, the cars backing up behind him, their lights at his neck. A Corvette passed him with sounding horn. A van followed, fish-tailing on the slick road. Where, thought Bunch, could they be going? It was cold and dark for early October. There would be no sun that day. He wondered what could be at the end of the line. A place like Helmsville? A sourness gripped his chest. Move as fast as you can, no matter where you end up, he thought.

He remembered a vacation, years before, with Jane and the children. A trip in August to the beach. The hatred was hardening then. It was past the festering stage. One hundred degrees by noon. The car's air-conditioning broke down. The kids screamed and the heat rose from the highway. He was hung-over, and every time he passed a car he pulled a bottle from beneath the seat. A cop spotted him in a town down near the coast, and he spent the night in jail. After the night in jail, she would not speak to him, at least directly. Instead, she spoke about him, to the children: "Your *father* is a drunk. Did you know that? Your *father* is wasting his life, and *mine*, and *yours*. Let's hope your father can stay out of jail so that the rest of the vacation won't be *ruined*."

It rained throughout the vacation. It rained as he hit her hard across the mouth as she boiled shrimp in the tiny kitchen of the beach cottage. The shrimp cooked to tiny, hard knots. Jane took the car and the children and hid from him. He stayed alone in the cottage for three days. When he was drunk, which was usually by eleven in the morning, he tried to find them. He made long distance calls. He searched the motels. His shoes rotted in the rain and steam of Myrtle Beach.

He turned left onto Charlie Justice Boulevard. The ass end of the city, he thought. No man's land. It had once been the main east-west highway, until the interstate pushed through. He passed an abandoned motel and an ancient, burned-out tourist court. A biker bar. A black club named The Third World Lounge. There were a couple of army surplus stores, a pool hall, and a battered, still-functioning old time market. The Helmsville abattoir was opening for the morning shift, and even in the rain Bunch caught a whiff of blood and offal.

The gay bars—The Brothers Club, and Wayne's—sat across the road from each other. As Bunch passed Wayne's, he tooted the horn. A large man, over six-three and wearing a dress, was engaged in a feverish conversation with a short, Mickey Rooney-type. They gaped at Bunch and turned once more on each other.

Half a mile or so beyond the bars and the abattoir, he saw what he had come for: Brenda's Health and Relaxation Center. All female staff. Open twenty-four hours. He pulled in behind the doublewide trailer.

"Well, Mr. Fitzgerald. Come on in. I ain't seen you for a long time."

"Hello, Brandy."

The employees of Brenda's Health and Relaxation Center knew Bunch as F. Scott Fitzgerald. They suspected that Fitzgerald was not his real name, but they were in the business of letting men be who they wished to be. At birth they had not been named Brandy, April, Angel, Dominique, Melinda or Valerie.

Brandy, forty-something, but still holding up, wore a pair of black, skin-tight jeans and a see-through pink blouse. Her hair was chiseled into a brassy column, like a photograph of a volcano's plume. Classy, Bunch thought. Marinates in perfume. Just right for me. The sourness did not recede, but there was something else besides. Bands tightened across his forehead, chest, and crotch.

Bunch followed her down a narrow hall to an eight by six foot cubicle. Centerfolds from *Playboy* and *Hustler* plastered the walls and ceiling. In a corner was a mattress and night stand. In another corner was a kitchen chair. The light in the cubicle was low and blue. The rain dashed like shotgun pellets on the metal roof. Brandy closed the door and rubbed against him.

"You're either up early or out late," she said.

"Yeah."

She thrust her tongue into his ear.

"You taste good today." Her hand went to the front of his pants.

"I guess you want the usual," she said.

"Yeah. The usual." What's so usual about it, he thought.

"You want to get comfortable?"

Bunch loosened his tie.

"Baby, ain't you forgetting something," Brandy said.

Bunch pulled his wallet from the jacket he had flung on the chair. He handed her two twenties.

"I thought maybe you'd let me have it one time for love," he said as he unbuckled his belt. Brandy cackled. A sputtering yawp.

"Mr. Fitzgerald, all the girls say you're the funniest customer we have. Don't go away now. I'll be right back." She smiled as she closed the door.

He lay on his back, filling the narrow mattress. Somewhere in the trailer a woman sang a song about her husband coming home with honey on his hands. The rain fell harder. Time, he thought, freezes. He saw himself on the mattress like a man in a coffin, cold in the blue light, his belly standing higher than his penis. Brandy returned and bolted the door. She folded her clothes neatly and laid them across the back of the chair. She kept her back to Bunch as she stepped out of her panties. Her ass sagged a little with age and wear, but it was still good. She turned toward Bunch and his eyes traveled down her body. A purple panther head, with barred white fangs and a blood red mouth was tattooed on her left, inner thigh. She dropped onto the mattress. Their faces were inches apart. Her breath, a mixture of cigarettes and cinnamon gum, hung in the air. She wrapped a leg across his belly.

"That's some tattoo, Brandy. It really looks good in this light." She slowly kneaded his body.

"Another customer said it seemed almost alive. That he could almost hear it roar. Some men don't want a tattooed woman, but most like it. Next time, I'm getting an eagle on my rear end. You about ready?"

Her head moved over him. The bands slackened and the sourness disappeared. Bunch knew that both would return. He closed his eyes and listened to the rain.

Bunch eased the car up the hill. He had been thinking of appointments during his cross town trip to the Fite's house. They were, he decided, the most useful of life's measuring devices. An appointment with Miss Brandy.

An appointment with Charles Fite. An appointment with Dr. Roland Pffippert. Six appointments could equal one day. Thirty appointments per week. A way to replace the clock.

He spotted the house. It teetered on the hill as if it were about to slide down into the Power House Church, or else ascend into the heavens. He parked the car beside a rain swollen ditch. On the front porch he shivered like a sick bear and knocked loudly. Something was on the other side of the door: electronic noises, shouts, squeals. He banged again. The wind whipped about him. Rain blew down his neck and into his shoes. The door knob turned.

The smell came out to meet him; a mixture of human grease, animal waste, smoke, old food, and alcohol—all riding on moist, thick air. With an involuntary reflex, he jerked his head away. When he turned back to the door, Tinka Fite motioned him in. Her face was heavily and inexpertly made-up, as if the make-up had been applied with a broom. Her smile made Bunch dizzy; a face in a dream had followed him out of his sleep into the sopping world.

"We was just fellowshipping a little. Been fellowshipping all night, and yesterday, and the day before. Seems like fellowshipping is all we been doing lately."

She stepped aside to let him pass into the house. He hesitated. I could go home, he thought, and go to bed. I could go to the office. I could go back to Brandy. I could even go out to the abattoir. Dread wiggled up his spine and turned the key on the bands.

In the front room, the only light came from the television set. Figures were spread out through the blue-gray dimness, the heads outlines against the glowing screen, the limbs cocked at broken angles as if tangled with each other. He almost laughed as he thought of one person with five arms. Two people sharing a single leg. All crammed into Charles and Tinka Fite's living room.

Basic self-protection told Bunch that laughter, at this moment, would be highly inappropriate.

Some of them squatted at Bunch's feet. The couch sagged with their weight. A monkey began to climb his leg. For a moment, Bunch did not know what it was. He imagined a new kind of infant, conceived in the house on a slick clay hill. A thing with the same gestation period as a dog, a hyena, a ferret. Bunch shook it from his leg and kicked at it, sending it bounding into the deep darkness that began just beyond the television. As it scampered away, he saw that it was a monkey, one of the chimps he had seen on the street with Charles. From the direction of the couch, came a low, drawling voice.

"Don't hurt the precious spirit. Charles says it came out of the sky and the earth and outta each of us. He says we got to be good to them. Better than we got treated. . ."

"All right," said another, deeper voice.

Bunch, squinting into the room, saw his client. Charles sat in a lawn chair raised above the floor on a platform of cinder blocks. Charles stroked the monkey that Bunch had kicked.

"Luther is right. Course he's right cause I told him about it."

The others nodded, murmuring. Bunch, his eyes accustomed to the room, could see them all. A couple of fat women, their faces smeared like Tinka's. Two men in baseball caps and plastic jackets. An old man stretched out in front of the television, his mouth opened in a snore. A younger woman, perhaps even pretty, sat with her arms pressed tightly across her chest, her body stiff, expectant, perched on the edge of a chair, leaning toward Charles. Two young men sat at his feet. One of them, shirtless, passed a liquor bottle up to Charles. The monkey leaped from Charles' lap and squatted upon the chest of the old man. Charles drank deeply.

"Charles, who are these people?" Bunch asked.

Charles' eyes narrowed. Bunch realized that questions could be a major mistake. He wondered if Charles could make the others turn on him: clawing, biting. Tinka and the fat women would do it. They could feed on me all day, he thought. A holiday feast. Another good newspaper story: LOCAL ATTORNEY DEVOURED AT CLIENT'S ORDER. Bunch felt their eyes. He tried to remember how far it was to the door. He saw himself being pulled down, twisting, bellowing. The television crackled. The old man groaned.

"These people," began Charles, "are the ones who *know*. They're the only people in the *world* who *know*."

The shirtless boy looked up at Bunch.

"There ain't nothing better than fellowshipping," the boy said.

Bunch took a couple of steps backwards. The floor creaked. Tinka fried meat in the kitchen. Charles climbed down from the lawn chair. He stood close enough for Bunch to feel the heat that came out of him. Bunch was surprised. There was no smell. Neutral.

"Fellowshipping is just a word. But we got to have some words. Got to be able to name things. Fellowshipping is doing what we want—together. Without nobody saying we wrong. Saying that we got to stop."

Charles reached down and ran his hands through the long hair of the shirtless boy.

"He knows what the spirit is. He's seen it. Lived with it. He's walked with me."

Troy spoke in a breathless rush, the words tumbling over each other.

"Spirit came down not like what others say the river people used to ask things that don't matter no more what they said made me feel bad grab a neck but a window wreck a car real fast don't worry now. . ."

The boy stopped. Charles patted him on the shoulder.

"See? Do you know that none of these people knowed

how to do what they wanted? They was knotted up tight. Now we all say and do. Say and do. I'm their guide. That's all. I'm not wanting a vote. I'm not wanting a prize. I want to do what they want to do. We been getting used to the idea of it. Been practicing for the way things gonna be forever."

Bunch tried to imagine all the things they had done. All he could think of was a bucket of eels.

". . . touching is part of it. We touched each other everywhere we could. When we started out, some of us didn't like it. At first Troy didn't want us to touch Darren. Wanda didn't want to touch Tinka. But after a while we wanted to. All our lives, somebody said no. Said I couldn't walk. Said me and Wanda and Tinka couldn't be naked in the same bed. Did they know us? Had people like us ever even been a face to them that runs the world?"

Bunch slowly shook his head and hoped he seemed sincere.

". . . and Marcelline thought about being fat. That's all she could think about. When she seen the precious spirits, she claimed they made her sick. But she started to hold them, to kiss them. And then she knew they was part of her. She used to be afraid. Afraid the world was a big laughing mouth. Afraid of quick things with fur. That old fear is gone. . ."

The monkeys nestled against Marcelline's big, spongy breasts. She cooed and slowly stroked them.

". . . we all live here. Nobody wants to go back to their old homes. Their people didn't treat them right. We get telephone calls. Eight, ten a day. It's the same thing. Tinka's momma. She cries, but Tinka won't go to the phone. Says she don't need her momma no more. That if her momma loved her, she wouldn't have to do what she thought somebody else wanted her to do. . ."

Bunch saw what it looked like, how it sounded. The touching. The leaping shadows. Shouts.

". . . and, Mr. Bunch, we know why you're here. I'm ready to go to the head doctor. . ."

Charles was through the door before Bunch knew he was gone. The others followed, spilling onto the porch. Bunch bolted by them to the car.

Charles stood in the yard by a concrete bird bath. Bunch ran through the rain. As he started the car, he saw Charles speaking, gesturing, to the others. Bunch rolled down the window, but could only understand a few words.

". . . spirit. . . we'll some day know the blood. . . Don't fellowship until I get back. . ."

They sang. Bunch stuck his head out of the window to be sure of the song. Charles climbed into the car. The car moved slowly down the hill. The singing receded behind it.

"Charles, how come they're singing an old McDonald's jingle?"

"It came to me on the Second Great Day."

Neither spoke again until they reached Pffippert's office.

Bunch had doubts about leaving Charles alone in the waiting room, but it was empty of patients and the receptionist, a blond in a tight nurse's outfit, seemed secure behind the glass cage that surrounded her desk. Charles sat erect, his feet neatly placed together, his hands folded in his lap. The receptionist's voice was high and musical.

"Dr. Pffippert would like to speak to you—alone— Mr. Bunch. You can go back now if you like."

Bunch read her name tag: Tammy. She was new to the office; part of Pffippert's re-decoration scheme, Bunch guessed. She wiggled a bit in her chair, her left leg bobbing up and down. Nervous energy, thought Bunch. I've seen a load of nervous energy today.

Pffippert bent over a stainless steel panel that contained a couple of dozen gauges, switches, dials, and toggles. The panel was attached to a large black box. Wires led from the box to a chair. Attachments were scattered about the office: stethoscopes, suction cups, gleaming rods with more wires attached to them. Pffippert, busily fascinated, adjusted knobs and checked gauges.

"Jesus, what is that thing?" Bunch said as he came into the office.

"Why, Roy. I didn't even hear you." Pffippert said. "I guess I was absorbed with the Anthus Board. I spent the entire weekend putting it together."

Bunch sat down across the room from the Anthus Board. He did not want to get too close to it.

"What does it do? I mean, it looks like a Goddamned electric chair."

"Really, Roy. You could be a little more receptive to revolutionary techniques. In fact, the Anthus Board hooks into the office computer system. Measures any sort of response: conducts basic tests, checks pulse rate, pupil dilation, motor and voluntary reactions. And all the information is reproduced on a print-out."

Pffippert flipped a switch. Green and red lights flashed on the board. Pffippert turned a dial and a soothing hum filled the room. Pffippert adjusted the knob and the hum turned into a static clicking.

"He's out there," Bunch said.

Pffippert tugged at wires, connecting and reconnecting them.

"Your client? Did you know that I'm the first clinical psychologist in the state to operate an Anthus Board! I received a letter from Dr. Anthus himself. A brilliant man. Also plays the cello beautifully. I studied under him you know. At the Productive Living Institute. Do you realize that I will revolutionize mental health in Helmsville? I can double my patient load within a year. Read the brochure on my desk. It will explain the whole thing."

Bunch picked up a slick-papered, elaborately illustrated booklet from the desk. The cover depicted a young, California-casual couple standing on a windswept promontory. They held hands, the pounding Pacific spread at their feet. Without reading, Bunch tossed the brochure back on the desk.

"Roland, there's been some new developments. Things I didn't know about until today."

Pffippert started down the hall toward the waiting room. Bunch followed.

"Like what, Roy? Surely Mr. Fite hasn't recovered from his personality disorder?"

Bunch wanted to tell him about the smell, Marcelline, Tinka, and the fellowshipping. But why bother, he thought. He may even find out on his own.

Charles had not moved since Bunch left him, but as Pffippert approached, he bounded forward to meet him.

"Have you ever sold orange juice or cameras on television?" Charles asked.

He took Pffippert's arm and tested the flesh by squeezing.

"You tanned, too. Got pretty hair. You ever told people to stop smoking or to send money overseas to the poor?"

Pffippert backed off a couple of steps and announced his name. He asked Charles to come into his office. Charles followed, still questioning.

"Did you ever tell people that they should get a car with front-wheel drive? Do you know about the coming of the blood?"

Bunch watched them disappear down the hall. Tammy looked up from a copy of *People*.

"What was he saying? That Mr. Fite. He mumbled, too, while he was waiting. You know?"

She must have been a cheerleader, Bunch thought. Smooth and creamy. Nice to everybody. Probably has a bedroom full of stuffed animals.

"He's a troubled man. He has suffered. Terribly."

Tammy shook her head in sympathy. He imagined her at a fellowshipping session. Charles would touch her until his hands fell off. She sighed prettily.

"A shame. Hey, did you see *The Devil's Servant* on the cable last night? It's so scary. It was about the devil taking over a whole town. Really. And the devil got control of everybody's mind. I could hardly go to sleep after I saw it. My boyfriend Jimmy, I don't think he's afraid of anything, bench presses three hundred pounds, he laughed at me. But it wasn't funny to me. I dreamed about the devil and heads rolling down stairs and arms in refrigerators and everything. . ."

Bunch liked her blue eyes and her pert, round breasts. Jimmy probably liked them too. You bet, sugar-crotch. The devil's in the T.V. He's on the cable. He's sitting in the family room eating popcorn and watching the Cotton Bowl. He's having a Tequila Sunrise with the homecoming queen. He's driving a Mercedes to Las Vegas for the weekend with a beautiful, rich poet. Bunch splashed back to the car, leaving Tammy, Pffippert and Charles. All the way back to the office he thought about the devil.

The head doctor talked for awhile about tests and getting to know and understand each other. None of it made much sense to Charles, so he stopped listening. The head doctor would pause every couple of minutes, as if he were waiting for an answer. Charles never spoke, but the head doctor went right on about understanding and being in touch with yourself. After that, Charles had to look at some pictures that did not make sense; just blobs on cardboard. The head doctor went through a couple of dozen before he gave up. Then he made Charles take another test; he had to mark five hundred little blocks on a piece of paper. Charles scratched the sheet with a pencil without reading the questions and finished in five minutes. He wondered what was going on back at the house; he would find out if any fellowshipping had been done while he was gone. He realized too that he had been fooled by the way the head doctor looked; Charles had thought that he was a T.V. man when he first saw him, the first real one he had ever met. It was possible, he knew, for a person to be a head doctor and a T.V. man at the same time. There were many such people. But no real T.V. man would ask him to take tests and answer dumb questions. It was Bunch's fault; only Bunch would expect him to put up with a fake T.V. man. He subtracted money from Bunch's share of the case, then wondered if it was right to do so. Bunch had been picked, too, before the Second Great Day. I don't know everything yet, he thought. Ninety-nine percent. He figured Bunch was in the one percent that was yet to be learned.

Once the tests were finished, Charles had a chance to study the office. He had never been in such a room. He realized that the head doctor must make a lot of money, or else was a winner on a quiz show. He decided that the head doctor wasn't so dumb after all. He remembered a couple of things from his past. They were in the one percent, too, he thought. There was the smartest boy in the fifth grade. He could name the capitals of all the states and the teacher had given him a mechanical pencil as a prize. He had once seen a man at a pool hall who could do card tricks; he won bets. Someone picked a card, and, without seeing it, the man could name the suit and value. Charles saw him win fifty dollars that way. And he did not even look smart; he was only a dried up, ugly old man with no teeth. The head doctor, he thought, must be smarter than that. Then it came to him; those tests had only been tricks, like when Monte Hall used to fool people in kangaroo suits into picking the wrong curtain.

"Tell me," began Pffippert, "about your parents."

He saw his father's wonderful dance again. His mother had cooked and prayed and cried sometimes. They were big and told him he couldn't do things.

"Daddy knew the dance. Momma died in the kitchen. Fixing beans. She had the cancer. Went right on fixing beans and cornbread every day. Been a long time."

Pffippert wrote down his answers in a small black notebook.

"Did they do anything bad to you, anything to make you not love them?"

Charles decided that he had been wrong about the tricks. The head doctor didn't really know any. The questions went on. Charles answered automatically, without interest. There did not seem to be any point to it. He thought of the others again, and wondered if they had dared to fellowship while he was away, if they had dared to disobey the blood. He imagined punishments for them. He would make Troy and Darren kneel on tacks and broken glass.

The head doctor questioned him about his marriage, his schooling, the place where he grew up. Charles felt dull and lifeless. He slowly realized that the head doctor's trick was to drain him; to take it all out; the voice, the power, to twist his legs once more. He debated whether or not he should run from the office before he became crippled again. He looked around the office and fixed upon the cockateels. Pffippert stopped writing.

"Do you admire my birds?"

"They in a cage."

"You don't approve of cages?"

"In a cage a thing can't breathe. Can't move."

"Would you feel better if I let them out?"

Pffippert opened the cage door. Tentatively, the birds edged their way to the opening. One flew to the top of a bookcase. The other fluttered back and forth across the room. Charles followed its flight until it lighted upon Pffippert's shoulder.

"You sure you never been on T.V.?" Charles asked.

"Positive. Most people know when they've been on T.V."

Charles could not decide if he was right. But he plainly saw that the head doctor only faked being rich so he could fool him and take away the blood and the power. If a person had enough money, he could be on television. In fact, once the money was gained, that would be the first thing any sensible person would do. Of course, those who were not rich were sometimes allowed on television. But most of these people were foreigners in wars, or else Americans who were accused of murder, or had been in train wrecks or plane crashes, or had some incurable or unusual disease. Often they were dead, piled up in mounds, or sprawled out beside flaming pieces of machinery. No, if a man was as rich as the head doctor pretended to be, he would have his own show. Charles decided to see if he could fool him.

"How do you know that we're not on T.V? Right now?" Charles asked.

Pffippert stroked the bird.

"There are no cameras here. No lights. No technicians. T.V. doesn't simply operate by itself."

Charles knew that this was a lie, but something had started to happen which was more important. It always came back to him when he needed it most. The blood moved again. He was no longer drained.

"Let's get back to the cages," said Pffippert.

"I freed the precious spirits from the cage by the river."

As the power and blood returned, Charles began to like the questions.

"And these spirits appear to you?" Pffippert said.

"You can come down to my house and see them. They're real pretty. There's three of them. All of them got fur and they run and climb anywhere they want. They live with me."

Pffippert stopped writing. He seemed to be thinking, his pen poised above the page.

"Mr. Bunch said they were monkeys."

"Bunch! He don't know nothing. They might *look* like monkeys. Oh yes. But you got to see. They're more than monkeys."

"Yes. Of course," interrupted Pffippert. "I understand. Let's go back to the cages. I can see that you don't like cages because they take away freedom. . ."

Charles still brooded over what Bunch had told the head doctor.

"Bunch. Now he wouldn't know that he's in a cage. People got cages, too, sitting in a cage and somebody throws shit and rotten food through the bars. My legs was a cage until the voice came to me. After that, I freed the precious spirits from their cage."

Pffippert turned on a tape recorder. Charles beamed. It was almost like being on television.

"Tinka got caged by the Power House Church. Believed everything the preacher said. Talking about Jesus all the time. Jesus is a cage put over everybody. She thought he was salvation. That's a cage, too. She believed in it. She wouldn't do what she wanted to do."

"She wanted to fuck, and paint up her face like a whore. She wanted to fuck men, women. She ain't had a chance to fuck a child yet. She tried to fuck the precious spirits, but it wouldn't work. They's too small. She tried and tried. Right there in the front room with all of us helping her. When it wouldn't work, she cried. Had to beat her just to shut her up. Someday, when we get us a bigger precious spirit, she's gonna do it. . ."

He spoke to the recorder, barely aware of the head doctor.

". . . and Luther was caged because he was by himself all the time. Now he says that life ain't ever been better. He drinks liquor all the time. We all drink. We all take dope. Darren and Troy get it for us. We ain't got a thing against dope. We ain't no *church*. Saying can't do this, can't do that. Like it used to be with Wanda. She loves it with us. Her husband caged her. Left her alone all the time with baby shit on the bed. She's going to get them kids. Gonna raise them up with a *real* family. . ."

"Charles, are you the father of this new family?"

Charles paused. He remembered the head doctor's tricks, but he was too strong now to be drained.

"I'm the daddy for all them that needs one."

The birds hopped back into their cages. The tape ran out. Pffippert closed the notebook.

"I think it's time for a little break."

A half hour later Pffippert plugged Charles into the Anthus Board. Pffippert sat behind the control panel. Electrodes were attached to Charles' wrists, temples, and chest. Wires criss-crossed the office. Charles locked into the power from within and without, as it circulated through him, from him, back into the machine.

"Now, Charles," began Pffippert, "when I ask you a question, I want you to give me the first answer that comes to mind."

"Home."

"No place."

"Woman."

"Gut."

"Man."

"Fool."

"Spirit."

"Dance."

"Touching."

"Blood."

Pffippert adjusted the knobs on the panel and made notations. He wet his lips and returned to his list of questions.

"God."

Charles laughed. The arrows on the dials waved. The print-out from the word processor spilled onto the floor and coiled like a gigantic white snake.

The Devil. Yes. Pffippert might even consider the possibility, Bunch thought. He wiped his mouth with a paper towel and put the plate on the coffee table. He had fixed a rare meal at home: quick fried cube steak and sliced tomatoes. He shook a cigarette out of the pack and watched the evening news. The President stood before a vast outdoor audience and said that everything was all right. That we no longer had to worry. Bunch sipped his bourbon and decided that the President had not looked in the right places.

When Bunch arrived to pick up Charles, the first thing he noticed was that Tammy was gone and that the couch in the waiting room had been turned over. Charles was quiet, sitting alone in a chair that looked like a vienna sausage. But Pffippert. His professional demeanor had been severely tested, perhaps the first such test ever. Pffippert was crying when Bunch arrived, standing amidst the white computer sheets and cockateel feathers. Pffippert could not speak at first, and when he did manage to put a sentence together he said something about Charles and the birds. Bunch asked him what Doctor Von Bey would have done in a similar situation, and Pffippert whined that Bunch was to get himself and his client out of the office. Bunch said he would call him next week.

So Bunch took Charles home through the autumn twilight. The house was as dark as in the morning, and noises still came from it. Bunch watched his client as he climbed the steps and opened the door. Cheers. Shouts of exultation. The door closed and the McDonald's jingle could clearly be heard.

The President went off the screen and was replaced by a laxative commercial. Bunch switched off the television and carried his plate into the kitchen. He deposited it in the sink with the rest of the dirty dishes. The phone rang.

"It ain't over," said the voice.

"No, Bobby," replied Bunch, "it isn't."

"You gonna be sorry some day."

"I'm sorry now."

"You gonna pay."

"When have I stopped paying?"

"You got a smart-ass answer for everything."

"No. I got questions. What do you think of the Devil?"
There was a long silence.

"Well? The Devil. What about him?" said Bunch.

"You trying to confuse me. But it ain't over."

"What ever is, you ignorant motherfucker?" Bunch slammed the receiver down. His hands shook. He poured more bourbon from a bottle on the counter, picked the receiver back up, and dialed Faye's number. Billy Junior answered.

"This is Uncle Roy. Are you feeling good?"

"Yes, Uncle Roy. When are you coming back over?"

"Soon. Oh soon. Billy, I'll bring you a football uniform. A brand new one."

"Really? Wait until I tell momma."

"Uh. . . Where is your momma?"

"She went out. Said she wouldn't be back until late."

"Tell her I called, will you?"

"Sure, Uncle Roy. When are you going to bring me the football uniform?"

"Soon. Everything happens real soon."

He sat down on the couch and tried not to think. But he couldn't stop himself. There was God and the Devil. There was Charles Fite and there was Goforth and Faye, and Trip Gant's boy arguing a summary judgment in a week. All this God and Devil business. I've never been able to tell the difference, so I never thought about it. He laughed to himself and lit another cigarette. Maybe Doctor Von Bey is right. But then that's just another answer, and nobody can really tell what the question is.

IX

Thurston "Ted" Cope came from a small town in the eastern end of the state. He had lived there all of his life except for time in school and the army. Occasionally, he had taken trips to larger, unsatisfactory places. He had not visited Helmsville in many years, but he expected to find little to approve of. There were many jackals there. He understood jackals and had fought them on many levels. He had practiced law for thirty years; he served as District Attorney in his empty, swampy county for twenty of those years. He had herded every jackal he could into prisons and reform schools, and onto death row. He prayed for their souls. In the morning he would begin to apply that vision on a larger scale than he had ever once imagined; he would begin his first day as Judge of the Superior Court of Darden County.

He registered at the Ramada Inn, ate dinner, and went to his room. Although it was early, he decided to change into pajamas and read before going to sleep.

Carefully, he placed his luminous blue suit on a wooden hanger and put on the purple silk monogrammed pajamas his wife had presented to him as a going-away present. Methodically, he brushed his teeth, working the bristles over the firm, pink tissue of his gums. He was a short, compact man with surprisingly broad shoulders. His hair was thick and shiny-white, and he was deeply tanned. At first glance, he appeared to be an ordinary, successful American—healthy, generous, with an honest, good-natured face.

He believed many things. He believed that communists had inspired and directed much that had transpired in America since the introduction of zoning ordinances. He believed in the existence of a conspiracy between Jews, Wall Street, the Rockefellers, and Moscow. He believed that bureaucrats had no right to tell the American people how to spend their money, raise their children, or where, when, or how to pray. He believed in the Bible (King James Version). He especially believed in true love, the cuteness of all children, and that sports taught young Americans valuable lessons about life. He believed that anyone who worked hard enough would be successful, and that anyone who took welfare money was a parasite. He believed that marriage was a sacred institution. He believed that foreigners did not actually have languages of their own. He believed in a firm handshake and a warm smile. He believed in sincerity. He was an American.

He knelt upon the gold shag carpet, beside the king size Serta posture-pedic bed, and prayed.

"Lord, tomorrow I become your judge. I will judge as did the good men of your book in ancient days. I will breathe the law and create irrevocable justice. Lord, it is right that you have given me this chance. I have long worked for decency. I have worked to stem the tide of jackal-dom and restore your will. Lord, the time of your promise is at hand. I thank you, and I know your thoughts are with me. Give me strength. Let your power work through me. I know, Lord, that there are great days ahead. That neither your work nor mine is yet done. I pray also for my wife Bitsy and my children, Bobby, Browning, Beatrice, Betsey, and Ted Junior. I ask this in the name of *your* son, Jesus Christ."

He settled into bed, his head propped upon two pillows. Praying usually soothed him, but his excitement was strong. For years, he had dreamed of being a judge as others dream of perpetual life and beauty. It would not have happened if he had failed in the Lord's work; if he had not labored to elect a decent man governor of the state; if he had not spent hundreds of hours organizing, planning, meeting with voters—the people—the real Americans who had suffered for years the sinister ways and crazed habits of the jackals. He tingled to think of it. Across the land, the people were rising. At the inauguration, he heard the governor's call to battle. Then, after the inaugural ball, came the governor's promise, rightfully earned.

He climbed from the bed and pulled a copy of the court docket from his briefcase. A murder trial, a rape sentencing, and an armed robbery were scheduled.

"Oh, boy," he said. Still, he would have to wait until the end of the week before he could get down to the real work. Mostly, the first few days would be spent reading files, motions, and pleadings. He had never enjoyed that part of the law, although he worked at it with diligence. It was not as much fun as trial work. And it often ended up confusing everyone and depriving the people of their due.

The only case set for the morning was a hearing on a motion for a summary judgment: *Fite vs. Loomis Trucking and Freight Company.* Civil law never appealed to him. *Fite vs. Loomis Trucking and Freight Company* would give him a chance, however, to size up the local lawyers. The case, his old torts professor had told him, is an extension of the man who argues it. Judge the man and you have gone halfway judging the case. T. Thurston "Ted" Cope nodded vigorously as he recalled the axiom uttered years before in a dusty lecture hall. He remembered almost everything that he had ever heard.

He yawned and slipped the docket back into his brief-case. Back in bed, he opened a book by Roy Rogers and Dale Evans on the joys of being a grandparent. He read a couple of pages, agreeing with Roy and Dale about the need for love and discipline, before he fell asleep.

Bunch let the telephone ring a dozen times before he hung up. He had tried for a week to reach Charles. He sent a letter, but expected no reply. Bunch yawned and lit a cigarette. It was nearly eight. Court would start in an hour and he would find out if *Fite vs. Loomis Trucking and Freight Company* had any life left to it. If Charles was alive, he thought. Such things happen every minute. Bunch pictured Charles in a forgotten spot; like a squirrel struck by a car. It would take a long time for anyone to notice. He could be in the river; or in a plastic bag at the dump in a pile of weeds and broken bottles. People were often found in such places. No one much cared. A man bleeds and wheezes while his neighbors in the next room turn up the stereo and dance.

It was a cool Monday morning. Bunch had spent the weekend alternating between preparing his arguments for the summary judgment and thinking of those bodies lost beside the highway; and of doomed men straining toward dirty windows for a last glimpse of the sky. It had occurred to him on Saturday afternoon, as he listened to his own breathing, the ticking of the desk clock, and the sparse traffic on Broad Street, that he was forty-three years old and that he might be closer to an end than a beginning. Some, he thought, lived to be a hundred and fifty. Whole towns in Russia eat raw wheat and drink goat's milk and can remember the last Czar's imperial progress through the province. They must, decided Bunch, keep it simple; no measurement of power, no contests, no ideas.

He thought also of his chances in court. He had never won a summary judgment. His clients were unlucky and careless. There were the slip and fall cases—fat men busting their asses on wet, slick floors. Violations of implied warranty—punks buy used cars; the engines fall out when the punks drive off the lot. Then there was the riding lawn mower that ran wild. Products. Many have faith in products—part of their expectation that they will not have to confront the unexpected. Charles does not want a car, or a boat, or a food processor. He wants to be God. And others want him to be God.

Bunch had called Pffippert on Friday and found him fully recovered from Charles' visit. Pffippert told him that the birds were fine, that the damage to the office was minimal, and that Tammy had gotten over her initial terror. Pffippert had decided that Charles presented a wonderful chance to prove the worth of the Anthus Board. Yes, indeed, Bunch thought. The Anthus Board must come with a terrific warranty.

Bunch read the name at the top of the docket. T. Thurston Cope. Bunch decided he needed to find out about the new judge.

Ed Snavely's office was two doors down. The door was open, the reception room empty of furniture. In the inner office, Snavely sat on the floor arranging and rearranging Bic pens into geometrical patterns. Bunch turned to leave, feeling like a man who has intruded upon a neighbor in a ludicrous, obscene posture. Too late. Snavely spotted him.

"Roy Bunch. Come in."

Snavely motioned for Bunch to take a seat on the floor. He sounded the same as always, genial, professionally cheerful. He was a large, basset-like man. With his thin hair combed back, his glen plaid pants and blue blazer, he looked like a sportscaster. As Bunch sat down, Snavely returned to his pens.

"Uh, Ed. What can you tell me about this new judge?"

"Ted Cope? A fine man. Very active in the last election. I don't know him personally, but everyone says that he'll do a wonderful job."

Bunch decided that the visit was a waste of time. Snavely never had a bad word for anyone with a title or more money. And there was something wrong with Snavely. Even more than usual.

"How is he in the courtroom? I mean is he tough to deal with? I got to be up in front of him at nine."

Snavely formed a trapezoid and smiled.

"Oh. He's new. First day out. But a fine man. Very moral. Clean living. Highly successful."

More wasted time, Bunch thought. He risked one more question.

"Say, Ed. Are you giving up on the old building? I heard there's some nice offices on Highland Street."

Snavely formed a pair of isosceles triangles. He spoke as if a tremendous pressure was forcing every word from him. The geniality half dissolved.

"Moving. Yes. I'm giving up."

"The law?"

"Yes."

"What will you do if you don't practice?"

"I'm leaving town. I can't stand it here anymore. Why. . . Helmsville is falling apart."

His eyes went cold and Bunch raised himself into a half squat, ready to spring and run.

"I never liked you, Bunch. I'll bet you thought I did. Didn't you? Everybody says 'old Ed. He's easy to get along with. He's got a smile for the whole world.' And you. This used to be a fine town until the day you set foot in it. You're. . . you're *negative!*"

Bunch ascended from the half-squat. Whatever had

happened to Snavely is contagious, he thought. Snavely subsided.

"Please. I apologize. You're the first person that's even come by for a visit since we decided to move. And you're not even a friend."

"Where are you going?" Bunch asked.

"To California. For awhile. My daughter, she lives there in an alternative community."

Bunch remained standing. Snavely's words poured out, the sound of a man no one had ever listened to.

"Dixie Anne and I decided that we should be near her. She is there with. . . this person she met while in therapy in Asheville. And while Dixie Anne and I have accepted. . . this relationship, we feel that we should be near her to help her *rationally*, and I emphasize *rationally*, with her problems. Stacy is exploring her options. That's what she calls it. Exploring her options. This person is not an American. The person she lives with in this. . . ah. . . alternative community. What do you think that means? Alternative community?"

Bunch shrugged. Snavely did not wait for an answer.

"I used to be respected around here. And now. . . and now. . . there's no reason to stay anymore. I'd advise you to get out. I don't know you very well. Haven't wanted to. . . But I do know there's no good reason for staying."

He paused to search for words. Bunch edged part of the way into the outer office. Snavely started up again.

"Dixie Anne and I sank most of our money into a Winnebago. With what's left we can live for six months. After that, I'm not going to think about Stacy or Dixie Anne, or foreigners, or alternative communities, or what I'm supposed to think about. Fuck it. Excuse me. I don't usually use profanity."

Bunch reached the door of the outer office. Snavely went back to his pens.

As he walked to the courthouse, Bunch thought of Ed. He thought of Charles, too. And of getting out. He could

see the road Ed was pointed toward. Whether it led out
of Helmsville or another city, whether it went north,
south, east, or west, it must surely be wide enough to
accommodate a multitude.

Raymer, the bailiff, exhibited his fast draw technique
to the new, good-looking court reporter.

"Split-second timing."

He whipped out his service revolver and crouched low.
The reporter giggled and crossed her legs.

"You oughta see me in my cowboy hat and chaps. I'm
mean."

Bunch spread his notes across the table.

"Hey, Raymer," he called.

Raymer paused in mid-draw.

"Don't call out to a man who's pulling his piece. Anything can happen."

Bunch stayed behind him, away from the muzzle.

"Where's the judge?"

Raymer holstered his thirty-eight and motioned toward the far side of the room.

"You ain't gonna get to bullshit this one. Can tell you
that up front. He ain't the type. You can go on back to
his chambers and get a look at him if you want to."

"What do you mean, look at him?"

"He's praying. Down on his knees. Been that way for
an hour. Left the door open so everybody could see. I
believe he spoke in tongues a couple of times. Go on
back there. It's a sight. All the boys from the Public
Defender's Office have been by."

"So the new judge maintains constant contact with a
higher authority. Think I'll get along with him?"

Raymer raised an eyebrow. He was a stumpy man
with a broken face who supported two ex-wives and five
children.

"What a dumb fucking question," he answered.

Raymer returned to the court reporter.

"You wanta see me twirl it?" he asked.

Bunch scanned Woodside's argument and answer one more time. Nothing unusual. I would probably say the same thing, Bunch thought. Damages too remote. Mental suffering did not spring from the accident itself. The clock above the bench said nine sharp.

The reporter uncrossed her legs. The clerk of court, a pumpkin-shaped woman, swallowed the last of a Snickers. Raymer stopped twirling his thirty-eight and called the court to order.

"All rise. Oyezz, oyezz, oyezz. The Superior Court is now in session for the county of Darden, the Honorable T. Thurston Cope presiding. All who have business come and be heard. God save this court and the great state of North Carolina."

Cope swept into the room, his new robe rustling. He motioned for all to be seated. He beamed, his smile a searchlight.

"Welcome," began T. Thurston Cope, "to a new day in Darden County. I want to tell you all that I will run an open, decent court. I love justice. I love truth. And I think you will agree with me when I say that these are the only standards worth applying. The jackals will not be given a full rein in my courtroom."

"Jackals," Bunch repeated to himself. Raymer tried to catch his eye, but Bunch refused to respond.

Judge Cope nodded to the clerk of court. She called the case in the high, sweet voice of a Baptist soprano.

"87 CVD 1241, *Charles Junior Fite and Tinka Arndt Fite versus Loomis Trucking and Freight Company.* Motion for partial summary judgment on the part of the defendant, Loomis Trucking and Freight Company."

At least, thought Bunch, I didn't have to bring Charles and his crowd along. He glanced at the empty defense table. Woodside will show in a minute, he told himself. Shining like a goddamned new penny. Spewing forth the law in a gracious and civilized manner.

Ten minutes passed. Judge Cope still beamed. The reporter picked at her nails. The clerk fussed with her hair. Raymer caressed the checkered grip of his thirty-eight. Bunch craned his neck every minute or so, checking the scarred brown doors at the back of the courtroom. At nine-thirty, the judge spoke again.

"This is unusual. It appears we have only one attorney present for the hearing. Traditionally, two attorneys are needed for this kind of proceeding."

He checked the others for assent. Bunch nodded with vigor. The judge went on. Bunch thought he sounded like Ozzie Nelson.

"You need two attorneys. Except perhaps in those cases involving jackals, such as murder, sexual crimes, armed robbery, and the like. I have my own theories on representation in those types of cases. Which I need not get into here. You do, however, have an idea what I mean?"

Bunch nodded again. I do, he thought. You bet I do. Judge Cope picked up his copy of the pleadings.

"It says here that the defendant's attorney of record is Mr. Ashley Woodside. Now I've read the complaint and answer and the motions and I think if Mr. Woodside were here, we could just go ahead and have the arguments. But he's not. And it's after nine-thirty. . ."

The brown doors opened. Bunch turned and saw a blue suit, a pair of handmade English shoes, and a striped regimental tie hurry toward the defense table.

"You must be Mr. Woodside," said Judge Cope.

The blue suit nodded.

"Yes, Your Honor. And I would like to begin by apologizing for being late. I mean no disrespect to the court. . ."

Bunch could see that the judge was lapping it up. Respect, he thought. I'll still respect you in the morning.

". . . I was playing racquetball with Trip. . . he's my boss, Mr. Gant. . . over at the Metropolitan Club. We play every morning. . ."

Judge Cope raised his hand. Woodside paused.

"Trip Gant? Why, he's one of the greatest athletes in the history of the state! One of the most gifted running backs Carolina ever had. Perhaps, Mr. Woodside, you're too young to remember the great mystery that surrounded Mr. Gant in his senior year. He did not play against Duke. I'll never forget that game. The crowd chanting 'Trip, Trip, Trip, Trip!' But he never came off the bench. Didn't even suit up. I've heard that he's a first-rate attorney. And you're one of his associates?"

Woodside fingered his Phi Beta Kappa key.

"Yes, Your Honor. I have that privilege."

"You must feel very fortunate working for such a man. Please continue."

"Very fortunate, Your Honor. As I was saying, we were playing racquetball. We play every morning. You feel great the rest of the day. And we'd each won three games. I almost never beat him. He's first in the city, you know. Anyway, we started the seventh game, and when it was tied at twenty I said to myself, why I've got to get to the courthouse. So I showered and dressed. And wouldn't you know it? My BMW wouldn't start. And I just had it tuned!"

Woodside shrugged helplessly, like a presidential aide who had just misspoken himself. Judge Cope furrowed his brow. When he spoke he sounded like a father explaining to his son why he must go to bed without dinner.

"Yes, Mr. Woodside. I've observed that many things we once took for granted aren't as reliable as they once were. Mechanics. Public servants. And young attorneys. And at the very threshold of your career. A shame. It could have been so easily avoided."

Woodside leaned forward, rapidly jiggling his Phi Beta Kappa key. To Bunch, he seemed frozen, like a man opening curtains to find a wrecking ball at the window.

"Ah. . . may I ask the court for. . . clarification?" Woodside stammered.

"I'm getting to that, Mr. Woodside. I'm going to allow you to argue today, but I'm also going to issue a contempt citation and a warrant for your arrest. Rules, Mr. Woodside. We must observe them or we will turn into jackals. God does not want us to be jackals. God wants us to be on time, and decent, and orderly. It is my experience that many are born jackals. Others, by small omissions that grow larger through carelessness, are transformed into jackals. You would not want that to happen, now would you? Can you see that I'm doing you a favor?"

Woodside sank into a chair. Judge Cope turned bright and cheery again.

"Ready to proceed, Mr. Woodside?"

Bunch contemplated the jackals. It was possible for a man to turn without even knowing. The whole of Darden county would be on all fours by morning. Jackals and devils and precious spirits. Bunch decided he must be careful. When Cope turns to me, he thought, he will see my ears come to points. Like Bela Lugosi in *The Island of Lost Souls.*

"Your Honor," choked Woodside. "I'd like a short recess."

Judge Cope switched from geniality to contemplation.

"This court has been waiting for you for over half an hour. However, under the circumstances, I think five minutes won't hurt."

Woodside shuffled over to the plaintiff's table. He moved like an old man.

"Ashley. Please. Have a seat," Bunch said.

"This won't take but a minute, Bunch." Woodside sounded broken inside.

"Trip won't like this. He won't like it at all. Why don't we go ahead and settle. I can get three thousand."

"Well, Ashley, I'll tell you how it is. My clients feel

that they have a pretty good case. They need the money. For philanthropic reasons. For their cause."

"I'll make it four. I can get away with four. I've got to settle. This guy hates me. Come on. Do you really want to try this thing in front of him? Contempt of court! He's crazy!"

Bunch took the cue. He raised his voice to a shout.

"CRAZY! WHY I THINK HE'S THE FINEST JUDGE WE'VE HAD IN THIS COUNTY IN TWENTY YEARS!"

Judge Cope, who had been silently praying, jerked his eyes open. Bunch turned his back on Woodside and pretended to read his notes. Woodside scurried back to the defense table. Bunch glanced toward the bench. A new expression emanated from the bench; righteous retribution. Judge Cope sniffed. Smelling jackals, Bunch thought.

"Mr. Woodside, you may begin. I will remind you, however, that no matter what you think of me, I still represent the court. And in that capacity, I can fine and punish, as I've already made clear."

Woodside mumbled out an acknowledgment. A rough day for the kid, Bunch thought.

Woodside spoke for ten minutes. Bunch listened to the first few words. Ah, tautology. The soul of the lawyer's art. We believe because we believe. Give me the gold ring because I've asked for it.

Woodside rattled off a list of case names, most of them much newer than those relied upon by Bunch, and which stated that precedent shows that a plaintiff's damages must bear a direct connection with the injury suffered. He closed by saying that the mental condition of Charles Fite could in no way be imputed to the automobile accident of the previous August.

Woodside sat down and stared at the table. A model of courtroom oratory, Bunch thought. Sounds like it came off a Goddamned computer.

Bunch lunged from his chair. Fuck the case law, he told himself. I'm going right for the judge's soul on this one.

"Your Honor, I see no need to cover all the cases that I've cited in the plaintiff's briefs. The law is, and should be, unsettled on the question as to what injury, physical or mental, may arise from negligence. In our state, mental suffering has been the end result of all manner of accidents, catastrophes, and disasters that can be caused by uncaring, even uncivilized, behavior. This we know. My point, Your Honor, is that my clients deserve, indeed they cry out, for a fair chance to be judged by their peers."

Finding a jury of their peers, thought Bunch, might involve shaking down every fucking mental ward in the state.

"That is why it is important, Your Honor, that this case go before a jury; that those points concerning the mental suffering inflicted upon Mr. Charles Fite not be merely swept aside because of the technical and oratorical brilliance of Mr. Woodside. . ."

He paused to catch his breath. What bullshit. Where do I go from here?

". . . but that the facts and ultimate conclusions of this case should receive a fair and open hearing in this court."

Bunch peered into Judge Cope's eyes. They were deep and brown, like a puppy's. Bunch reached forth his hands in a gesture of supplication. This is shameless, he thought.

"Your Honor, may I say a few words about Charles and Tinka Fite?"

Woodside stirred from his stupor. He rose to object.

"Your Honor, this is irregular. Motions for summary judgment are confined to the law, not the character and personality of the litigants."

Woodside wanted to say more, but Judge Cope raised his hand.

"Objection denied, Mr. Woodside. What is heard here is at my discretion. Read your rules of civil procedure."

Bunch felt the benevolent heat from the bench.

"Judge Cope, Charles and Tinka Arndt Fite are plain people, poor people. They are without education. They do not have rich families. They could not afford to hire an expensive, capable law firm such as Mr. Woodside is associated with. I am a poor man myself."

Mendacious. Keep it mendacious, thought Bunch.

"Your Honor, Charles and Tinka Fite are, if you will, symbolic of the millions of our fellow citizens who come before the courts of our land each year. They do not come expecting handouts. They do not come expecting the court to *give* them *anything*. They come only with the humble expectation of receiving a hearing, and having the results of that hearing judged by people like themselves: good, decent, honest citizens. Citizens, I might add, to borrow a term of yours, your honor, who would never stoop to running with jackals."

Bunch lowered his arms. The judge stared intently at him. Bunch spoke in a subdued, thoughtful tone.

"As Mr. Woodside pointed out, and as you have read yourself, the question of mental suffering in negligence is one of remoteness in relation to the harm suffered. Charles Fite, if he was present today, could tell you that there is nothing remote about the agony, about the affliction which he has borne since the accident of last August. Mere words cannot begin to tell what he has gone through."

At last, thought Bunch, a bit of truth does come out.

Woodside started to raise an objection but Judge Cope silenced him again. Bunch was prepared to go on, but Judge Cope signaled that he wanted to ask a question.

"Mr. Bunch, are your clients practicing Christians?"

"Your Honor, Mrs. Fite has been a life-long church-goer. Devout and pious. And as for Mr. Fite, I believe it is safe to say that he has more intimate and detailed

114

knowledge of the workings of the Almighty than any man that I've ever encountered. Indeed, Your Honor, it is fair to say that the precious spirit works daily with them to ease their pain and comfort them."

Judge Cope left for his chambers to review the pleadings and make a decision. Raymer served the warrant and contempt citation on Woodside. Bunch packed his briefcase. Raymer sat next to Woodside, who looked as if he had been forced to swallow a plate of fiberglass.

"Hey, Bunch," said Raymer. "You think I need to put the cuffs on old Ashley here?"

"Naw. He's a good boy."

Raymer whooped and laughed.

"Not like you was them times. Fought all the way back to the lock-up."

Bunch snapped his briefcase shut.

"Careful, Raymer. You'll destroy my new image."

Judge Cope returned to the courtroom. Raymer told everyone to rise. The judge was beaming once more.

"Mr. Bunch, I'm going to enter a decision denying the summary judgment. I assume that you're agreeable."

"Your Honor, defendant serves notice of appeal," Woodside managed to croak.

"Very well, Mr. Woodside. It is duly noted. And I hope the events of this morning have been a lesson to you."

Woodside did not answer. Raymer led him toward the brown doors. Bunch heard Raymer laugh once more as he told Woodside that the county jail was serving fried bologna for lunch. Bunch started to leave, but Judge Cope called him back.

"And there's one more thing, Mr. Bunch. The next time you appear before me, I want to see your shoes shined, your hair combed, and your suit pressed. Mercy me. You're an officer of the court. You may be the finest lawyer in the world, but if your appearance is that of a tramp, no one will listen to you. You might even be taken for a jackal. On rare occasions, that happens to entirely innocent persons."

Judge Cope turned up his smile until it nearly blotted out the rest of his face. Bunch grinned meekly.

"Take my advice," said Judge Cope. "Appearance as well as convictions are important in this world."

"I will, Your Honor. I can tell that you're a man who understands human nature. A valuable asset."

Judge Cope lit up like a video game.

"It's good to see an attorney take friendly advice in the right spirit. So many lawyers today are rude and ungentlemanly. You'd think they had no principles or good, plain common sense. They don't know how to listen to constructive criticism. I can tell that you're not that way."

"I try my best, Your Honor. That's all anyone can do."

He'll love that one, thought Bunch. And when the going gets tough, the tough get going. If the shoe fits, wear it. Early to bed and early to rise. If you're so smart, why ain't you rich?

Judge Cope pondered Bunch's words.

"That's deep, Mr. Bunch. And so true."

Bunch paused at the front entrance of the courthouse. The Confederate soldier stood erect above the mob on the front steps. Bunch felt the soldier's power and courage, and knew he had no right to meet his calm, brave gaze. Bunch made his way through the silent, squatting figures, not bothering to avoid their stares. Brothers, sisters, he thought, we are gathered together for what nameless purpose?

Bunch drove across town in the lunch-time traffic. He had debated with himself whether or not to tell Charles and Tinka of their success. They would not understand. They would not understand unless they saw money. But they did have a right to know.

The street was empty, the house silent. The front door gaped open. A section of chain length fence was flattened—as if a great weight had struck it. Scraps of paper and clothing littered the yard.

In the high noon sun, Bunch squinted toward the house. He saw no reason to leave the car. He could see enough from where he sat. Bunch began to believe in curses. The tomb of Tut and the blood-sucking flies that fastened upon those who knew too much. There was a squeaking in the wind. In the far corner of the yard, upon a stunted apple tree, a thing with hinges creaked. The thing was fleshy-pale and extended from the tree to which it was strapped. It owned a boot and a white sock. Bunch realized it was an artificial leg, rocking back and forth; like a field goal kicker warming up at the Super Bowl.

He lit a cigarette and hit the gas. They're moving, he thought. He tried to think of a way to find them. Ten years ago the trail would have been wide. It would be tougher now. There were too many ways they could blend into the environment. He watched the empty house through his rearview mirror as he bounced away.

Gant lowered himself onto the new, specially-designed Swedish toilet. The plumbing contractor in Atlanta had taken almost six months to get it for him. The bowl was elongated and pointed, lit a ship's prow. The specialist at Duke had told him that such a toilet might help relieve his problem. But the specialists never seemed sure of what might be wrong with him. Still, the toilet was worth a try. To Gant, knowledgeable as he was on the subject, the toilet was an elegant thing. When he sat on it, he felt as if he were climbing into a sleek fighter aircraft, or placing himself behind the wheel of a high-powered Formula I racer.

The office was closed and empty, the time of day which Gant usually chose to work on his problem. But, despite the Swedish toilet, he could not concentrate properly, and concentration was all important. Other matters pressed upon him, intrigued him.

There was the business with Woodside. A shame, certainly, he thought. Woodside would have to be taken care of soon. Then there was the new judge. The judge would be somewhat more difficult than Woodside, but a challenge worth the effort. Gant smiled when he thought of Bunch. He had decided years before that other lawyers presented the easiest problems of all. Bunch would be amusing. In fact, there had not been nearly enough amusement in his life for quite a while.

He grunted, but there was no movement. He sensed that there would be no reward this day. He opened the file on the Loomis case, which rested on his legs. I need something like this, he thought. For too long my art has been predictable—summary judgments, settlements, cheap victories. But here. Here is a real question for the law, my law, to decide.

As he read through Woodside's arguments, he ceased straining. The hard thing inside of him would stay there. He had many days ahead of him to work on it. But in front of him, on the white paper, was this business with voices and God. It was not a question worthy of Woodside. His arguments were sound and banal, the work of a small mind that slips easily into routine and predictability. He scolded himself for not recognizing the absurd grandeur of the thing from the beginning. As he read through the file, he forgot about the hard thing inside of him. He made plans.

Later, he raised his pants and left the office. Nothing had been achieved through the elongated Swedish toilet. But everything was different. He felt good as he drove home through the autumn twilight. The Loomis file rested snugly in the briefcase beside him on the seat. He would, he decided, carry it with him for a long time to come.

X

L unch at La Petite Chateau. Gant had suggested dining together, but left it up to Woodside to pick the restaurant. Gant ignored restaurants. Anyone interested in food, he believed, had a strong streak of the trivial in him. It was akin to an interest in modern dance or films.

Gant did not want to take care of Woodside in the office. He had learned that it was better to handle such things at a neutral site. The waiter, who had announced on their arrival that his name was Allen, appeared from behind a wall of ferns and refilled Gant's water glass. Woodside folded his napkin, leaving the spinach salad half eaten. Pale, thought Gant, as the waiter slipped away. Allen and Ashley. Pale young men, anxious to please.

"I think you know why I asked you to lunch," began Gant. Woodside nodded, his eyes widening a bit.

"In fact, there are several reasons; not simply the unfortunate incident in the Loomis case. First, though, I want you to tell me about Judge Cope."

119

Woodside, who had been sitting board-straight, unstiffened a little.

"I've never seen anyone like him. There is a kind of. . . wildness."

Gant sipped the water. It tasted cold and clean, although he realized that cleanliness was an illusion. There was no substance pure enough to enter his body, to filter through his system.

"Wildness?"

Woodside hesitated.

"Yes. I mean, I guess that's the right word," answered Woodside.

Allen appeared to refill their glasses. Gant waved him away.

"Cope's very religious, right?" Gant had heard of the praying, of the pronouncements.

"Maybe. . . there is a kind of unearthliness about him."

At least, Gant thought.

"Roy Bunch didn't do a bad job with him," Gant said.

Woodside flushed. The spot of pinkness on his cheeks made him look like an English school boy.

"How do you think Bunch pulled that off?" Gant said.

Woodside drained his glass of wine. Gant watched Allen float across the room.

"Bunch is unethical."

"Describe his tactics."

Woodside poured the last of the carafe. His hand shook a little.

"He appealed to Cope's worst instincts. He didn't argue the law. Just went on about how poor and decent and godly his clients are. It would've made you sick to hear it. And the tone of voice he used. You'd think he was. . . preaching."

Gant had to acknowledge a little admiration for Bunch.

Allen cleared the table and handed Gant the check.

The waiter smelled starched and sweet. A thin, pale boy with long tickling fingers. Gant dropped money on the tray.

"Keep the difference," Gant said.

Allen's voice was high and melodious.

"Thank you, sir."

Gant watched as Allen floated away. Where do they come from, he thought. The last of the race, primping and pleasing in the twilight. Father-fearing boys. He returned to the problem of Woodside.

"Responsibility," he began, "is powerful, but ambiguous."

A light film of sweat covered Woodside's high forehead.

"The idea of responsibility makes some men limp. Other men relish it. It forms the basis of their character. For those men, the greater the responsibility, the greater the sense of joy and accomplishment."

"Yes, Trip. Very important."

"I knew you'd agree with me."

Then it was Woodside's turn. He chose his words carefully.

"The incident the other day. It was unfortunate, Trip. Very unfortunate. I'll never let anything like that happen again."

Gant smiled.

"I know you won't."

"Trip, we can win an appeal. When the Appeals Court gets a chance to find out what went on, they'll reverse. They'll have to."

Woodside's blue eyes begged.

"There's not going to be an appeal. I withdrew notice this morning," Gant said.

"Why? Don't you want me to handle it? I'll handle it."

"That's another thing. You're off the case. I'm going to take it myself. For the good of the firm."

"Trip. . . I hope you haven't lost confidence in me."

Woodside blurted out the last few words in a rush. That's what he wanted to say, Gant thought. He's been waiting for affirmation while eating his Goddamned spinach salad.

"It's more serious than that, Ashley."

"More serious?"

"Yes. You have until the end of the week."

Woodside's voice was low and distorted, like a record played on the wrong speed.

"More serious?"

Gant shrugged. I guess he's hearing what I say. If he isn't, the letter is on his desk.

"I understand," Gant said, "that there's a paralegal instructorship opening up at the community college. I'll put in a good word for you if you want."

Gant stood and put on his overcoat. Woodside remained seated. Gant patted his shoulder. Thin, he thought. Beneath the suit's padding, there's a skinny, half-developed body. Funny. He looked strong enough when we played racquetball. Some men shrink. You can see them settling inside their clothing, their chins drawing closer to their collars until only half the face is visible. Then, one day, there's nothing left.

"Why don't you take the rest of the afternoon off?"

Woodside did not move. Gant decided to leave. Allen passed him, pushing a dessert cart.

"I hope you enjoyed your meal with us. If you come again, ask for Allen. I'd love to serve you."

"You bet."

"Judge Cope, do you have a moment?"

"Yessir. I don't believe I've had the pleasure."

The smiles met. A force field rose between them.

"I'm Trip Gant. I'm sorry I haven't had a chance to introduce myself. When we're too busy, we tend to forget our manners. I'm afraid, too, that the bar association hasn't been as hospitable as it should be. Since I'm the president, I guess that's my fault."

Cope rose from behind his desk and shook Gant's hand.

"A pleasure. Trip Gant. You're a very famous man. I recall the Wake Forest game in '61. Three touchdowns. Two hundred and seventeen yards."

"Longer ago than I care to remember."

Righter's old office. Gant noted that every trace of the former occupant had been eradicated. The walls were freshly painted a startling shade of yellow. The ashtrays were gone. The carpet was a blinding green, the color of a June Bug's back.

"Sit down, sit down." Cope motioned toward a chair. Gant took a seat, and noticed that Cope wore his robe, even in chambers. A tiny cross and an American flag lapel pin were fastened over his heart.

"What can I do for you today, Mr. Gant?"

"Trip, please."

"Good. Men should call one another by their first names. I'm Ted."

"Ted, I mainly come by to ask you to dinner tomorrow night. I imagine you haven't had a home-cooked meal since you've come to Helmsville."

"Yes, I'm afraid that's true. But I suppose that I'm spoiled. My wife, Bitsy, is a marvelous cook. The best biscuits and fried chicken in the state. And her casseroles. It makes my mouth water to think of them."

At the mention of such food, Gant's lower tract rumbled slightly. Judge Cope clicked his tongue and chuckled.

"The wives. What would we do without them?"

There would be a splendid silence, Gant thought. And the space in my life would double.

"As soon as I get settled into my duties here," Cope said, "Bitsy will join me. We miss each other very much.

Forty-one years together. I take it that you're a family man?"

"No. Martha is infertile. One of the great disappointments in my life."

Judge Cope shook his head in sympathy.

"I can imagine," Cope said. "Children are your only real treasure."

Could he possibly believe that? Gant thought.

"I take it you're proud of your children," Gant said.

"Oh, yes. They have their own problems, like all of us. I love them deeply. They're grown and out of the house now, but we stay in close contact with all of them."

Gant did not want to hear about Cope's offspring. If he was not careful, Cope might bring out pictures and read from the large white bible on the desk.

"Trip, there is, I know, another reason for your visit today. Ashley Woodside?"

"I suppose it is necessary to bring up poor Ashley. I want to thank you for your actions in the Loomis case. At the firm, we had our doubts about Ashley. I think he has the ability to be a fine lawyer. His training and background are excellent. There is, shall we say, an attitudinal deficiency. I've just come from lunch with Ashley, and I believe we've found a satisfactory solution for his problems."

Judge Cope sounded wise, his voice double-dipped in the vat of responsibility.

"I felt I had no other choice. I'm sure, Trip, that you understand. Suppose, when you were playing at Chapel Hill, you had decided not to abide by the rules of the game. Let's say you lined up off-sides on every play because you just happened to feel like doing it that way. Then where would the team be?"

"Ted, you've done Ashley Woodside a favor. He might not see it that way now. He will, however, come to realize the correctness of your actions."

"That's the problem today, Trip. Too many people

think that they have the right to act any way they please. That's when they start turning into jackals."

"Jackals?" Gant said.

"Exactly," Judge Cope said.

"I see. That's something worth thinking about. Jackals. Yes. Will seven tomorrow night be convenient?"

"I look forward to it."

Gant left the judge's chambers and walked briskly back to his office. There would be plenty of time for his daily run, and maybe even another go at the bathroom. And time to think about the judge.

In Gant's house there were five bedrooms, three bathrooms, a huge living room, a study, and numerous other rooms that Gant had probably not visited more than a dozen times since he moved into the house.

He did, however, approve of the driveway. It wound through an alley of oak trees that led up to the house. Anyone coming to visit had only one approach, and could be seen and heard for quite a distance before reaching the house.

The lawn was wide and neat, stretching around three sides of the house. On the fourth side was a patch of woods which screened the house from the golf course. The golf course was too close to suit Gant, but the property was prestigious and the neighborhood the most expensive in the city; mock-colonial houses rearing forth amid boxwoods, oaks, and gardens.

Martha rarely, it seemed to Gant, left the house. She no longer bothered with the Garden Club, or the Great Books discussion group, or any of the dozen or so activities which once filled her time. She watched television, and spent hours dressing and putting on make-up. She made long distance telephone calls to people who barely remembered her as Miss Helmsville, or Maid of Cotton, or as a debutante. When Gant told her the judge was coming for dinner, she seemed more lively than usual. She chirped and capered, and Gant halfway expected her to dance. When she was younger, she had loved to dance.

Through the window of the study, Gant saw Ted Cope step from a silver Cadillac. The judge's metallic blue suit seemed to be in competition with the Christmas lights and decorations which covered the city. I might have guessed that much, Gant thought. The total metal look, like an astronaut.

Gant had gone to the study as soon as he returned from the office. It was in a part of the house most distant from the kitchen and the cooking odors. Martha seldom cooked, and had never been much good at it anyway. The maid had been paid an extra fifteen dollars to prepare the kind of food Ted Cope enjoyed.

As Gant answered the door, he met Martha as she came down the stairs. She was a tall woman, with the face of a girl. Even at Christmas time, she was deeply tanned. She smelled strongly of perfume and various preservatives, her flesh soaked in non-biodegradable solutions.

Introductions were gushed. Gant studied Martha as she fluttered about the judge. He approved of her training. When I have to bring her out, she at least knows what to do.

"Why, Judge Cope. Trip tells me that you're from Eddneyville. Do you know Walter Bewley? He's an old beau of mine."

Cope goes for that sort of crap, Gant thought. He's wiggling.

"Of course," said Cope. "I've known Walter for years. Of course, he's a good bit younger than I am. . ."

"Why you could fool me, Your Honor," trilled Martha. She giggled like a cheerleader.

"Please call me Ted."

"That's the cutest name. I always loved it. Does your wife call you Teddy?"

The living room was furnished in antiques of varying degrees of ugliness. A ten foot Christmas tree loomed in one corner. Ted and Martha sat chattering next to each other on the love seat. Gant stood, waiting for a break in the conversation.

"Walter was the handsomest thing. He came down from Carolina to take me to the May Day cotillion at Agnes Scott. The other girls were so jealous. Of course, that was before I met Trip."

She can, thought Gant, go on this way forever. And Cope was taking it all in: Martha, the house, the furniture.

"Drink?" Gant said.

Cope beamed at Martha, not hearing Gant's question.

"The usual dear," Martha said.

A pharmaceutical cocktail, Gant thought.

"Ted?" Gant said.

"Ah. . . what's that, Trip?"

"A drink. Would you care for one?"

"Do you have buttermilk?"

I might have guessed, Gant thought.

"No. I think we ran out this morning. Didn't we, Martha?"

Cope grinned shyly as Martha batted her eyes at him.

"Well, ice tea would be fine. With four teaspoons of sugar," Cope said.

Martha patted Cope's knee.

"Why you know, I do believe that you're a very wholesome man."

The judge grinned a little less shyly this time.

From the hall off the kitchen, Gant listened to the sound of their voices, undulating in harmony, rich as fat, thick gravy. Back-slapping, flirting and other forms of oafishness. The customs of the county, Gant thought.

The talk continued through dinner. Martha knew hundreds of people across the state, as many as Cope and Gant. She reported on their health, the fate of their children, the demise of their marriages, how they furnished their homes, and where they took their vacations. Occasionally, Gant poked at his food, shoving it around his plate; fried chicken, okra and tomatoes, mashed potatoes, turnip greens. Cope took seconds and thirds and, finally, a large slice of pecan pie. He belched frequently, attempting to hide the noise behind his hand. And he talked nearly as much as Martha.

"I can't wait for Bitsy to meet you. You'll have so much in common."

Martha leaned toward the judge, who inhaled deeply of her scents.

"You must miss her. All those things a wife can do for a husband."

Cope swallowed a chunk of crust.

"It's been hard. But with the Christmas recess, we'll be together again."

"Make up for lost time, eh, Your Honor?" giggled Martha. She winked at Cope, who paused in mid-chew, flecks of crust on his lips.

Gant began to see the avenue that led most directly to the judge's heart. I'm surprised. Who would have thought that Martha could be so directly useful?

The maid cleared the dishes away, and they returned to the living room. Martha and Ted pressed tightly against each other on the love seat. Gant excused himself. They hardly noticed that he had gone.

From the bushes outside the living room window, he heard the maid walking down the driveway toward the bus stop. He crouched low until he was sure that she was gone. Slowly he raised his head until he had a good view of the living room.

Martha and Ted, entwined, gyrated, and pawed as can only those who enjoy the excitement of momentary surprise and discovery. Cope lunged up toward her face, thrusting with his mouth, their tongues wrestling. His hand flashed under her dress. They spoke between kisses. Gant strained to hear them.

"Trip. . . good to me."

"Best halfback in Carolina history."

"Careful. . ."

"I'm sorry. . ."

They groped and licked, their eyes turning now and then toward the door.

"I love my wife. . ."

"From the minute I saw you. . ."

"I'm in room 2103. . . 5:30 tomorrow. I'll recess early."

In the light from the window, Gant wrote the time and room number in his address book. I wish I could be there, he thought. It will be like two different species of insects mating. There will be time enough, though, and I will see it. He slipped the address book back into his jacket. Watching others in secret. What a good game, he thought. Father in the study. Mother in the bathroom. Women of all sorts. Men talking to themselves, their faces slack with fatigue, lack of suspicion. The glances toward the door grew more frequent. The kissing and rubbing subsided.

"I'd die if he saw us."

"It would be. . . most embarrassing."

Martha smoothed her dress and hair. Cope straightened his tie and brushed the hair back from his face. Elastic-like, it popped into place. Gant crept from the window and soundlessly entered the back door.

The living room smelled of the Christmas tree and human heat.

"Sorry to be gone so long," Gant said. "There were a couple of phone calls I had to make."

He sat down, facing Ted and Martha.

"You know how it is, don't you, Ted?"

Gant's eyes met the judge's. The red leaked through the tan. The judge was out of breath.

"Oh, yes. . . if you follow the law, you're always on duty."

Although it was not yet eleven, Cope made his apologies.

"Really must be going. A tight schedule. And I must call Bitsy. We talk to each other every night."

"I look forward to seeing more of you," Martha said. "And when Bitsy moves down from Eddneyville, you be sure to bring her over too."

"I will. . . I will. I must be going. This was like. . . almost like. . . being at home," Cope said.

Gant watched him climb into the Cadillac. Do you feel Bitsy up after dinner? he thought.

Gant returned to the living room with a copy of the *Advance Decisions of the North Carolina Court of Appeals*. He flipped pages, occasionally reading a comment from the opinions. Martha curled up in a wingback chair and took a deep swallow from a fresh drink. With her legs tucked under her, she reminded Gant of the first time he had ever dated her. There she was, in the lobby of the dorm, with the other girls, waiting for their dates. When he saw her there, he realized he wanted her. He knew she was pretty and rich; he had not quite guessed that she was also mindless and good-natured; that she did not give a good Goddamn about anything.

"What do you think of Judge Cope?" he asked.

She slurped her drink.

"He was. . . not quite at ease when he arrived. He loosened up though. He could use a new suit, but I guess it's difficult to get really good clothes in those little towns down east. I like him. He reminds me of lawyers around the courthouse when I was a girl. They loved my daddy."

Her father had hired Gant. He dropped dead while arguing a contested will. Gant thought of other men he had seen her with. There was the surgeon she danced with for hours at the yearly Heart Fund Ball. The full-back he played with who coveted her: a strapping Polack from New Jersey who was impervious to pain. And how many others? He suspected Daddy. He used to ask her to sit on his lap a little too often. Other lawyers certainly. She adored lawyers, and understood, probably while still a child, that they run the world.

"I'm going to bed," he announced.

Martha drained the last of the scotch.

"And I'm going to catch *Mommie Dearest* on H.B.O."

Gant kissed her on the forehead. It had been a long time since he had kissed her, but she did not seem surprised.

"I thought I might get home early tomorrow, say around 5:30. We could go to dinner."

"I won't be here. Shopping."

Gant admired the ease with which she spoke. I must learn not to underestimate the purely ornamental.

"I hope you haven't lost the gift list this year," he said.

She walked to the bar and poured another drink.

"I'm halfway through it. I should finish in plenty of time."

He listened as she padded downstairs to the T.V. room. The set blared and shouted. Upstairs, he changed into jogging shorts, did a hundred push-ups, a hundred sit-ups, showered, and got into bed. He relaxed and took a reading of his lower tract. All was smooth and cool.

XI

The Palomino Motel, on Charlie Justice Boulevard, once boasted an electric stallion. The stallion disappeared, along with the plumbing, light fixtures, furniture, and midnight customers. Ten or fifteen years ago, the Palomino had been a whorehouse. Luther had worked there, handing out soap and towels to the girls, and cleaning up. He said that it had been the cleanest whorehouse between Richmond and Atlanta.

Charles was disappointed to find that the stallion was gone. The concrete base upon which the neon horse reared and kicked remained. He had envisioned the perfect, snorting horse, vivid and beautiful.

The house had become too small for the family. When Luther mentioned the Palomino, Charles decided the need was answered. Now there would be room for the precious spirits and for Wanda's children, Shane and Misty Marie. Charles had brought the children to their mother, leading them away from a day-care center while their father was at work. They were his special interest and he watched for signs of the precious spirit in them. For surely, he thought, if any human in the family, besides himself, had the spirit, it must be the children. By the time a child was six or seven, he reasoned, the spirit had turned cold and the don'ts of the world controlled it. He encouraged the children to play with the monkeys and to learn from them. They went naked as often as possible, even in the cold of early winter. No adult was allowed to correct or touch them, except for Charles and Wanda. The two children called Charles Daddy. So did the rest of the family.

Charles had decreed, before the miracle of the Palomino, that those who could must return to work or find new jobs. Smith was exempt; he barely moved, even during fellowshipping. Marcelline stayed home too. Her real job was tending the precious spirits. First Wanda was hired at a Seven Eleven. Then Thelma found a job at a packing-house, stirring the vats containing the ingredients for hot dogs and potted meat. Tinka tried, as she had wanted for so long, to become a whore. One evening, she set out for an interstate truck stop. She wore an ancient prom gown and a bright red wig she had recovered from a Salvation Army clothing bin. She returned near dawn, the gown ripped and smudged. She had made twelve dollars.

Troy and Darren could not find jobs, but they could steal. In this way, they brought in much that was needed by the family. And much that was not; tape decks, hub caps, and two lawn mowers. Thad and Henry hired on with the cable T.V. company.

For a while, things had been good. There was money and nightly television and fellowshipping. Charles had been almost content. The children climbed upon him each morning and he stroked and cuddled them. The voice was mellow and kind. As these easy days went on, the voice changed. It questioned the contentment. Things were good, but should not more people know of the blood, the precious spirit? Should not the world become as the family had become? The more the voice questioned, the more irritable Charles became. He withheld fellowshipping some nights. He had to beat Tinka more often than usual. Then Luther, who stayed drunk most of the time, and who, like Smith, was incapable of working, mentioned the Palomino. And Charles know that it was the place. The house seemed cramped and remote, hidden from the great, teeming streets and the people who would be a part of the family if only they knew of him. The miracle of Cumby's church could be repeated daily, thousands of times.

They had moved at night. It was clear and cold, and the stars blinked above the city lights. Smith's Ford was loaded with food, toys, and clothing. Smith crouched in the back seat with Misty Marie and Shane. He pressed his face against the window, straining to see the moon and stars. He did not know where he was going, and the voices around him were faint and ghostly, like out of a dream. Soon, even before the car got underway, he fell asleep, the warm, naked children pressed against him.

The move did not progress smoothly. One of the Precious Spirits was lost for awhile. After much searching, Marcelline discovered it under the house. She crawled between the supporting cinder blocks to coax the monkey to her, but became wedged there. It took most of the family to pull her out.

Charles did not help in the freeing of Marcelline. Instead, he watched Thad and Henry as the twins loaded their pick-up truck with furniture.

"Thad," called Charles.

"Yes, Daddy." Thad answered shyly. He was not used to being addressed directly by Charles.

"We're gonna leave a sign."

"A sign?"

"Yes. So anybody that comes by can know what we mean."

Thad nodded.

"What kind of sign, Daddy?"

"Your leg."

Thad sat on the half-frozen ground and rolled up his pant's leg.

"It don't bother me like it did. Before I met you," Thad said.

He slowly undid the brace which held the leg to his stump. When the leg came loose, he passed it up to Charles.

Charles held it out before him, inspecting it.

"It ain't real. It creaked when you fellowshipped. But it can be a real sign. I know what you're thinking. How am I gonna walk? But you done taken care of that. You can hop. We know about spirits that can hop. Now you can be like them."

"Yes, Daddy," answered Thad. Henry helped him up. They followed Charles to a pine tree beside the house, Thad leaning on Henry. They watched as Charles worked the leg's strap around the trunk.

"There," said Charles as he tightened the straps, "that's a sign from the family. Them that come later will know we been here."

The Palomino sat in a hollow, half obscured from the road. It was covered with dead kudzu vines. A faded "No Trespassing" sign was posted where the horse had once reared. The motel office smelled of damp, rotting carpet. Charles stood atop the registration desk. Troy had pulled the Ford to the office door, and the headlights lit up the room, which was crowded with the shivering family.

"This is it," said Charles. "We're home now."

Slowly, in his deep voice, he sang the first words of the McDonald's jingle. The rest joined in. They sang with solemnity. The moon settled over the Palomino and the clouds retreated toward the west.

Henry, with Thad's assistance, used the tools provided by the cable company to hook into a power line. Television returned, reigning over the office, where Charles spent most of the day in a lawn chair mounted upon the registration desk. In a padlocked room they found several beds, as well as another television set. The set did not work, its insides having been torn out long ago. Nevertheless, Marcelline watched it from time to time. Water was a problem at first, but Troy and Darren stole enough hose to hook up to the service station next door. Tinka cooked beans on an open fire in the back parking lot. At dawn each morning the family assembled in the office to hear Charles' message of the day. Sometimes he shouted at them, and they hung their heads in shame and fear. At other times Charles cried and then the family howled with him. When he smiled, they smiled back. In the evening, when they returned from their jobs, there was singing and dancing, concentrated television watching, and fellowshipping, when Charles allowed it. Sometimes there were punishments, too. Luther had to sleep outside once because he talked when Charles was telling the family more about the blood. Darren and Troy had to fellowship with Marcelline and each other in front of the family after they were caught peeing into the beans that Tinka had fixed for dinner.

This was the way things were for a couple of weeks. It was as good as Charles thought it was going to be. He liked sitting on the registration desk as the family waited for him to say and do. He liked the heat which radiated from him to the others. But eventually he grew frustrated. The new people did not come to the Palomino. A police car came by now and then, lingered a moment, and left. No one bothered them, but no one seemed interested either.

One morning in mid-December, Charles was studying the Christmas commercials. He enjoyed the Inertia Nutcracker best, especially the way the shells fragmented. The egg scrambler was good too; he liked the expressions on the T.V. children's faces when they were forced to eat gooey egg whites. As he watched the commercials he felt that they were going to mean something. Then it was there before him on the screen. A happy voice told everyone to come to the Darden Grove Mall for Christmas shopping. A happy family arrived at the mall and piled out of a station wagon. Mom, dad, and the kids went from store to store, discovering perfect presents: for dad, a power saw; for mom, Chanel Number Five; for the kids, computer play sets. The happy voice spoke to Charles, and he saw.

Darden Grove Mall was multi-leveled and fully-enclosed. It contained two theaters, four restaurants, fifty-two wholesale and retail outlets and a two hundred foot long arcade and game room. It rose out of what had once been a pine grove. The city had built a high school nearby. Housing tracts and apartment complexes had followed fast food restaurants, carpet outlets, and auto parts stores.

Two weeks before Christmas, the shoppers hurried through the mall, their arms loaded like a looting army at the fall of a great empire. On the first level, next to the penny-filled reflecting pool, the mechanical boys choir sang "O Holy Night," "The First Noel," and "The Little Drummer Boy."

Beside the choir, on the far side of the Orange Julius stand, sat Santa's castle: a wall-board fortress draped with fiberglass snow. A line of children and parents stretched from the castle's low door, past the choir, past the J. C. Penny's dancing elves, past the windows decorated to resemble packages and Christmas trees and angels.

Former Superior Court Judge Claude Righter sat on a bench near the castle. Since retiring, he spent most of his time in the mall. His wife had left him. The children no longer called. He still, however, possessed his judicial robes, and he always wore them in public. Occasionally, someone stared or laughed. He did not hear them. He had heard almost nothing since he signed the resignation letter that Trip Gant had shoved across the desk at him. The line of children and parents moved slowly past. Vaguely, he wondered why the children entered the castle's low door. He thought of asking one of the adults, but that would be a waste of time, he decided.

On the third level, behind the Morrison's Cafeteria steam table, Reverend Leon Cumby scooped up mashed potatoes, carrots, rice, and peas. He prayed for deliverance. He no longer had a church, and had been fired from his job as the fry cook at the Steak and Egg Kitchen because he preached to the customers. Since coming to Morrison's he had been warned twice, once just as he was convinced that he had saved the soul of a woman who had ordered the Friday seafood special. Once more, the manager told him, and he could look for another job. He cursed the godless and prayed for them beneath his breath.

He dished out another vegetable platter. The line grew short. The dinner hour ended and he could take his break. He wandered onto the mezzanine. He snorted as he observed the line leading into Santa's castle. He hated the trappings of Christmas. Something else caught his eye. Three or four men began to set up a platform across the narrow, packed floor space between Santa's castle and the Frederick's of Hollywood outlet. One of the men was Henry. The Reverend Cumby leaned over the railing to get a better look.

The platform, six two-by-fours mounted on concrete blocks, would not provide much of a view, but Charles knew his voice and presence would be enough. He began in a shout, his words rising above "O Come All Ye Faithful." The family gathered around the platform. The monkeys frolicked and danced.

"You got Fab, Tide, and Cheer. You got Ford, Chevrolet, and Chrysler. You got spatter screens, vegamatics, and bamboo steamers. And you got this Christmas thing. You gotta wait for Christmas? You gotta wait for your birthday? Thanksgiving? The Fourth of July?"

"NOOOOO!" answered the family.

"See? Hear'em? I'm talking about SATISFACTION. Not just at Christmas. Not when whoever set everything up calls for SATISFACTION. I'm talking about SATISFACTION RIGHT NOW. EVERY DAY. FOR AS LONG AS YOU LIVE! HOW'S THAT SOUND?"

"GOOOOOD," roared the family.

Claude Righter left the bench and moved closer to the platform. He began to nod. Leon Cumby forgot about the steam table and the souls of diners.

"YOU HEARD OF FELLOWSHIPPING?"

"YEEESSSS!"

Charles gestured toward the crowd at Santa's castle.

"MOST OF YOU AIN'T! IT'S TOUCHING AND FEELING RIGHT! WHO TELLS YOU THAT IT AIN'T RIGHT TO FELLOWSHIP? WHO TELLS YOU THAT YOU GOTTA DO THIS OR YOU GOTTA DO THAT? YOU DON'T EVEN KNOW!"

Charles slowly danced as he spoke. The monkeys swayed at his feet, as did the family. It did not occur to Charles how one word flowed from the other, or how they came out of his mind and mouth. But he could see the words, a silver mist, floating upwards to the high, concrete ceiling of the Darden Grove Mall.

"WHO TELLS YOU THAT YOU CAN'T DO WHAT?

THEM THAT MAKE UP THINGS! YOU GOT TO TAKE WHAT YOU FEEL. TAKE WHAT YOU FEEL!"

Claude Righter was soon at Charles' feet. He had not heard words for a long time.

"THAT'S WHAT YOU GOT TO DO! NOW YOU TAKE OLD SANTA CLAUS OVER THERE. . ."

Charles' arm shot forward, pointing toward Santa's castle.

"THERE AIN'T NO REAL SANTA CLAUS! THE IDEA OF HIM AIN'T BAD! SOMEBODY TO COME DOWN A CHIMBLY EVERY YEAR AND GIVE YOU A TOY! I HOPE YOU CHILDREN OVER THERE ARE LISTENING! PARENTS TOO!"

A few stared. Most tried not to notice the little man with the big arms and the hoarse, deep, powerful voice. A couple of punks from the arcade jeered and clapped.

". . . I'M TALKING ABOUT WHAT'S REAL! ABOUT WHAT BOILS UP INSIDE AND YOU GOTTA LET OUT! NOT SANTA CLAUS OR JESUS AND ALL THEM OTHER MEN LIKE THAT! IT DON'T BELONG INSIDE! IF IT STAYS THERE TOO LONG, YOU GONNA BUST LIKE A GODDAMNED BALLOON! I KNOW WHAT I'M SAYING!"

His arm moved like a rifle searching for a new target. Charles pointed toward the punks.

"I'VE SEEN LOTS OF BOYS LIKE YOU! TROY AND DARREN USED TO BE THE SAME AS YOU! THEY HAPPY NOW. THEY GOT FAMILY! THEY GOT REASONS! YOU COME WITH ME AND YOU'LL KNOW WHAT YOU ARE! YOU'LL HAVE THE VOICE. . ."

The family chanted responsively. Claude Righter joined them. There was no retirement. There was no mall.

". . . AND THE BLOOD!" bellowed Charles.

". . . AND THE BLOOD. . ."

". . . AND THE PRECIOUS SPIRITS. . ."

". . . AND THE PRECIOUS SPIRITS. . ."

Charles picked up the female monkey.

"LOOK! ALL OF YOU! AT THE SPIRIT! WE AIN'T GOT IT HIDDEN! SANTA CLAUS WON'T LET IT OUT! JESUS WON'T LET IT OUT! I'M HERE TO FREE YOU! DO YOU WANT A MAN IN A RED SUIT AND A WHITE BEARD? DO YOU WANT A SKY GOD? OR DO YOU WANT AN *EARTH GOD*?"

". . . EARTH GOD," shouted the family.

"DO YOU WANT A GOD THAT KNOWS HOW YOU FEEL OR ONE THAT LETS MEN TELL YOU HOW TO FEEL?"

"WE WANT YOU!" the family roared.

The Reverend Cumby, posted between Santa's castle and Toy World, had heard enough. He knew the Lord would not let him lose twice. He elbowed his way closer to the platform. The heat blew in from his heart and head.

"THIS *MAN*," began Cumby, "THIS MAN THAT CALLS HIMSELF GOD IS A DRUNKARD, AN IDOLATER, AND A WHOREMASTER!"

Charles paused, handing the monkey down to Marcelline. He had seen Cumby heading toward the platform, his mouth already moving even before the words came out.

"AND THIS MAN," shouted Charles, "IS FROM A TIRED, OLD WORN-OUT *CHURCH*. HE AIN'T. . . HE AIN'T. . . *MODERN*!"

Charles was not exactly sure of the word's meaning, but it was a special television word. The T.V. men always meant something good whenever they used it.

". . . AND IF YOU AIN'T MODERN, YOU AIN'T SHIT!"

Cumby's face colored like a radish. He did not know what modern meant either, but he felt it was akin to calling a man a son-of-a-bitch or a bastard.

Smith, who had crawled under the platform for a little rest, was at eye-level with Cumby's battered work shoes. Modern. Un-modern. Not up to date. Up to date. Acquainted with the latest methods. Old fashioned. Not old fashioned. His eyes grew heavy.

"WHAT I AM," sang Charles, "IS WHAT YOU'LL NEVER BE! YOU AIN'T GOT IT, AND YOU CAN'T GET IT! YOU AIN'T GOT WHAT IT TAKES! SOME GOT IT, AND DON'T KNOW HOW TO USE IT! SOME, LIKE YOU, CUMBY, AIN'T GOT IT, BUT PRETEND THEY DO! THEN THERE'S ME! I GOT IT AND I KNOW WHAT TO DO WITH IT!"

Charles leered down at Cumby. There was laughter in his voice.

"AND YOU KNOW YOU AIN'T GOT IT! I WALKED INTO THIS POOR FOOL'S CHURCH AND TOOK AWAY HIS PEOPLE! IN FIVE MINUTES THEY GIVE UP ON HIM! YOU KNOW WHAT I TOLD THEM? THE SAME THINGS I'M TELLING YOU! THE VERY WORDS YOU BEEN LISTENING FOR, HOPING FOR, ALL YOUR LIVES! BRING YOUR PACKAGES! BRING YOU VEGAMATICS! YOUR CHEVROLETS! BRING YOU BABIES, AND YOUR HUSBANDS, AND YOUR WIVES! BRING WHATEVER YOU GOT! COME TO CHARLIE JUSTICE BOULEVARD! COME TO THE PALOMINO WHERE THE ELECTRIC SPIRIT OF THE PRECIOUS HORSE ONCE DANCED! FORGET ABOUT BEING SCARED! I'M OFFERING YOU EVERYTHING! NOW!"

Cumby shouted that Charles was against Jesus, the Bible, and the Holy Word. No one listened. The family and Claude Righter chanted.

"Everything. . . now!"

"Everything. . . now!"

"Everything. . . now!"

Charles danced faster, chanting with his people. All would follow. The stores would empty. A solid mass of people would pour over the cloverleaf of the interstate, diverting traffic, leading a nation of cars and shoppers and gifts toward the Palomino. The T.V. men would have to come too. They would have to come to see.

Santa Claus and a squat, sweaty man wearing a silver tie and a nameplate that read "Bert-Manager" worked their way toward Charles. Two security guards followed along behind.

Cumby still shouted, and he felt the rage, but he knew it was the same as when the church died. Or like since then, when he tried to preach in restaurants, on street corners, in bus stations. No one heard him. He offered hell and truth, and no one wanted to listen. But he could fight the devil still.

Santa and Bert whispered, conferring. Bert cleared his throat and yelled up to Charles.

"Say, you got a permit for this. . . this talk you're making?"

Charles still danced, his rifle-arm in Santa Claus' face.

"HE COME OUT! YOU HERE TO FIGHT WITH ME? I DONE WHIPPED JESUS' MAN TWICE NOW! YOU CAN'T WIN. YOU AIN'T GOT A CHANCE."

Bert motioned the security guards forward.

"This mall," yelled Bert at the dancing, gesturing Charles, "is private property. You can't come in here and do this sort of thing. Now you just come on down from there and we'll forget all about this."

Charles buck danced, leaning forward toward Bert. The chanting continued.

"FORGET THE WHOLE THING? YOU MEAN FORGET LIVING? A MAN LIKE YOU. A LITTLE OLD FAT-BELLIED MAN. YOU DON'T KNOW WHAT LIVING IS!"

The security guards started to climb onto the platform, but Leon Cumby, boiling with holiness, blind on divine fury, burst past them and sprang at Charles. He had watched the devil for too long. Cumby missed, his feet hooking on the edge of the platform, and he belly-flopped the little female monkey, and crushed the life from her. Its overfed body splayed outward under Cumby's weight. Cumby tried to rise and charge again, but Marcelline was upon him, biting and punching. They rolled from the platform, taking Claude Righter's knees out from under him. The three of them, in a loose ball, hurled about the floor.

Cumby's leap had been a signal. The arcade punks went for the shoppers, stripping them of gifts, smashing what they could not carry. Darren and Troy cornered Santa Claus in his castle. Tinka screamed. A monkey bit a security guard. Bert, his name tag and tie ripped away, crawled from the crowd, shouting for someone to call the police. Smith awakened for a moment. Feet and faces boiled by at eye level. He rolled onto his side, away from the fight. The shopping crowd tried to keep away from the platform. Little bits of it were chewed off and sucked into the struggle. Charles danced, shaking the boards, dancing as he had never danced before. Sirens could be heard above "Silver Bells."

Bunch leaned back in the beanbag chair, watching Ella Fitzgerald live from Harlem. She sang "What Month Was Jesus Born." A two hundred voice choir backed her up.

Ella: "WHAT MONTH WAS JESUS BORN?"

Choir: "IT WAS THE *LAST* MONTH OF THE YEAR!"

Ella: "WHAT MONTH WAS JESUS BORN?"

Choir: "IT WAS THE *LAST* MONTH OF THE YEAR!"

Ella: "WAS IT *JANUARY*?"

Choir: "NOOOOO, NOOOOO!"

Ella: "WAS IT *FEBRUARY*?"

Choir: "NOOOOO, NOOOOO!"

"IT WAS THE LAST MONTH OF THE YEAR!"

He tended to forget Christmas. As he watched Ella and the choir, he guessed that Christmas was a big deal when he was a kid. If he drew deeply enough from his memories, usually an unpleasant experience, he could recall images. At nine he stood in the yard of his parent's house, clutching the handlebars of his new bicycle. It was a good Christmas morning with dead, tawny grass and bare trees. His parents told him to smile as they argued over how to operate the new camera. They bickered for a good while about the angle and exposure.

Then there was Christmas with Jane and the kids. From the first couple of years of marriage, he recalled a kind of tepid glow. Later, there was the traditional Christmas morning shouting match, fueled by hangovers and bills. He remembered pulling down a Christmas tree, the green and silver and red balls shattering amid the toys, ties, and pajamas. His kids were old enough then to hate him for it. Maybe that happened, he thought. If it did not, it was still the kind of thing I probably would have done.

He decided to stop remembering. It only made him feel bad. That's always what's wrong with memory, he thought. I can't remember anything good. Humming along with Ella and the choir, he picked up the evening newspaper. Gant's face spread across the front page of the local news section. Bunch had seen Gant's picture a good bit lately: Christmas benefits, charity drives. And there he was, presiding at the Bar Association banquet in honor of Judge T. Thurston "Ted" Cope. Gant and the judge, and their wives Margaret and Bitsy, smiled with warmth and sincerity. It was easy to see what Gant was up to with the judge. The same as every other judge Bunch had ever seen in town. Bunch had avoided Cope since the summary judgment, except for smiling hellos in the courthouse corridors. Then, one day last week, Cope had not returned his greeting. Instead, the judge glared at him.

Bunch tossed the paper toward the fireplace. Ella Fitzgerald and the All-Harlem choir still inquired as to the month of Christ's birth. Bunch went into the kitchen for a beer. He stood by the refrigerator as he drank. Gant had put the word out on him, he decided. But why, was the question. Why make all this trouble? He could have appealed the summary judgment. He could have filed a dozen motions to slow the case down. Hell, thought Bunch. He could get it put off forever. But all Gant wanted from him was the medicals and Pffippert's report.

Pffippert had called him that morning. The reports on Charles would be ready in early January, in time for the deposition. Dynamite and innovative was what Pffippert called the material. Of course, thought Bunch. Pffippert believes that everything he does is dynamite and innovative.

Bunch had begun to believe that none of it mattered—the judge's animosity, Pffippert's pretensions, Gant's schemes. He had not seen his clients in weeks, could not even trace them. The last thing he had seen was the artificial leg dancing in the wind. And that had been enough. He had gone home that night and had three drinks before he realized that the bourbon had no effect on him. And he remembered the devil again and had laughed. For a couple of weeks he had not cared where they had gone. But when he thought of Gant and the big score, he wanted Charles and Tinka to come back, to get on with it, wherever it was going.

Ella Fitzgerald and the All-Harlem choir roared into a stomping, shouting rendition of "Hark, The Herald Angels Sing." The telephone rang.

"Who is this?" asked a shaky, redneck voice.

"I'm whoever you want me to be," answered Bunch.

"I'm trying to get ahold of Roy Bunch, the lawyer."

"You're lucky. I can be Roy Bunch. Who is this?"

"Luther."

Bunch finished off the beer and placed the can next to the other empties on the counter.

"Luther, huh? What do you want?"

"I'm down at the jail," Luther said.

"A tough break. What'd you do?"

"Nothing. I'm calling on the jailhouse phone. The police missed me."

"That's good," Bunch said. He debated whether or not to hang up.

"I bet you don't remember me, but I've seen you," Luther said.

Bunch grew wary. He thought Luther might be one of Goforth's friends. He had not heard from Goforth for a long time, but he expected him to re-surface at any moment. The Goforths of the world always re-surfaced, he thought. Maybe with Charlene. Maybe with Charlene and a sawed-off shotgun.

"So what do you want with me?" Bunch asked.

"It's about Daddy. He's in jail. And most of the family too!"

"Your daddy? Look, you can go to a bondsman's office. There's a whole string of them right across the street from the courthouse. But first, you got to wait for the magistrate to set bond. . ."

"You're a friend of Daddy's. He said right before they took him away to call you."

"What's your daddy's name?" asked Bunch.

"We call him Daddy. He's our real daddy now. He shows us what we need, what we want. . ."

Bunch reached for another beer. Ella and the choir were screaming their version of "Angels We Have Heard on High."

"No. No. Hell no. Your Daddy's got *another* name, hasn't he? Nobody's just named Daddy."

"He's daddy to us, but some call him Charles."

"Charles Fite?"

"That's his name to those that ain't in the family. But

someday everybody will be in the family. See, people got to understand. . ."

Bunch pulled on his shoes, hopping as he spoke.

"Don't leave. Don't move. I'm coming right down."

"Daddy said the T.V. men would come any day. And pretty T.V. women, too."

Luther stroked the dead monkey. The animal's head dangled to one side, as if connected to the body by a piece of string.

"He was right," Luther said. "He ain't been wrong yet."

He held the monkey close. Its tail and feet hung straight down.

"As soon as I get back to the Palomino, I'm gonna get me a jar and some rubbing alcohol and pre-serve the precious spirit. That's the last thing Daddy told me before they put him in the po-lice car. Besides calling you, I mean."

Bunch handed Luther a five.

"Go on home. Take the bus. Spend the rest on the alcohol."

Luther stuck the bill in his shirt pocket.

"Thanks, Mr. Bunch. I can tell that you're a friend of Daddy's."

Luther disappeared down the alley that ran between the courthouse and the county jail.

The Channel Nine live-action mini-camera crew had set up just outside the jail doors. Bunch shaded his eyes from the lights. A young woman thrust a microphone toward him as he started up the steps.

"And you, sir. Are you associated with the Daddy Fite Family?"

Bunch tried to look into her face, but the light was too strong.

"I'm here on other business. I have to take a piss and this place looks like it's open."

The lights died. The microphone jerked away. He saw the woman a little more clearly. She was not young.

"A smart ass," she rasped. "I'm trying to get a story and I run into a smart ass."

Bunch felt a little sorry for her. It must be tough coming up with a new act every day. It must be tough being new and relevant each moment.

"My mission is urgent, but I am acquainted with Daddy Fite."

The microphone lunged toward his mouth.

"Harry! The lights!" shouted the woman.

"O.K." began the woman. "Tell us what you know. But don't say anything inappropriate. This is T.V."

"I'm Charles Fite's personal attorney, Roy A. Bunch. I plan to have him out of jail in an hour or so that he may return to his mission."

The woman seemed pleased.

"And what is his mission?" she asked.

"Why spreading the wisdom and truth of his teachings. Thank you. I must see to my client's interest."

Bunch turned away from the camera. As he headed toward the jail, he caught some of what the woman was saying.

". . . new religion. . . riot tonight at. . . shoppers beaten. . . continuing coverage. . . news at eleven."

The visitor's room contained two metal chairs and a scarred table. The floor was concrete and looked wet. The walls were a history of men's lives:

Pussy.

Vernon Wright was railroaded here in 1974.

Judge Carver is a son of a bitch.

Danny will suck your dick. Cell block three.

Charlotte, N.C.

Motherfucker.

Macon.

Bunch lit a cigarette and waited. He listened to the singing that came from another corner of the jail. The

jingle was loud, defiant. Other prisoners bellowed for
the singing to cease, but the singers did not seem to
listen. Bunch heard a male voice shouting what sounded
like bible verses. He shrugged. You could never be sure
in jail. The sound is tricky.

He had spoken to many men in the visitor's room;
frantic boys, who could barely stay alive in the county
jail, worrying about their chances in the Raleigh pen.

Then there were the terminally numb, who hardly
knew they were there. So many, thought Bunch. I have
waited for so many; furtive, whispering, afraid to know
what their chances were, desperate to hear the right
thing.

A deputy brought Charles in. His clothes were dirty
and torn. A zig-zag lightening bolt of a cut ran across
his forehead. Bunch slid a pack of cigarettes across the
table.

"Are you hurt much?" asked Bunch.

Charles inhaled deeply, turning a third of the cigarette into ash. He shook his head.

"He's gonna pay."

"Who?"

"Somebody. None of your business."

Charles finished the cigarette and flipped the butt
into a corner.

"Somebody that murdered a precious spirit. That's
who," Charles half-shouted.

"A monkey?"

"*You* might think it's a monkey."

Bunch decided to change the subject.

"I've talked to a bondsman. I'm going to have you and
your friends. . ."

"FAMILY!" screamed Charles. "THEY MY FAMILY."

"O.K. Family. You'll be out in an hour. I need to talk
with you first. I've been trying to find you for weeks."

Charles shook another cigarette out of the pack. He
smiled.

"We gonna be on T.V."

"Yeah. I know. Me too. But for once, you're going to have to listen to what I have to say. We won the first part of the case. That's what's really important. Now that we. . ."

Charles began to shake his head.

"We got on T.V. and we didn't even need you."

Bunch studied the cut on Charles' forehead. What was the point in telling him, he thought. I may as well tell a tree or a dog.

"You know something, Bunch? If you hadn't been picked as the instrument, I'd got us another lawyer a long time ago. You ain't got no money for us. At the rate you was doing things, I'd been old before I got on T.V. Had to do it myself. Had to go out and take care of business. Spread the word."

Bunch noticed that the cut stopped a quarter inch or so above the deep darkness of Charles' left eye.

"You mean preach at the mall?" said Bunch.

"I DON'T PREACH! I TELL THE TRUTH!"

XII

The deposition began at two o'clock in Gant's office. Gant and a new blond associate who closely resembled Woodside sat on one side of the long, highly-polished conference table. On the other side were Bunch, Charles, and Tinka. A stenographer typed in a corner as Tinka went through her testimony.

Gant let the associate handle the questions. He would conduct the examination on Charles Fite. Besides, he could see now how everything would be. In his private bathroom, the plan had taken further shape, and its details had presented themselves to him.

First, he hired a detective from Atlanta. Akins, the detective, supplied him with a steady stream of photographs and video tapes. And Gant was pleased with the results—so pleased that he had installed a television and VCR in the bathroom.

The earliest tapes had been shot at the Ramada Inn. They consisted mostly of medium shots of Cope and Martha pawing and grunting across the room. After Christmas, Cope's wife, Bitsy, had moved to Helmsville.

Ted left the Ramada Inn and purchased a brick neo-colonial with skinny white columns in Yorktowne Heights, a development a cut or two below Gant's in status.

The tapes continued to come, delivered by Akins every Friday. After the delivery was made, Akins, a small, neat, terrier-like man, always asked Gant if he had enough evidence. And Gant always gave him the same answer—that there was never enough evidence. Akins would shrug and return the next week.

As for the photographs, they numbered well over a hundred. These too were kept in the bathroom. Gant spent much time arranging them in chronological order in family photographic albums that were like those which Ted and Bitsy kept on their coffee table. Gant planned to present them to the Copes at the proper time. But the video tapes were the main thing—a triumph, Gant thought.

The ones from Yorktowne Heights were the best. They were done when Bitsy was out shopping or away visiting her children for the weekend and Ted and Martha had a chance to arrange their trysts. All the action took place in the living room. Gant especially liked a sequence on the emerald-green shag carpet. Cope and Martha used the carpet because Cope insisted that it was a sin to defile the marriage bed. And there, on the tape, was Martha, naked—except for a gold crown—on all fours, her face aligned directly with the camera, with Cope puffing and blowing behind her. It was the first day they had played dress-up, which was Martha's idea. She began the session in a prom gown. Cope wore a football uniform. By the time their coupling began, after their version of the crowning of the homecoming queen, Cope wore only the helmet, so it was difficult to see his face. Later, there were other costumes: the cowboy and cowgirl, the general and the WAC. At the end of each session Martha would suggest an outfit for the next.

When they finished, Cope always made the same speech. His subject was sin and the failings of the flesh, and about how much he admired Gant, and how what they were doing was wrong. Martha yawned and smiled and told him that he was cute. After she left, Cope prayed loudly, down on his knees, naked but for a football helmet, or a cowboy hat, or a general's braided cap.

It had cost Gant quite a bit to get the tapes and pictures. Akins did not come cheap. Goforth did. A couple of thousand took care of him. Akins had discovered him living in a trailer park, and it took little convincing to make him see that he and Gant had a common cause. Goforth was in Florida, but he would be back soon. If things went according to the plan—and they would—he would bring back the woman named Charlene. But on the evening before the deposition, Gant saw the final, necessary element in his creation.

It had come to him as he strained and sweated at stool, watching Martha in a belly dancer's costume and Cope in a jeweled turban. He saw that the trial should be televised. He had been on television in the past, when he played football, or later, when he was interviewed about some public issue. But he had never performed for the whole public at what he did best. The trial would be his moment, a moment when even the faceless and nameless would grasp his power and indifference. As the vision came to him, his lower tract had given him a small, hard reward which struck the porcelain with a tiny ping.

The associate finished questioning Tinka. Charles had not taken his eyes off Gant since the deposition began. Before the Day, Charles could not have spoken to such a man, would not have been noticed by him. The man was beautiful—like a blond-headed Dan Rather,

Charles thought. Bunch, who was not beautiful, asked Charles the same questions that he had answered so many times before. Charles gave the same answers, his eyes never leaving the face of the beautiful lawyer. Finally, Bunch finished, and the beautiful lawyer started to ask questions.

"Now, Mr. Fite, since the wreck last August you've felt good about life? About yourself?" Gant smiled.

"Good. What do you mean, good?" asked Charles.

"I think you know what good means. Are you happy? Do you have what you want in life? What you need?"

"I got it."

"You've got what you need?"

"I got it and everybody else wants it."

"I see. And what do you have?"

Charles could tell that the beautiful lawyer was interested. He hunched forward, his hands twisting and untwisting in his lap.

"I got my family, a good place to live, the Palomino Motel. I got my legs and I got power."

"I believe you were once disabled?"

"Couldn't walk."

"That's it. And after the wreck you could walk?"

Bunch interrupted before Charles could tell about walking and the river and all the other miracles.

"I want the record to be clear on this. He walked, for the first time, a full six weeks after the wreck. Walking is one result of the wreck, but not the only one."

Gant smiled and Charles smiled back. Charles felt as if he had a kind of gleeful conspiracy with this man.

When Bunch finished, the beautiful lawyer started back on the questions.

"Would you say that you're better off now than before the wreck last August?" asked Gant.

"Hell yes! I didn't have no family, except for Tinka here, couldn't walk. . ."

"So you consider yourself better off?"

"That's what I'm saying. Listen, you'd be better off too, and so would everyone else, if you was a little like me. Of course, ain't nobody can be *just* like me."

"Why is that?"

"Because I'm the earth god," Charles said.

"Yes," said Gant. "The earth god. Did you know immediately after the wreck that you were the earth god?"

"Naw! It wasn't right off. It come to me gradual. There was a voice, then I walked. Then me and the voice was the same. Then. . ."

"I understand," interrupted Gant. "Let me ask you an important question. Did you decide you were the earth god before or after you met Mr. Bunch?"

Charles tried to answer, but Bunch cut him off again, saying words to the beautiful lawyer that Charles did not, at first, understand. The words changed and Charles understood them. Bunch called the beautiful lawyer a sneak, and that he did not have to sit still for anymore bullshit questions. The beautiful lawyer said that the record should show that Mr. Bunch used an obscenity. And Bunch said that was fine by him, since the whole day had been one long obscenity. Charles liked the way the beautiful lawyer handled Bunch. He did not get excited, and acted as if, instead, that Bunch was just a jabbering idiot that had gotten in the way of his conversation with Charles. Bunch quieted down, but Charles felt him tense again when he answered the beautiful lawyer's question.

"I knowed I was the earth god after I met Bunch. I became the god on my own. But I got to say this. Bunch, he was picked. But he ain't helped a bit. When I got on T.V., it wasn't because of him. And I ain't got a dime yet."

Bunch did not interrupt for awhile. He sat between Charles and Tinka like he was angry or thinking hard about something.

The beautiful lawyer talked to Charles for a long

time. Charles told him about the family, about fellowshipping, about the miracles. The beautiful lawyer
asked Charles about the booze and the drugs and
Charles told him how important they were. He asked
Charles if everybody in the family drank and took
drugs and he said that all of them did. Except for Smith.
He was too old to like it much and that it only took a
couple of sips to lay him out so hard that he wasn't even
good for fellowshipping. As the questions continued,
Charles felt his excitement grow. The beautiful lawyer
was on the verge of joining the family. These questions
might sound like they had something to do with getting
money. But he could see what the beautiful lawyer was
up to. And he smiled and nodded all the time, as if he
really liked what he was hearing. And Charles needed a
man like him.

Things had not been good. After the dancing at the
mall, the T.V. people only came to the Palomino once. He
tried to tell them about the show he would have, but
they did not listen. After he asked the pretty T.V. woman if she would like to fellowship, they did not come
back. That night, the family watched the six o'clock
news. Charles spoke to the camera, shouting about the
blood and the truth. The precious spirits and Marcelline
appeared and Charles explained how there had been
another spirit that got smushed flat by Cumby. Then
the family came on and sang the jingle.

It had turned out all wrong. To begin with, Charles
and the family weren't even the main story. They had to
wait until the very end of the show before they got to be
seen. There was a plane crash, and a couple of car
wrecks, a liver transplant, the weather report, the opening of a sewage plant, and basketball and football men.
And finally the Palomino. But the T.V. people acted like
the family was a joke. They sat behind their big desk
and laughed and laughed.

After the news went off, Charles did not have much to

say. The others knew better than to speak—except for Tinka. She whined about not being seen and how she should've been on instead of Marcelline because she was the earth god's wife. It ended up with Charles beating her for a long time, so long that she stopped crying before he had finished. Later, he punished Troy and Darren because they did not sing the after-meal jingle loud enough. Shane and Misty Marie started to get on his nerves, running through the office, screaming, fighting, constantly changing channels on the T.V. He told Wanda to whip them. She did, but he could tell that she did not like doing it. The children cried afterwards—until Charles shouted for them to shut up.

Not a single new person had tried to join the family. A couple of the sissy-men from one of the bars down the road came in one evening. They left when Tinka, Marcelline, and Thelma took off their clothes. Charles had stood in the parking lots of the Third World Lounge and the biker bar, shouting, dancing, ordering the family to sing the jingle. But the people of those other families, the black men in their pimp suits and bikers in denim and leather, only jeered and threw beer cans. They did not even take the trouble to run Charles off.

The beautiful lawyer stopped asking questions and began to read from some paper that the other head doctor had written. This was not the fake T.V. man that was Bunch's friend, the one that got so upset when Charles tried to take his birds on the day Charles found out he was the Daddy. This other one was fat and bald and sounded like a foreigner. Charles liked this other head doctor even less than Pffippert, who at least was pretty. The fat head doctor made him answer the same dumb questions, and he did not even have precious spirits in his office, or a T.V.-like machine.

As the beautiful lawyer read, Charles grew sleepy. He closed his eyes, and could see the beautiful lawyer fellowshipping with Wanda and Darren. And a man as beautiful as he was probably had a beautiful wife.

The beautiful lawyer stopped reading and the questions started again. Instantly, Charles was awake.

"Do you love people?" Gant asked.

Charles placed his large hands on the table, his palms flat on the polished walnut top. He liked the way they looked against the deep shine.

"You know, when I get on T.V. regular, I'm gonna get me a table just like this one. Where'd you get it? They places where you can get T.V. furniture?"

Gant smiled.

"I'm sure I don't know. And I want to get back to how you feel about television. I want to understand where you picked up such an idea. Perhaps Mister Bunch could illuminate us on this point. . ."

"All of the illumination in the room is pouring out of Mr. Gant," said Bunch. It was the first time Bunch had spoken in a while, and Charles was surprised to hear his voice, irritated that his conversation with the beautiful lawyer had been halted. There was a question coming, Charles felt, an important question.

"You're right this time," said Gant to Bunch. "By the way, Mr. Fite, my wife Martha picked out this table, as well as all the other furnishings in these offices."

The time had come.

"You and your wife want to fellowship sometime? Come on down to the Palomino Motel!" Charles shouted.

"Fellowshipping," Gant said. "I believe we've heard a great deal about that subject today. I don't believe I'm interested. . ."

"Ain't interested?" Charles said. "How come you ain't interested? There must be something wrong! A beautiful man like you! Why you could fellowship more than Burt Reynolds."

The room was silent. A tiny smile creased Bunch's face. The beautiful lawyer's tone was still friendly.

"I'll ask the questions," Gant said.

The beautiful lawyer finally finished. All Charles could think about was how bad things were going. The

beautiful lawyer did not have to think twice about turning him down. Dimly, he sensed that someone was to
blame.

The deposition ended. Charles made a final effort. He
grabbed the beautiful lawyer's hand and shook it. He
squeezed hard to show his power. The beautiful lawyer
shook him off and left the room. Later, as Luther drove
Charles and Tinka back to the Palomino, Tinka began
to whine again. She complained of the cold, of having
nothing to eat but grits, and of how Luther had hurt her
in the last fellowshipping session. When she said that
there was not enough money for make-up, Charles told
Luther to pull over. In a Kroger's parking lot, Charles
yanked Tinka from the car and began to beat her.

"Who is Doctor Frederick Von Bey?" asked Gant.

After Charles and Tinka left, Gant had invited
Bunch into his private office for a "friendly discussion."
Bunch wondered if he was going to make an offer. The
signs were against it, he thought. It won't be anything
I've expected. That's the problem with tricky bastards
like Gant.

"You read Dr. Pffippert's report. Von Bey's the noted
German psychiatrist," Bunch said.

"I've never heard of him. Neither have my experts, or
any other reputable shrink I've talked to."

Gant flipped through the report, pausing to read to
himself every few pages.

"Is Pffippert sound?" asked Gant. "I mean professionally of course."

"I have great faith in him," Bunch answered.

That's a good one, Bunch thought. Von Bey's Syndrome. It had all been right there in Pffippert's report.
The twelve hundred dollar report. Besides extolling the
hitherto unknown contribution of Doctor Von Bey, the
report had included many other interesting bits of information that Pffippert must have considered highly

relevant. For example, Bunch learned that Charles Junior Fite represents a revolt of the modern sensibility against the monolithic structure of industrial-technical civilization; that Charles also represents the Dionysian side of western man, which has been in perpetual conflict with the rationalistic since the rise of Greek civilization. Or something like that. There was also a very long printout from the Anthus Board. Bunch did not understand it, but he got it admitted into the transcript of the deposition anyway.

Pffippert had refused to see Charles again because of the business with the birds, the receptionist, and the furniture. But the Anthus Board, according to Pffippert, had made further visits a waste of time. The Anthus Board was the key to the future. That was also in the twelve hundred dollar report. The report also stated that Charles had the most unusual readings ever recorded—readings which showed Charles Fite Junior to have become mentally unbalanced as the result of the automobile accident of August, 1987. Bunch was grateful at least for those few words.

When Bunch received the report, he read it several times, trying each time to determine exactly how it was supposed to be of any use to him. The letter that Pffippert attached was, on the other hand, quite clear. Pffippert was happy with what he had turned out. Eventually it would make him more famous than the guy who wrote *The Three Faces of Eve*. When properly documented and tested, his study of Charles Junior Fite would prove to be as valuable as anything done by R.D. Laing. He was also starting a book on Charles and wanted to know if Bunch would serve as his legal advisor in securing an agent and publisher.

After Bunch read the letter, on the morning of the deposition, he called Pffippert's office. Pffippert's mellow, well-modulated voice told him, through the answering service tape, that he, Roland T. Pffippert, would be out of the office all week. He would be attending a conference on para-psychology and sexual repression at the Productive Living Institute in Santa Barbara, California, where he was reading a paper based upon original research.

Gant slid Pffippert's report into the file.

"Why do you think I wanted to have this conversation with you?" Gant asked.

It's the Gant treatment, Bunch told himself, coming back after hours. The office deserted. Just the two of us. Man to man. Or lawyer to lawyer. Very cozy.

"No idea," Bunch said.

"You've done a good job with Charles. My compliments."

"What do you mean?"

"Sometimes he sounds believable."

"Charles believes every word he says."

"I don't doubt it. If you believed you could get a million bucks, you'd sound authentic too. I particularly liked the fellowshipping business."

"Listen, Gant, I didn't dream up anything. I don't have to."

"You don't have to put on *your* act with me. You're a good actor, though—like when you appeared in front of Judge Cope on that summary judgment. The judge was impressed."

"That's the idea I got. I won."

"And I'm glad you did. It made me realize that there was more to this case than I first thought. Much more. . ."

"Besides the million bucks?" Bunch asked.

"The money means little to me. Anyway, you won't get more than a couple of thousand, and that's because the truck driver clearly screwed up. More importantly, this case interests me. It has, shall we say, a certain esoteric appeal. Judge Cope is deeply interested too, much more so than when you won the summary judgment."

"Interested, huh?" Bunch said. "What's got him interested?"

"I believe it all started when he saw you on T.V. Your interview at the jail? I was with him that evening. Martha and I see a good bit of Ted and Bitsy."

"Yeah," said Bunch. "I take the paper. Are you a jackal-hunter yourself now? Been giving money to Christians for a Lobotomized World?"

"Judge Cope felt. . . somewhat deceived by your actions. Especially after he got a good look at Charles and his family. The judge was shocked about the fellowshipping. He's something of a prude."

"Why are you telling me this?" Bunch asked. "It's not your style. I've had a couple of cases against you in the past. You probably don't remember them. . ."

"You're right. I don't."

"Well, I do. And you were the slickest, trickiest bastard that ever got a dismissal. You soothe and goad. You win, no matter what. Only this time you act like you don't want to win. You could have delayed and waited me out."

"That's not what I'm after," Gant said. "I want you right where you are, and where you're going to be when the trial starts. By the way, things turned out well for your clients on the riot charges, didn't they?"

Bunch had expected Charles and the family to draw time. After all, they were dirty and crazy. But the district attorney asked for a dismissal and Judge Carver quickly agreed. Santa Claus and the mall manager had been furious, but what could they do? The only defendant who was found guilty and sentenced was a guy named Cumby, a preacher. He got three months in the county. When Charles heard the sentence, he danced and the rest of them sang the McDonald's jingle and

Bunch thought the whole crowd would be slapped in for contempt. But Carver only picked at himself and called the next case.

"So what?" answered Bunch. "Even the truly lost can get lucky."

Gant laughed. Bunch had never heard him laugh. To hear Gant laugh was frightening and disorienting. Like the day he saw Charles walk for the first time.

"That's very good, Roy. Very good indeed. In fact, I've come to believe that you have an excellent, cosmic sense of humor. I re-read your complaint this morning. A masterpiece."

"Everything in that complaint is true," Bunch said. "There's something very important here that you don't understand."

"And what's that?"

"Charles is for real, no matter what he calls himself. The family is for real too. If we lose it, it will be because Charles is not crazy enough."

"And you will lose," Gant said. "The truly lost got out of the riot charges because I fixed it. Thing are easy to fix here—most of the time. I didn't want any petty criminal matter standing in the way of my trial. You see, Roy, the reason I always win, and you always lose, is because I can see the whole picture."

"Tell me about the whole picture. I've been practicing law longer than I like to think and I've never seen the whole fucking picture."

Gant's eyes widened in mock amazement.

"Really? It's unusual for a lawyer to make such an admission."

"Yeah. Most of us aren't too fond of admissions."

"This case is absurd on its face. Your client isn't any crazier now than before the wreck. It won't be difficult to show."

"What makes you so sure?" asked Bunch. Bunch felt a small surge of hatred and envy for Gant. But there was something else—something he could not immediately identify. Gant smiled his smile of pity. Bunch felt a sudden urge to reach across the desk, to muss his hair, to yank at his tie, to make him less perfect than what he was.

"You like this, don't you?" Bunch asked.

"I do. I enjoy the sport of lawyering. And so do you."

Gant stood and began to pace around the room. Gradually, as he paced, his manner, his appearance were transformed. He gestured emphatically with clenched fist and pointing finger. To Bunch he sounded like a carnival barker.

"This case," Gant said, "has more possibilities than any I've ever been involved in. Even though I'm sure to win, there is the doing of the thing. That's what matters. . ."

The urge to grab at Gant faded. It came to Bunch, as he watched Gant's progress back and forth across the room, that Gant was like Charles in at least one way. Both of them had an idea of how the world should be. It was not enough, for either of them, to take the world as it is. There had to be more. Bunch felt a little sorry for them, for the world.

". . . your client claims he is God," Gant said. "You claim that he is crazy. In his eyes, not only is he sane, but he has the answer to all the questions which have puzzled and frustrated the human race for centuries. Where do I fit in? I'll tell you. I can show that Charles Fite has as good a claim to being God as can be found, only he is entitled to nothing for that claim. . ."

Gant clapped his hands.

"And it all came about by accident. If Woodside had not been late for court that day. If Cope had been sent to another district. If you had not made the right moves, put on the right act during the summary judgment. It all would have ended even before I got the chance to see what splendid possibilities it offered for me! I would never have had this chance! I would still be progressing from one mundane triumph to another. Eventually, I would have grown stale and fat, and I would have begun to slip. I would be like everyone else. I should thank you."

Bunch realized that Gant could go on like this indefinitely. It was as if a statue, or a machine had suddenly began to dance and sing. It was time to leave.

"Well, Trip," said Bunch, "when it's time for the fucking show, I'll be there."

Gant stopped pacing. Bunch saw that he had become Gant again, at least for a moment. But he could sense something stirring within. Gant's eyes weren't right yet. They were a little too wide, a little too moist and swollen. He smiled his old smile of triumph. Bunch paused at the door.

"How many scores do you think a man is entitled to?" said Bunch.

"All he can get," answered Gant.

"None," answered Bunch. "He's entitled to none."

Then Bunch was gone. Gant sat down. The faces in the photographs on the office wall still gazed down at him with good humor and comradeship. He sensed his superiority to them, those who had been his mentors, his heroes, or his peers. Would any of them had tried such a case? Would any of them have tried to prove that God deserved nothing? Privately, of course, most of them believed this. God does not make decisions. God does not reach into a human life and re-arrange it. No one in the photographs had dared to prove it publicly.

He opened the desk drawer and removed a brown papered package. Another of Akin's tapes. Soon he would retire to the bathroom to enjoy it. First, however, he called Goforth to see if the Florida trip had been successful.

XIII

"Tonight temperatures in the Piedmont will break a fifty year low. We can expect more snow and sleet by morning. . ."
The precious spirit hung in its jar, suspended in alcohol. To Charles, it seemed almost happy, much happier than he was. The office was the only warm room in the motel. A single kerosene heater sat on the reservation desk, between Charles, on his lawn chair, and the jar. The family sat at the foot of the desk, facing the television. Beyond the streaked windows and the broken "No Vacancy" sign, snow fell.

Charles was tired of waiting for better days, for a larger family, for his show to start. He still felt the power as the blood flowed forcefully within him. Still, nothing seemed to work. He had gone to the mall once more, but two policemen ordered him out. He had even gone back to the bars on Charlie Justice Boulevard. The bikers and the sissy men had not even bothered to come out and laugh at him as he shouted and sang in the cold.

For a little while, though, there had been a reason to hope.

He had gone to the middle of the city, where he walked on the second great day. He spoke for an hour on the courthouse steps. The people there were like his family. He could tell they had been lost for a long time, that they were waiting. They even looked like the family. They were not pretty, like T.V. people and the happy children and parents in the mall. They wanted to be beautiful, but did not understand how. They listened, but none of them showed up at the Palomino. He had not done exactly the right thing, or said the perfect word. They were waiting; he could tell.

It wasn't his fault that he never found the right word. A deputy came out of the courthouse and told him to leave. Charles refused, and the deputy came back with a short man with a tanned face and silver hair. The man said he was a judge and that Charles had thirty seconds to leave, that he would not tolerate jackals shouting in public, blaspheming all that was decent. He called Charles a jackal, a name he did know. The crowd on the steps became restless and began to murmur. Two more deputies showed up and the judge said a riot was about to start and the deputies drew their guns. The mob backed away from the steps and Luther and Darren and Troy led Charles away. He let himself be taken. The little judge had ruined his chance.

He had thought about the judge as Luther drove back to the Palomino. There were many men, he decided, like the judge. They had been put in his way, and he did not yet understand how to get around them.

Everyone but Wanda was out of work. Henry and Thad had been fired when the cable T.V. company found out that they had wired the Palomino. The abattoir went on half-days and Thelma had been laid off. Darren and Troy tried to steal, but it was too cold. All they had gotten lately were two weed eaters that had been left in unlocked sheds, some hubcaps, cartons of cigarettes, and four jars of Penrose Hot Sausages. More than once they were forced to flee when store managers spotted them shoplifting. And it was impossible to break into homes. People stayed in their houses at night, close to the heat. Tinka could not find customers at the truck stops. The money from selling the weed eaters and the hubcaps was nearly gone. There was only one jar of sausages and enough grits for another week. Then there was Righter.

Righter once had some money. It had lasted into the first couple of weeks of January—until his children, or some other meddlers, had gotten their hands on it. The money had made things good. There had been plenty of liquor and drugs, and the Palomino went on regular electric service. Righter's money, Charles thought, was only a little taste of how life would be when he got his million dollars. Now, it might never be his. And without it, nothing else could follow.

Righter did not seem to care when the money dried up. In fact, he did not care about anything. All he did was sit around in that robe. Charles brooded about the robe.

The rest of the family was nearly as worthless as Righter. They sat below the throne, whispering. They whined too much and expected Charles to fix whatever was wrong with them. He had given them the word and the Precious Spirits. He had taught them how to fellowship. That was not enough for them. He had to listen to them. They were cold. They were tired of eating grits. They could not find jobs. They did not get to fellowship as much as they wanted.

"Darren! Turn down the T.V.!" Charles' voice was harsh.

Thelma yelped in disapproval. *I Love Lucy* was coming on. It was her favorite show.

"Outside Thelma! Go stand in the pool! Where the shit is deepest!"

Slowly, she struggled to her feet. After she had gone, Charles marched back and forth on the registration desk.

"There's gonna be some changes made. You ain't been doing right. I try and try. You can't follow the way I lay out for you. You're weak and sick and won't ever get even a little bit of the power. You want it to be easy. You want to fellowship every minute, but you don't know what fellowshipping is for. You watch T.V., but you don't understand it."

He pointed toward Marcelline, who cradled one of the surviving monkeys.

"I seen you watching one of them T.V. preachers the other night. I come in from spreading the truth, and you tried to change the station real fast so I couldn't catch you at it. But you ain't quick enough. None of you is quick enough to fool me. I SEE EVERYTHING! YOU SUPPOSED TO KNOW THAT IF YOU DON'T KNOW NOTHING ELSE!"

Charles ordered Marcelline to the pool. The cold flooded the room as she left. Charles did not immediately resume his speech. He wanted what was happening, and what was going to happen, to sink in. He searched the faces of the family, and they did not meet his gaze.

"Luther," he said in a low, matter-of-fact tone. "You been sneaking down the road to that bar where the sissy men live; the ones that come here, but wouldn't stay."

Luther began to stutter.

"Daddy. . . I been. . . I been trying to get them for the family. . . some of them. . . some of them was interested. . . They said. . ."

"THEN WHERE ARE THEY? I WORK TO BRING IN NEW FAMILY! YOU GONNA BE BETTER THAN ME? I WAS ON T.V.! I WAS AT THE MALL! I WALKED!"

Tears came to Luther's eyes.

"I've. . . I've tried to do right. I swear. . . if I done something wrong. I'm sorry. I. . ."

Charles' voice was powerful with contempt.

"You been fellowshipping with them men—they ain't family."

The hum was loud now. It had been soft at first. The more Charles told the truth, told the things he had seen and those things that Darren and Troy had reported to him, the stronger it became.

"And then we got the judge."

At first, Righter did not realize that Charles was speaking to him. He smiled. He had been smiling since Christmas at the mall.

"YOU! JUDGE! THERE AIN'T ROOM FOR BUT ONE JUDGE IN THIS FAMILY!"

Charles leaped from the desk. The family scrambled out of his way.

"I want that robe," said Charles.

Righter did not seem to understand.

"The robe? My robe?"

"That's right. From now on, I wear the robe."

Righter stood.

"I can't be without my robe. The state gave it to me. The robe is important. I'm a college graduate. I have a law degree. You see, I really am a judge, even if I don't hear cases anymore. I feel like a judge. . ."

Charles grasped the zipper at Righter's throat and gave it a downward jerk. The robe opened to reveal a filthy white shirt and a stained striped tie. Righter tried to get his hand back in the zipper. Charles slapped him hard across the mouth, leaving a deep red mark against the pallor of Righter's face. Righter's arms fell to his sides and Charles shucked him of the robe. Charles climbed back atop the desk.

"I been watching you for a long time," Charles said. "What you think is important ain't shit. You ain't shit and neither is being no judge up in court. I'm the real judge!"

Charles pulled the robe around his body. It was several sizes too large. He looked like a child in adult's clothing. Righter did not move. He stood rock-like, his arms at his sides. Charles took his seat in the lawn chair.

"You can sing now."

None of them had moved during the taking of the robe. It was a kind of miracle. It excited them in a new way. Tinka thought Charles looked good in it, like a preacher. Troy and Darren wished they had taken the robe and given it to Charles as a present. They had been a little afraid of Righter. He was large and imposing, and they understood that he once had the power to send people to jail. Now, Charles had made him less than nothing. Henry and Thad did not understand what had happened, although they sensed something would come of it. They rubbed their hands on their legs. Luther was relieved. Charles had forgotten about him. Smith, huddled under an old quilt, had seen such things in the past. The taking of the robe vaguely disturbed him. This feeling passed, and he pulled the quilt tightly around his thin body. It was important to stay warm.

They sang the jingle. Shane and Misty Marie climbed the desk so that they could be closer to Daddy. Charles applauded as they danced and sang in their high children's voices. The family sang with upturned faces. The cold did not matter so much now.

Righter did not sing. As the jingle ended, he started toward Charles. He came on slowly, swinging his arms and shouting. Before he could get on the desk, the other men of the family were upon him. Quickly, they pinned him to the floor. The rush toward Charles had taken the last of his energy. He lay still, without struggling, beneath the men.

Charles stood at the edge of the desk, his hands on his hips, his legs spread wide. He could tell that Righter had once been a happy man. He had gotten to do pretty much anything he wanted.

"You ain't part of us no more," Charles said. "You done missed out on the chance of a lifetime. That's right. You can't fellowship no more. You ain't got a robe. The road that leads outta here is empty and cold and you gotta walk it. I walked it. You might find a thing worth having, but you ain't ever gonna have what you had here."

The men pulled Righter to his feet and pushed him through the door. He vanished into the snow and the night, carefully taking one step at a time, his head bent into the storm. In a couple of minutes he was gone. Charles gave the signal and the singing started again.

Charles felt a little better. He let Shane and Misty Marie stroke the robe. They marveled at how silky it felt. The family sang loudly, with hot, red faces. We been needing something like this, Charles thought. He tapped his foot to the song. Might have a little dancing and fellowshipping tonight. It'll be good for them, except for Luther. He tried to decide whether Luther should go to the swimming pool or kneel in the parking lot. I'll figure it out later, he told himself.

Wanda and her children disappeared three days after Charles took the robe. She came home early from the Seven-Eleven and said she was taking Shane and Misty Marie to get new shoes. By the time the *CBS Evening News* was over, she had not returned. Later that night, while the family watched *The Bill Cosby Show*, Charles walked over to the service station across Charlie Justice Boulevard and telephoned the Seven-Eleven. The manager told Charles that Wanda brought the children to the store, where she met a man who drove a new, yellow Chevy pick-up. The man left with the children. Later, he came back and picked up Wanda. She said that the man was her husband, which surprised the manager because he didn't know she was married. The manager thought it wasn't right for her to leave without giving notice. She even left her car—Smith's old blue Ford.

Later that night, Charles sent Troy and Darren to recover Smith's Ford. Each morning that followed, Charles left with Troy and Darren in the Ford, and they searched the city and surrounding countryside. Each night, when they returned without Wanda and the children, Charles held court. The members of the family gladly informed on each other and on themselves. After they reported, the punishments were handed out. All, except Smith, were guilty of something. As Charles pronounced sentence, they felt the power of the robe and understood that things were as they were meant to be.

For Charles, the nightly judgment and punishment was small compensation for the loss of Wanda and the children. It was not just that Wanda brought in a small, but steady income. She had been one of the first to join the family, and she was easily the best-looking. Charles had plans for Shane and Misty Marie. They were approaching an age when fellowshipping was possible. More importantly, they were not tainted with a past, like the rest of the family. They could have been made right, he thought, if it had been left up to him.

They tracked back and forth across the city and suburbs for two weeks. The search only made the disappearance harder for Charles to bear. As they drove the streets, the people—people who should have been in the family—spread out before him, going through their useless lives, oblivious to him, as if he did not exist. There were still the people on the courthouse steps, and he often wished he could stop to speak to them. He could too, if it had not been for the little judge, the man who called him a jackal. Smith explained to him what a jackal was. It seemed to Charles a kind of precious spirit, but the little judge meant it in a bad way. And then one evening on the late news, he saw the little judge and the beautiful lawyer. They were with their wives in a glittering place of lights and music. A T.V. man asked them about the United Way and both of them said that it was a good thing. In the dimly lit, stinking cold of the Palomino he saw that the little judge had what he, Charles, deserved. He was only a man, yet there he was with the beautiful lawyer. There he was showing the beauty and power. It was more than Charles could stand. He snapped off the T.V. and gave Tinka a good beating.

They traveled many streets and knocked on many doors before they found the trailer. Charles felt that Wanda and the children might be behind a certain door, or about to walk out of a certain house. Sometimes they waited for as long as half a day before they gave up. When he saw the trailer, however, he knew that it was different from all the other trailers he had seen during the search. It was not far from where he met Wanda, out in the pines and fields.

Charles ordered Darren to stop the car at the top of the long, rutted drive. The yellow pick-up sat out front. As Charles waited for another sign, Shane and Misty Marie emerged from the trailer, carrying bright dolls, rocketships, and spacemen. The children began to play in the mud of the yard. Darren eased the Ford to the bottom of the hill. He and Troy waited by the car. The robe rustled in the wind. The children smiled.

"You're the man that had the monkeys," Shane said.

Charles patted the boy's head. His corn-silk hair was clean and freshly cut.

"Not monkeys. Precious Spirits—like you. Don't you remember the talks we had about the Spirits and the television, and the dancing?"

"Monkey," giggled Misty Marie. She cuddled a Cabbage Patch doll.

Charles frowned.

"No. Precious Spirits."

Shane shook his head.

"Daddy says that they was monkeys."

"I'm your Daddy."

The children looked to each other, then back to Charles.

"Daddy's in the trailer," Shane said.

I oughta just take them, Charles thought. Wanda would come back then. She'd thank me for saving her again.

"Whoever is in that trailer ain't your Daddy. The Daddy is the one that cares most about what happens to you. That man in there don't know who you are."

Shane held up an X-wing fighter.

"He give me this," the boy said. "And lots of other stuff. A bunch of Star Wars things. I got Darth Vader and Luke Skywalker and Chewbaca. Misty got that Cabbage Patch doll and Barbie and Ken and Ken's car. And he give Momma an electric guitar."

The boy was dreamy with toys, trips to McDonalds and a promised bicycle from this other man who had so much.

"He's got this truck, too. He takes us for rides. Took us to Charlotte yesterday. Says he's gonna take us there tonight to hear momma sing. She sings so pretty and all the people like her."

"Sing?" said Charles with genuine astonishment. "Sing? About what?"

"I don't know," said Shane. "People clap their hands and holler though."

The idea of Wanda singing in front of people instantly consumed Charles. I got to get her back, he thought. I got to have her. Charles took the boy's hand.

"You better come with me. That man in the trailer is fooling you, giving you things that don't matter none. I got what you need. Me and you and Misty Marie, we'll walk. We'll walk all over the world."

They were his children, and so was she. He had made them. They had lived among the precious spirits. He had given them everything, and they had been taken away. Shane tried to jerk his hand away, but Charles held it tightly.

"I don't wanta go with you!" the boy shouted. "I don't like where you stay! It's cold! It stinks!"

Charles lifted Shane to his feet. The boy howled, twisting and turning like a fish on a line. Misty Marie did not bother with her brother and this funny man in his funny dress. It was another game. She cast aside her Cabbage Patch doll and picked up Ken and Barbie. This game Shane and the man played was not as much fun as the Ken and Barbie game. She dressed and undressed the dolls. Ken told Barbie that he was going to bring her a diamond ring from Dallas, where he would eat dinner with J. R. Ewing.

Charles called Darren and Troy. They shuffled half-heartedly away from the car. The radio was playing good music—rock and roll about blowing up houses and slaughtering people. As they reached Charles, the door to the trailer opened.

It was Wanda. She wore black, skin-tight leather pants, velvet vest and a ruffled red blouse. Her hair was piled in an elaborate mound, and her make-up was thick and heavy. Darren and Troy moaned. They had never seen a more beautiful woman—outside of television.

When Charles saw her, he released Shane's hand and the boy ran to his mother. She was a T.V. woman, he realized. She had gotten some of the power. Slowly, with Shane clutching her arm, and with a great swaying of breasts and haunches, she approached Charles. She stayed a good ten feet away from him—out of grabbing distance.

"I didn't know you'd turned out this way," Charles said.

Wanda smiled. It was a performer's smile, automatic and designed to convey instant warmth.

"It ain't too late," Charles said. "I'll take you back. When I get on T.V. you'll be up there with me."

"You done a lot for me, Charles. . ."

"You mean Daddy."

The smile never wavered.

"No. My daddy lives in Gaffney. He's got a bad back and he used to work in the mill."

"You're wrong. You got to admit that I'm the Daddy."

The smile left Wanda's face. She backed up a couple of feet. Then she was bright and nervous, changing the subject.

"Do I look all right? This is the way I dress when I sing at the Country Palace. Two shows nightly. I just started last week, but I can tell that a lot of people like me. Cecil set it up. He's friends with the manager. I used to sing in the choir. I used to sing in the kitchen. I had all of Barbara Mandrell's records. Cecil says I sound as good as her. If it weren't for Cecil, I'd never had this chance. He took me back. . ."

"You used to sing with the family too," Charles said. He decided that even though she had been re-tainted by Cecil that she was very close to being a precious spirit.

". . . I was gonna tell you how much I appreciated what you done for me, about the fellowshipping and. . . uh. . . all that. It changed my life. I feel bad about sneaking away, though. See, Cecil had been coming to the Seven-Eleven for a long time, ever since he seen me on T.V. after that trouble out at the mall. At first, I wouldn't listen to him, but he kept coming and crying and going on about Shane and Misty Marie. And they *are* his kids too. And he seemed different, like he'd changed as much as I had. Then he told me about the Country Palace and it come to me that I had to go back. I mean, we never got divorced or nothing."

"Them that is family should never leave," Charles

said. "That's the one thing you can't do. I'll take you back, and the kids too. I'll teach you the right way to live. You can sing at the Country Palace too. You won't have to fellowship with nobody but me. You won't have to stand in the swimming pool. . ."

Over Wanda's shoulder, Charles saw a man appear in the trailer's doorway. Despite the cold, he was shirtless and wore a pair of jeans and cowboy boots. He was a powerful man, with a big belly and heavy arms. He had just gotten out of the shower and was damp and slick, his skin red from the heat and water. He regarded the scene in the front yard for a moment, then disappeared back into the trailer. When he returned, he had pulled a jacket over his shoulders and he carried a shotgun, long, black and glowing dully with oil.

Charles watched Cecil closely as he came across the yard. The hum was suddenly high and wild. The gun seemed to grow out of Cecil's body. Darren and Troy retreated behind the car and crouched low. Cecil stood beside Wanda, the shotgun pointing toward the ground.

"That's him, ain't it?" Cecil asked Wanda.

Wanda nodded and told the children to go inside and watch television. Shane ran, abandoning the toys. Misty Marie grabbed the Cabbage Patch doll, but left Ken and Barbie.

Cecil curled his lips, showing long, yellow teeth. Charles smelled him, the hot, washed odor like charred beef.

"You made my wife be untrue to me, and my kids got nightmares on account of you."

Cecil spoke as if he were addressing a thing instead of a man or a god.

"They didn't get nightmares from me," Charles said. "They got them from being without me, from not having the right things. This, what they got now, is the nightmare. Can they dance? Have they got a word?"

The shotgun came up slowly, until the muzzle was

level with Charles' throat. Charles' speech did not slow down, nor did he acknowledge that the gun was there.

". . . and you done made Wanda give up her happiness. And for what? She can be on my show. We'll be on television every day."

He turned to Wanda.

"You done lost your real family," said Charles. "You give up the best thing you ever had. Look at me! I got a robe now! This man here, he might have helped you a little. But would you be a singer if it wasn't for me? If it wasn't for the family? You would be like you was when I found you—after this man here run off and took your kids. You didn't have a voice. You didn't know what fellowshipping was."

"I ought to kill you," Cecil said. His voice was flat and cold.

Wanda backed toward the trailer.

"Cecil. . . please don't shoot him. Things is just starting up right. Please. . . he'll go."

The hum was high, undulating with electric rhythm.

"He can shoot me if he wants to," Charles said. "But he won't. If he shoots me, he'll be shooting you and them kids. He'll blow a hole in everything."

Charles looked into Cecil's pale blue eyes. The red from the shower was fading. Cecil was slick and white, like a fish belly. The eye told Charles that this man could not kill him. Cecil looked away from him.

"Go on!" shouted Charles. "Pull it! You ready to kill the world?"

Cecil's voice shook.

"Don't make me do it. Get out!"

Charles laughed, long and loud.

"You can't. You won't."

Wanda turned to run to the trailer. The heel of her Texas, rhinestone, high heel boot went through the plastic of the X-wing fighter. The toy whistled and flashed one last time as Wanda lost her balance and fell into the mud. She was up in a second, her leather pants split, her ruffled blouse smeared.

"It's ruined!" she cried as she frantically tried to brush the mud from the blouse. "And my pants! I can't go on tonight with split pants."

She began to cry, her shoulders heaving, her make-up melting under the tears.

"Look what you done!" yelled Cecil. "Coming to a man's house this way. . . I oughta. . . I oughta. . ."

The shotgun muzzle flashed white, then orange, then red. The rush of its force skipped just past Charles' head. The Ford's windshield exploded, peppering Troy and Darren with glass. They hurled themselves into the tall grass beside the driveway.

Cecil pumped another shell into the breach.

"I. . . I don't know why I missed. But you ain't getting a second chance."

Wanda leaned against the trailer, still weeping.

"Don't kill him! I used to love him so!" she shouted.

She disappeared into the trailer. Cecil leveled the shotgun at Charles. Then he slowly backed away, like an infantryman in orderly retreat. Twice, before he reached the trailer, he halted and took aim. But he never fired.

The wind whipped around them, making their eyes water, setting their teeth to chattering. Troy drove and Darren, who had caught most of the glass when the windshield was blown out, sat in the back and picked at his bleeding face.

"Goddamn, it hurts. Man with a shotgun. Coulda got my eyes."

Charles, who rode beside Troy, could still see the muzzle flash. It was a kind of miracle, he decided, even though he had lost again. The blast had been invigorating. But this would not be like the day he walked or when he found out he was the earth god. What it meant would not be shown immediately. He leaned over the seat.

"Can you steal a gun?" he shouted above the wind.

Darren worked a particularly long shard of glass from his cheek.

"Yeah. I reckon. My uncle Delbert's got a pistol. I fired it last Fourth of July. You remember that little old gun, Troy?"

Troy shouted that he did, and that it wasn't any good outside of fifteen feet. Charles did not care. To have it was the main thing.

"I want you to get it tonight," yelled Charles.

Darren let out a whine.

"But, Daddy, I need to go to the hospital. I got to get this glass out. It hurts like a motherfucker. . ."

"You ain't going to no hospital until I get the gun. You hear?"

"Yes, Daddy."

"Troy?"

"Yes, Daddy. I hear."

"You take Henry's truck and don't say nothing about what you're up to. And keep your mouth shut about Wanda too."

"But, Daddy," shouted Darren. "She's so pretty and the family would be so glad to find out. . ."

"Shut up, Darren. Shut your Goddamned mouth."

XIV

Bunch was not sure that Charles and Tinka would make the ten o'clock appointment. He had given Alda the morning off in case they did; he had decided that there was no reason to involve an innocent party. He had not seen or heard from them since the deposition. He had driven by the Palomino a couple of times, though he could never quite bring himself to stop. Still, they had to be informed about the trial, and he had hoped that the last letter had somehow convinced them to come.

The trial would start in three weeks. It should not have been up before the end of the summer term, but Cope had insisted, clearing the docket of murders, rapes, and armed robberies. It was Gant's doing, Bunch thought. Gant understood judges. He had probably understood Claude Righter very well: former judge, former member of Charles Fite's family. He was a member of no one's family now. There had been the headline right after the city's yearly snow fall: RETIRED JUDGE FOUND FROZEN IN VACANT LOT.

Not that I had much use for him, Bunch thought. According to Raymer, who had been detailed to the sheriff's office after Cope heard him tell a joke about a sailor with a twelve-inch dick, Righter was naked and blue all over. Peaceful, though, said Raymer. Curled up like a baby.

The last time Bunch had seen Righter was in district court, when the charges had been dismissed against Charles. He grinned and sang like the others and would not speak. Retired judges aren't supposed to end up in vacant lots any more than they are supposed to fellowship with Tinka Fite. None of my business, Bunch thought. Could happen to anyone these days.

Bunch lit a cigarette and exhaled deeply. Righter had been, despite his brutishness, too old-fashioned. Cope was different, an expert practitioner of the new style—hysterical self-congratulation. The new style had merely, however, been re-cycled from the past. Cope might once have been an illiterate Christian in Rome, howling at the emperor in hopes of martyrdom. Such a style came naturally to Cope; only he did not have his own martyrdom in mind.

Raymer had also told him of the encounter between Cope and Charles. Cope had raged about jackals for days afterwards, and sentenced two eighteen year olds to twenty years apiece for stealing a video game. Cope gave the sheriff's department standing orders to keep the mob off the steps. But it was still there. It scattered when the deputies came out to shoo it away. Like a flock of starlings, it always returned to its nesting ground.

Bunch had big news for Charles, news that would be celebrated with much fellowshipping and dancing. Gant had called the afternoon before. The trial would be televised on the local public station. According to Gant, it was Cope's idea, which would not have been surprising. Except that Bunch was sure that Gant, too, wanted it televised. Part of his plan to show that God deserved nothing.

He fought down the urge for a drink and lit another cigarette. I have my own plans, he thought. And there are those with plans who are supposed to be on my side. Pffippert, for instance. He had visited Pffippert's office the day after his expert had returned from the conference on para-psychology and sexual repression. Bunch found him doing some sort of gerbil-like exercise on the office floor.

"You fucked me over, Roland. The report isn't worth shit. You shouldn't get a dime out of me, much less twelve hundred."

Pffippert paused in his exercise.

"I hear your pain, Roy. And I understand."

He resumed the exercise, rotating his legs from the hips.

"Understand my pain? The report is what I'm talking about. It has no substance. It makes no sense. Can you hear that? Hear this too. At the trial I don't want anything about the Dionysian face of western man or the Bermuda Triangle or any similar horseshit."

Pffippert had risen from the floor and toweled himself off.

"Don't I look great? Sun and relaxation. And stimulating ideas, I might add."

"And a couple of sixteen year old girls?"

Pffippert's smile became enigmatic.

"I haven't seen a dime, Roy. I doubt you have the money necessary for my services."

While this was true, Bunch had not wanted to hear it.

"Don't worry about the fucking money."

"Besides, it's not twelve hundred. It's fourteen. Damages to the office. Not to mention the mental suffering inflicted upon my receptionist and birds. A most disturbing, but interesting experience. By the way, how *is* Charles?"

"He's nuts. I can't even talk to him."

"I understand your position, which sounds quite desperate and depressing."

"You could say that."

"Roy, you have my sympathy. And I will do my best for your client, which will be the best you can get in this town. Just this morning I was working up my notes on Von Bey's syndrome."

"I don't care whether you use Von Bey or Oral Roberts."

"By the way, have you thought about my offer? The book? There will by something in it for you, of course. Perhaps you can even come up with my fourteen hundred. I'm trying to help you, Roy. Help you to understand yourself and. . ."

Then there was Ms. Williams, the social worker. Bunch could not remember her first name. Most social workers did not have first names anyway. She was, or had been before the wreck, Charles' case worker. Bunch had met her at lunch time in her basement office in the court house. The office was tiny, shabby, and institutional. Bunch would have felt right at home if it were not for the posters. One announced that "If life gives you lemons, make lemonade." Another presented a quotation from Emerson superimposed over a sparkling river at sunset.

Ms. Williams was probably thirty, but looked forty, with thinning brown hair and oversized glasses. She wore a polyester pants suit that was a size or so too small. When Bunch had entered the office, she was eating a salad from a styrofoam bowl and drinking a Diet Coke.

"I hope you don't mind," she had gestured toward the salad. "This is my lunch hour."

Her voice was high and melodious. Like a girl's, Bunch had thought with surprise. When she smiled, her teeth were small, white and crooked. It had not been a Gant or Cope smile.

"So you're Charles Fite's lawyer. Well, I must say that Charles is difficult to find. He's missed his last three meetings and his checks have all been returned to us. . ."

"He's changed his address."

"He should notify D.S.S. He stands to lose his benefits if he doesn't stay in contact with us."

"It may well be that he's no longer qualified."

"How's that?" She had speared an olive and popped it into her mouth.

"He can walk now."

She had been sipping from the can of Diet Coke when he had told her this. She had belched softly.

"Oh! Excuse me!"

She had blushed then. Bunch had not been able to remember the last person he had seen blush.

"He can walk?" she said.

"I've seen it."

He told her about the wreck and the precious spirits and the Palomino Motel. About fellowshipping and the McDonalds jingle. He tried not to leave anything out.

She finished the salad and dropped the bowl into the trash can.

"He can walk. Just like that." She had shaken her head slowly.

"I'm sure," she said. "I can't do anything more for him. Neither can D.S.S. I had wanted to believe that we could help him. He's distant. Charles was very distant and. . . well. . . very uncooperative."

"I've read your reports," Bunch said. "Charles is at least uncooperative."

She does not, he had thought, have much to do with the world. Maybe somewhere she inhabits a perfect

187

world where all people do the right things, where there are no lunatics, or cripples, or mean, vicious bastards. But how could she, given what must pass through her door every day?

"What do you want with me? Is Charles in some kind of trouble?"

"Not with the law. In fact, he stands to collect a good bit of money. I represent him in a civil case—personal injury. And you, well, you have a special knowledge of Charles, of what he was like before the wreck. That's the basis of this case, that the wreck caused certain. . . tendencies in his character to become more pronounced. And caused him to go. . . crazy."

He regretted the use of the word crazy. Like Pffippert, she probably did not believe that people were insane, only she might be honest enough to say so on the stand. She did not have Pffippert's shields. All she had was two posters. She must be crazy herself, or very brave, with her high girl's voice and clear brown eyes.

"Poor Charles," she said. "He was so hostile. Sad and lonely, without a way of coping. It must have seemed to him that no one cared. The weak don't get much understanding. I guess I should take some of the blame myself. D.S.S. is cold, impersonal. We have so many clients, and so little time for them. . ."

Bunch had started to stop her, to say that Charles was not what she imagined. Her voice had halted him, however.

". . . and then this wreck. He's probably more confused and lost than ever."

She smiled at him again and Bunch avoided her eyes.

"I'll be happy to testify, Mr. Bunch. You know, most lawyers won't represent the poor, the disadvantaged. I often work with lawyers. I know. Oh some are sensitive to the needs of the poor. There's Legal Aid and the public defender's office, but they're just a sop, a little window-dressing for the middle class. All those so-called nice people who want to forget about the Charles Fites of the world. You just tell me what you want me to cover. I must warn you, though. I'll only tell the truth."

"Of that I'm sure. Of course there'll be an expert's fee."

With her small, white hand she waved aside the suggestion of money.

"You can donate it to the Sierra Club. My favorite charity."

At ten-thirty there was still no sign of Charles and Tinka. Bunch leaned forward in his chair, resting his arms on the window sill, the city below him. The city's colors, grays, reds, and whites, were muted. Sleet had fallen a couple of days before, but had quickly melted. The sky was pale, washed-out, clear; the sunlight weak and brittle.

There was one more expert. Bunch had read about him in the paper a month or so before. His name was Father Babbington, a professor of philosophy at the local Catholic college. Father Babbington, according to the article about him in the paper, believed in devils. In fact, he had written several mildly controversial books on them.

Bunch had driven out to see him at the college, which was green and red-bricked and quiet. It doesn't belong here, Bunch had thought as he entered the driveway that lead past the administration building. It was one of the Vatican's outposts in a heathen region.

Bunch had expected to find a thin, aesthetic type in a book-lined study, pouring over Aquinas, or at least grading freshman essays on Plato. Instead, he found a fat young man with a face like a pie, who peered at Bunch over a copy of *The National Enquirer*. The headline on the cover read:

MICHAEL JACKSON SEES DEMONS IN MALIBU!

"Mr. Bunch?" Babbington's mouth was full and pouty,

his smile slightly out of focus. Bunch extended his hand and the priest shook it with a surprisingly firm grip. Bunch guessed that it had been practiced for years.

When they settled into their chairs, Babbington had tossed the *Enquirer* to one side of the littered desk.

"Original research?" Bunch asked.

"In my line, you take your information where you can find it. I subscribe to tabloids from all over the world. Those from the Philippines, Africa, and the United States are particularly useful."

Babbington's voice was high and lilting. Higher even than Ms. Williams'.

"I must keep up," Babbington said, "with the public's perception of the devil. Not all demonic possessions are real. In fact, few are. Some might even be migraine headaches or constipation."

"The devil in the fundament, eh?"

"The devil's not anywhere in most cases. That's why we have psychiatrists, judges, policemen. There are, of course, exceptions. Sometimes those who don't believe in the evil cannot begin to help. . ."

Bunch decided that Father Babbington really liked the devil.

". . . have you seen my latest book, *The Devil in History: A Philosophical Reconsideration?* It's sold more than ten thousand copies, which isn't bad for a book from an ecclesiastical publishing house."

"I don't have time for too much outside reading."

"I'll give you a copy."

"Yes. . . thanks."

"I write not only for scholars, but for laymen too. I want my books to say something—and they do. The humanist believes that men are responsible for history. But what about those men who loom larger than life? Who wield power for evil? Martin Luther? Darwin? Marx? Stalin? Who can account for their powers? They were not normal men in any way. Consider, for example, Luther's sexual excesses. . ."

As Father Babbington went on, he grew more animated. His small, button, stuffed-toy-dog eyes seemed larger. Babbington finally paused for breath, and Bunch had raised a hand, like a student asking his teacher a question.

"Like I said on the phone. I need an expert witness in religious matters."

Bunch described the case and Babbington nodded as he spoke.

"So," Bunch said, "your testimony could help to show that my client has, shall we say, developed delusions which tend to show. . ."

"To show that the devil's in him," interrupted Babbington.

"Not until after the trial."

"Of course. Yes. But here. Right under my nose in Helmsville. You know, fewer Southern Protestants have demonic possessions than any other group. Then again, my figures aren't complete. Perhaps I could do an exorcism? I wanted to try one for ever so long. Do you think your client would consent?"

"I wouldn't try that one just yet. Charles is easily offended at times."

"If the devil is there, he will show himself sooner or later."

"Yeah," Bunch said. "Sooner or later."

At a little after eleven, Bunch knew that the Fites would not show. He reached into a desk drawer and found the bourbon. He took a quick, shallow sip. The liquor was warm and comforting. He recalled how Righter enjoyed a drink. I suspect Righter usually had a few in the morning, just to get primed for the power exercising. His face gave him away—red hot. Probably gray before the morning belts, texture like parchment, before he got the blood flowing.

At eleven-thirty, after a couple of more sips, Bunch locked the office. He drove through the noon traffic, fighting that little ache in his stomach that came from wondering about life at the Palomino.

Bunch parked close to the door. Through the window, the glow of the television was faint. He recalled his first visit to the family, back in the fall, and the ache in his stomach turned to full-fledged queasiness. Gently, he knocked at the door. Finally, he heard a shuffling noise. The door opened a crack and an old man's face appeared. Bunch recognized him from the hearing.

"They're out back. There's a pool there," the old man said.

"What're they doing there? It's too cold to swim."

"I don't know. People do things that. . . don't make sense."

The door closed.

The swimming pool was set in a U-shaped yard. As Bunch rounded the corner of the building, he saw Charles standing on the diving board, wearing an oversize robe that fluttered in the wind.

The two punks and the two men in nylon coaches jackets and baseball caps stood behind Charles. One of the men leaned on the shoulder of the other, the empty leg of his pants floating gently behind him. The two monkeys shivered and chattered and hugged themselves. Charles spoke into the pool. The closer Bunch drew to him, the slower his steps became. Finally, he could go no further. He stopped a good thirty feet from the diving board. Charles and the others did not seem to notice him. Bunch heard heavy coughing from the pool.

"It ain't got better," said Charles. "That's because you won't let it. You don't listen. You don't care. The power comes from inside. If you only get a little bit of me inside of you, you'd be all right."

"Yes, Daddy," said a faint voice from the pool. Bunch barely heard the words because of the volume of the coughing. Finally, the coughing reached a crescendo of hacks, sputters, and tearings, and stopped.

Bunch began to back away from the pool. He did not want to see what was in the pool Then, one of the punks spotted him.

"Look, Daddy!" he shouted.

Charles slowly lifted his head.

"What do you want?" he asked. Still backing up, Bunch told him about the trial.

"Then I'm gonna get the money?" shouted Charles.

"If we win," answered Bunch, picking up his pace.

"Win?"

"Win the case."

Bunch reached the corner of the building and paused. Charles and his buddies returned their attention to the pool. The coughing resumed and there were also moans and squishing noises. One of the punks laughed and passed a bottle up to Charles, who took a long pull.

"There's something else," shouted Bunch. "The trial is going to be on television."

The punks and the men in the nylon jackets looked at each other, and then at Charles. The noises in the pool ceased. Charles began to laugh, the kind of laugh, thought Bunch, that might go on forever. Bunch walked rapidly toward his car. Then he was running, his tie whipping up around his shoulders. Panting, he started the car. From the direction of the pool, he heard the McDonald's jingle.

When Bunch left the Palomino, he did not return to his office. Alda would be back. There would probably be clients in the waiting room. Instead, he drove east on Charlie Justice Boulevard, past the bars and Brenda's Health and Relaxation Center. He slowed down a little there, but did not stop.

He did not know where he was going. It was still fairly early in the day. Despite the chill, he rolled down the windows and let the wind wash over him. He was moving fast—seventy most of the time. After ten miles, he slowed down. He gulped in the wind, cold and burning, and was a little dizzy.

Around a sharp turn was a white-washed church, old for that part of the country. A funeral was in progress. A black, shiny hearse was parked in front of the church door. Two men leaned on the hearse and smoked. Bunch pulled into the church driveway and cut the engine. It was quiet there, and the wind had died down. In a little while, the crowd began to file out of the church. Behind it came the coffin, brassy and glowing, the pallbearers laboring under its weight. The crowd was silent and Bunch could hear their feet crunch through the gravel as they followed the coffin to the cemetery beside the church. When the coffin was under the awning above the grave, he drove on.

There are rituals and there are rituals. This was the first clear thought he had had since he left the Palomino. And there are questions: like what the fuck am I doing?

The road lay straight before him, like a highway in a dream stretching to the horizon. He had taken the case as a kind of joke, one of a long series of absurdities he had either instigated or been a party to, or, sometimes, victim of. Jokes and tricks. These things are what I've put my faith in, he thought. If you look very long at the world, you think it makes no sense at all. That's why men make their plans. Only the plans don't make the world any better. Most of them only prove what they set out to be against. You believe the world is ridiculous and go right on acting as if it made sense.

The highway was an old one, once a major east-west route. If I drove long enough, he thought, I would strike the Atlantic somewhere south of Wilmington. I could drive straight through, get there by nine.

He did not think for a few more miles. To be moving

away from where he had been was enough. He felt cool, deserted, like a bottle washed by the ocean, burnished by the sand, and cast upon an empty beach. The feeling did not last.

"There are patterns," he said aloud. "Terrible patterns."

He lit a cigarette as he passed a hand-lettered sign advertising collards. A mile later another similar sign said "Repent." The Methodist minister, when he was a boy, had spoken about sin like a meek and gentle Christ, polite and diffident. There are, he thought, sins enough to go around. He remembered Righter again, whose frozen image he had tried to ignore since he fled the Palomino, but which had been beside him in the car the whole way.

He took a last pull from the cigarette and flipped it out the window. Miracles, stains, sins, the devil, and the big score. And of course, the unalterable law. Plans and patterns. It came to him that he should quit Charles, turn the whole mess over to another lawyer. He could not think of one desperate enough to take the case. His imagination failed. I cannot find a way to be more than what I am, he thought. He made a wide turn in the road and headed back toward the city.

XV

At dawn, Charles, upon his throne, watched a *Star Trek* re-run. A gang of space hippies demanded that Captain Kirk take them to a planet called Eden, where the air was forever balmy and the trees heavy with fruit. Kirk attempted to persuade them that Eden did not exist, and that they could not flee their responsibility to the universe. The hippies refused to listen. Paradise was what they wanted.

Charles had been awake all night. The power was not strong. Even after Bunch had told him about the T.V. show the power had only flared up for a few days.

Then the commercials started. There was Wanda, singing about cowboy hats and love in Texas and the pleasures to be found at the Country Palace. At first, he had said nothing to the family about Wanda's disappearance. When the commercials started, though, he felt their unspoken doubt. Later, they begged him to let them go to the Country Palace. Charles had ordered them to shut up and to forget Wanda. They had remained docile for nearly a week, until Saturday night when Wanda appeared with her band. It was more than a commercial: she was part of a real show called "Metrolina Country Jubilee."

She sang a song about a man named Daddy. It was meant to be funny, and she said she had written it herself. She sang about monkeys and motels and pick-up trucks. When she got to the part about the funny little man in a robe, Charles ordered the channel changed. Luther and the women had protested, so Charles put them in the pool. He did not let them out for two days.

He had barely slept since then. Failure was thick upon him. He rarely spoke, and he paid little attention to the screen. Wanda had tainted it with her presence and her song. The image of what his own T.V. show would be like was no longer clear. There was still no money. And there were those who would try to keep it from happening—like the little man who got the law to run him off the courthouse steps.

The light in the east grew brighter. Charles pulled his robe around him in the cold. The space hippies reached Eden and died; the fruit was full of poison. Soon the family would awaken and expect him to give them something good, something that they thought they deserved. They would think about Wanda and their old homes.

Charles reached under the robe and stroked the grip of the .22 It was still a secret. He would wait, showing it at the right time. When Wanda had appeared on the screen, he had thought of using it, of blowing her image away.

The sun was up, its light falling upon the slack, heavy faces of the sleepers below him. He pulled the pistol from beneath the robe. He liked the way it looked. It was a cowboy's gun. John Wayne and Matt Dillon carried guns just like it. He aimed it at targets beyond the window. Over the front desk he could see a figure moving with long, rapid strides, heading down Charlie Justice Boulevard, straight for the Palomino.

The Reverend Leon Cumby got off the city bus five blocks from the Palomino. He could have ridden to the door of the motel, but he liked the idea of marching to the Palomino, like a standard bearer in God's army. He wished for a horde behind him, prepared to do more than march and preach. The Lord had been working with him, though, preparing him for his lone mission, a mission of conversion.

Cumby had gotten out of jail a week before. While he was inside, he had tried to minister to the other inmates, but they had refused his promises of heaven. He had thought, for a time, that he had saved one of them, a boy charged with breaking into a Dairy Queen. The boy had listened to him, and had even prayed a time or two. The boy's mother, however, made bail for him and he left. He never even said good-bye. Cumby had worried over the boy's soul and whether or not he had actually been saved. One morning, a few days before Cumby's release, the boy re-appeared in the cell block. He had been caught robbing a Kentucky Fried Chicken. He had laughed at Cumby and said that he was headed for Central Prison in Raleigh. And that anybody with half a fucking brain knew that there was no God in Central Prison.

The failure with this boy disappointed Cumby, and he did not feel happy even when he got out of jail. He had taken a room at a cheap hotel near the bus station, which was nothing like the bit of heaven which the Ramada Inn once promised. He was so dispirited that he only made half-hearted attempts to convert the other tenants, who, drunks and whores that they were, were sorely in need of the Lord's mercy. Mostly, he lay on his broken-down bed and thought about Charles and Tinka and the family. After three days, his heart had risen, and he understood what his mission was to be.

Cumby carried a placard which read:

THE DEVIL LIVES ON CHARLIE JUSTICE BOULEVARD

It had taken him a long time to figure out what he wanted the sign to say. He had prayed over the need for a proper message. At first, he had written verses from Revelation on the sign. Then the Lord told him that there must be a more direct message. He had been up most of the night waiting for the right words. Finally, they had come to him, and he slept with contentment.

He shifted the placard from his shoulder and held it straight out before him. The cold was intense and he marched with his head surrounded by the frozen vapors of his breath.

"I have suffered," he prayed aloud. "Like Job of old, I have suffered."

He shouted his prayers as he marched. He reached his station, the parking lot at the Palomino Motel.

Cumby paraded back and forth for an hour in the parking lot, shouting until his voice grew hoarse. His heart was flushed with longing, and he wished for sweet victory. As he went on about the seven-headed beast and the seventh seal of heaven and the angels of darkness, the door of the Palomino's office opened and Charles stepped outside, alone. Cumby tightened his grip on the placard. Charles smiled.

"Reverend Cumby, you must be cold. Come in and warm up."

Tinka yelled that the grits were ready as Cumby followed Charles into the office. The family watched the *Today Show*. Troy leaped to his feet.

"What's he doing here?" he shouted.

Henry, Thad, Marcelline, and Thelma had turned from an incomprehensible report about the MX missile. They looked from Cumby to each other with astonishment.

"Who's the Daddy here?" Charles asked.

No one answered.

"That's what I thought. Today, I'm gonna make good things happen."

Cumby leaned his placard against the reception desk. The longing in his heart was draining out, being replaced with joy. He would get his people back and more besides.

"Can I say something, Charles?" Cumby asked.

"His name's Daddy," yelled Troy.

"Go right ahead, Reverend Cumby," said Charles.

"Thank you. I don't understand why God has put me here among you—you who have denied Him for so long. I am here in peace and I will let the Lord's will work upon me. . ."

Cumby gave a good-natured chuckle.

". . . I been believing you folks was demons. The Lord is showing me another picture, though. I believe that, deep down, you are going to be the way God wants you to be."

Charles slapped Cumby on the back.

"That's the truth, Reverend!"

Tinka ladled out the grits onto paper plates, leaving a good portion for the family's dinner. They ate in silence, furtively eyeing the reception desk, where Charles and Cumby sat side-by-side, Luther having brought in a second lawn chair. Charles ate slowly, his eyes on the family. Cumby spoke loudly, his preaching voice at times drowning out the news reports about the terrible American defeat in the Middle East.

"These is the last days. Don't you believe the end of time is coming?"

He did not wait for an answer.

"We got to get ready, put our heads right and make our hearts pure. Get rid of that sin and devilment. You think I could have some more grits?"

"Give him some grits," Charles said.

Tinka emptied another ladelfull onto Cumby's plate.

"Thank you. I've loved grits all my life. To bad you ain't got a little fatback to go with them. You folks pray much? I hate to say it, what with the way you been so nice this morning, but that television there is full of the devil. It is. Now, there *are some* good shows—*The 700 Club*, for instance. I don't get to watch much, though. When I was in jail, after that little misunderstanding we had back at Christmastime, I tried to get the other men to watch them shows, them good shows, but they wouldn't have it. No sir. They wanted sex. Just nothing but sex. . ."

The family had stopped eating and were weighing Cumby's words. They pretended to fix themselves upon the screen.

". . . I live down at the Hotel Nylon now. Ain't but ten dollars a week. But you all got a *whole motel*. Think of what we could do with a whole motel. Could I have a little more of them grits? Too bad you ain't got no butter. Red eye gravy. That's a little bit of heaven for your taste buds, ain't it? Anyway, the police come in the Hotel Nylon last night and took away a couple of boys that was selling dope. . ."

As Cumby spoke he felt happy for the first time in a long while. He shoveled the grits in, leaving little flecks of white on his lips and the corners of his mouth. He would tell them soon of what the Lord wanted, and they would listen, and they would be his.

". . . I hope God can help them boys. I've tried to help people, but they won't listen. Now I ain't saying anything against you folks. You been mighty good to me this morning. But you got to remember. You can't ignore the Lord's word. The end of time, though; that's what we need to think about. The time of tribulation is gonna be upon us before we know it. Of course, the rapture's gonna come first. . ."

It was time Cumby told them what the Lord wanted.

He was so excited, he feared the words might not come out of his mouth the right way.

"Now I got a message and I want you to hear me out. The Lord wants me to set up a Rapture Center. See, we could get a crowd of true, born-again Christians and could work and pray together and wait for the rapture to come. And. . . well this motel is perfect. We got the room. People would come here from all over the world. Sanctify this motel. Make it a holy place. The World Rapture Headquarters. That's what we could call it. How's that sound to you?"

He did not direct the question to Charles, but rather to the family. In his excitement, he stood and leaned forward from the edge of the desk. No one spoke or moved.

"That's real good, Reverend," Charles finally said.

Cumby was instantly filled with the power of the Holy Spirit. He could see all that would follow.

"Children," said Charles. "It's cold. We need to get warm. We gonna fellowship, and our guest will fellowship with us. Bring out the Precious Spirits."

Marcelline disappeared. In a moment, she returned with the monkeys, who ran and skidded around the office. Luther hauled the jar containing the dead precious spirit from beneath the desk.

Cumby started when he saw the dead monkey. The power of the holy spirit abated a little when he remembered that he had killed it.

"I hope you don't hold it against me. The way your monkey died and all," Cumby said.

When no one answered him, he felt better. And he wondered what role the monkeys would play in fellowshipping, which to him meant good Christian praying and singing together as one. He had been to churches where snakes were handled, but he had never quite approved of it. It took people's mind off the Lord's word.

202

"Lock the door," Charles commanded.

Darren sprang forward. Thelma stepped out of her dress and stood waiting. Luther, pantless, embraced her. Henry, naked except for his baseball cap, pulled Tinka to the floor. Marcelline hugged a monkey. Clothes dropped all over the office.

Cumby was about to shout the evil out of the room, but Charles booted him into the cold, squirming flesh before he could open his mouth. Quickly, they stripped him. Soon, his shouts of protest were muffled under their flesh. Only his large, yellow feet could be seen protruding from the pile of bodies.

By the time the news at noon came on, they had finished. They lay exhausted, too tired to dress despite the cold. Cumby lay on his back, his arms and legs tightly trussed. His eyes rolled like a frightened hog's. He swallowed deep breaths when he spoke.

"The Lord. . . will not forgive you. . . The Lord does not allow his servants to be. . . mocked and reviled."

Charles, who had stayed on the throne, directing the fellowshipping, smiled down at him.

"Where's the Lord? Is he gonna change what happened to you?"

"He. . . He will not suffer it," gasped Cumby.

"You *liked* it!" Charles shouted. "You pretended that you didn't. I can see inside of you, though. Even you got a little bit of the precious spirit in you. Not enough, though."

The family roused itself as Charles spoke, nodding and affirming his words.

"If old Cumby here has a little of the precious spirit, what you got?" Charles asked.

Cumby struggled until his head came up from the floor.

"There ain't but one truth! Jesus Christ. Today! Yesterday! And Forever!"

"Is this man right?" asked Charles.

"NOOOOO!"

"Has he ever been right?"

"NOOOOO!"

Charles climbed down from the throne. With a foot he forced Cumby's head back to the floor.

"Some of you used to be with him. He'd tell you about dead things. He'd let you sing a little bit. There weren't no dancing. No fellowshipping. He wasn't one of you. In fact. . ."

Charles paused. The hum was strong, and the family had tapped into the power.

"In fact, *he is dead*. He even smushed one of the precious spirits so that it couldn't dance no more. He don't stand for nothing but death. He walks and talks and waves his Bible and his signs around. None of that matters. He's still dead. And he wants to kill everything that ain't like him. Even when we let a little of the spirit and truth into him that old deadness is still there. If you're dead, you can't feel nothing. Ain't that right?"

"YESSSSS!"

"It's right and it's true. See, he pretends he's alive, like he pretends that them words he says mean something. Coming in here, going on about a Rapture Center, eating our grits. Trying to make us look like fools. That's what the dead do. They want to fool us into being like them. If you was to poke him in the belly, he'd yell like he was alive. That would be a trick. Tricks is all there is to him. He's a fake. And fakes and the dead are out to pull us down. They want to take away the power! And I ain't gonna have it!"

The room was silent, except for Cumby's breathing. His voice was cracked and dry when he spoke.

"I'll. . . I'll go. I won't bother you no more. I mean. . . God wants me to do what I do. . . anyway. . . just. . . ah. . . untie me and give me back my clothes and I'll leave."

"Bring me a knife," said Charles.

Tinka handed him a paring knife. Charles pressed the point against Cumby's left cheek.

"It's time you got to be real," Charles said.

He pulled the point slowly along Cumby's face and a trickle of blood ran down Cumby's neck.

"You'll burn in Hell!" screamed Cumby, suddenly, finally accepting that there would be no souls saved, no World Rapture Headquarters, that the devil might win now and then. Charles raked the edge of the knife slowly down Cumby's thick chest, leaving haphazard red gaps.

"Burn in Hell?" said Charles. "I done been in Hell and it ain't there no more."

Cumby begged for Jesus. The family gathered around him. Luther turned up the volume on the T.V. The Three Stooges cavorted as a gigantic birthday cake exploded in the faces of a roomful of rich people.

Everyone, except for Smith, took a turn. He watched through the afternoon, wrapped in several old quilts, not stirring. Cumby recited verses from the bible as they worked, until Darren poured a dish of grits down his throat. Cumby gurgled and sputtered and no one understood what he said. After the first couple of slashes, Charles directed. More knives were brought in. At three, when *Bowling for Dollars* came on, Charles knew that it was time to show the .22. The family gasped in admiration when the gun emerged from Charles' robe. He held it with both hands, the muzzle a foot from Cumby's forehead. Cumby opened a pale, unseeing eye.

"You oughta be glad you got to see the truth this one time," Charles said.

Cumby tried to speak again, but before the words came out, Charles fired. The round hit Cumby between the eyes, and he skidded and twitched from the impact.

Charles stuck the .22 back under his robe. It was warm, and it felt good there.

"He got to dance one time," Charles said.

"OOOOOOOOOO" said the family.

XVI

Gant's heart was steady, the beat regular and strong, as he jogged up the long hill on Beaumont Street. The pumping seemed to him a counterpoint to the slap of his running shoes on the sidewalk. A healthy music.

It was late afternoon on a day which had been unexpectedly balmy; a day of false spring in early March. The cold would return, and there might even be snow. However, today the lawyers went about their courthouse business in shirt sleeves and men in the mob on the steps removed their shirts.

The sun lapped at him and he stretched his limbs in its warmth. The preliminaries for the trial would start the next Monday. By Friday, the trial would be underway. He picked up his pace, the steepness of the hill melting beneath him.

The motion that I conceived will have form, he thought. According to Akins, Goforth had Charlene safely tucked away. He had never seen her, and did not want to, until the right time. When she was needed, she would be as new to him as she would be surprising to Bunch. She had cost a little more than he anticipated. Goforth had wanted more money and a used Trans-Am. Little enough for the exact, perfect moment. After the trial, Bunch would be invited to the office. There he would discover Goforth, Charlene, signed and attested affidavits, and a copy of his letter of resignation from the state bar. Bunch would have an immediate understanding. He might even, thought Gant, appreciate the beauty of the moment, the structure and symmetry.

And Martha had dumped Cope. Akins had recorded the final scene. In the first few minutes of the tape, Cope was alone, awaiting her arrival. He wore a Confederate general's uniform, complete with patent leather boots and a clanking sabre which dragged behind him as he paced about the living room, moving in and out of the camera's view. He checked his watch every few seconds, and struck poses before a six-foot long gilt-edged mirror that stood behind a plaid couch. He cocked his Jeb Stuart be-plumed cavalryman's hat first on one side, and then the other.

Martha arrived. Instead of a hoop-skirt and crinolines, she wore one of her L. L. Bean suburban matron outfits. Cope asked her where her costume was. There was no time to waste. Bitsy would be back from the mall in a couple of hours. He called her his little Martha-Baby and embraced her. She was stiff and unyielding. She smiled and said she was no longer his little Martha-Baby. Nor was he her little Teddy Bear. Gant recognized the firmness in her voice. She used it only on special occasions, or when she wanted something that might require a little trouble in the getting. She told him that she would not see him again—at least in the way in which they had grown accustomed to seeing each other. Of course, there would still be social occasions. Bitsy and Trip must be considered. Why not, he asked, the sabre jingling. She was bored, she answered. Spring was coming and, for her, spring was, she said in a little-girl-filled-with-wonder kind of voice, "a time for new beginnings." She had to get in touch with her needs once more. She was thinking of starting tennis lessons and spending a few weeks at Hilton Head. She kissed Cope on the cheek, told him to take off the sword before he hurt himself, and walked out of the camera angle. After she had gone, Cope sat for a long while with his hands in his lap. Then he knelt and prayed and asked God why he had taken his little Martha-Baby away from him.

Gant ordered Akins to stay on the job and record anything that went on in Cope's living room. The tapes, he realized, had become their own justification, and he eagerly awaited the new ones which Akins mailed to him each week. It did not matter that many of the subsequent tapes were boring. It was enough to have them.

Cope, except for the times with Martha, was as much the same in private as in public. He engaged in long monologues about jackals, communists, the news media and the good old days in America when everyone had values and ideals. Bitsy, a tiny woman with an enormous, bell-shaped permanent and a whippet's face, knitted, watched television, and absently agreed with him. Gant had never heard her speak directly to anyone. She was capable, however, of general comments on the weather, food, and prices at the Darden Grove Mall.

Gant was present in a number of the tapes. At least twice a month there was dinner with the Copes, which were followed by television viewing—usually sporting events, presidential addresses, religious entertainment, or Bob Hope specials. Bitsy served angel food cake. Martha and Cope, after the scene with the Confederate uniform, seldom spoke. Before, there had been a great deal of what was supposed to pass as innocent horseplay, touching, tickling, and good night kisses. Martha was usually the instigator, but Cope followed along quickly enough, the longing and fear bright in his eyes. Once, after Martha decided to get in touch with herself, Gant left them alone in the living room to see what would happen. Bitsy was busy cutting cake, and Gant excused himself and went to wait in the bathroom. As soon as he was gone, Cope went for his little Martha-Baby. She shoved him away, and he sprawled on the floor. He got back into his Lazy Boy recliner just as Bitsy brought the coffee and cake into the living room.

Sometimes, when the television showed only what Cope termed ultra-liberal filth, the screen was left blank and conversation was attempted. Gant found one subject which was potentially dangerous: The Case. Cope wanted to get the Fites and Bunch. Each time the subject came up, Cope retold the story of how he had driven Charles Fite from the courthouse steps. Bunch, he said, was even worse than his clients. Bunch had fooled him into believing that he was a good, Christian man. Such jackals would be dealt with when the trial began. Slowly and carefully, Gant calmed him down. Fairness, Gant would convince him each time, was the best course. Let the Fites and Bunch rage and howl. It would do them no good. Fairness and legal decorum were the key to the Lord's victory. Reluctantly, Cope seemed to accept the idea, although Gant could see that the urge to wreck the case was still strong within him. It would be necessary, he knew, to keep a close watch on Cope throughout the trial.

Each time he drove away from the Copes, Gant searched for Akins' van on the street. When he spotted it, he was satisfied with his secret knowledge. When the tapes came to him, the pleasure was deep when he saw himself with the others. They could not know what he knew. When he watched himself in the tapes, casting a quick glance in the camera's direction, the thrill was powerful. His bowels would rumble then, but usually nothing came of it.

Those evenings of television watching, those hours of listening to Cope's rubbish, would soon come to an end. The tapes would be the only reality. When the trial was over, he would ask the Copes over for dinner to view *Gone With The Wind* on the VCR. It was one of Martha's favorites. The technician from Greenville that Akins had referred him to was busy preparing Gant's own version of the film. Interspersed with scenes of Rhett and Scarlett would be scenes of Ted and Martha. The first segments would last for five to ten seconds, working up to fifteen minutes toward the end of the film. Just before Rhett tells Scarlet that he no longer gives a damn, Ted and Martha complete a happy afternoon on the living room rug. Their sections of the film had been selected from the six weeks worth of tapes. Gant thought of it as a kind of tribute to them, "A Best of Ted and Martha."

All three of them, Cope, Bitsy, and Martha, would protest, squalling and whining, threatening to leave. Of course, he would not allow that. He would make it clear that the originals of the tapes, the complete works so to speak, would be available for whoever might want to see them, such as Ted's good friend, the Governor, who would, no doubt, be shocked by his actions. The Democrats in Raleigh would also love a private, or public, viewing. As for Martha, she would surely understand the implications of the tapes in terms of her continued financial security. They would then quiet down and watch the film. During the intermission, the photograph albums, a chronologically arranged record of Ted and Martha's passion, would be presented. Examination would be required. Throughout the evening, iced tea, angel food cake, and scotch would be available.

Gant stopped in front of the museum. The brass plaque glowed in the late afternoon sun. On impulse, he bounded up the brick steps and crossed the wide porch. The house was turreted, gabled, and rambling, with porches on three sides and additions that covered much of the once-spacious lot. Gant's family—his grandfather's—had been numerous, but only a few children had been produced by his father's generation. Gant was the only one still in Helmsville.

The exhibitions were housed in a few of the downstairs rooms. The rest of the house, except for the director's small office, was empty. No one greeted him as he softly and quickly closed the door.

He browsed through what had been the dining room, library, and sun porch. Within the glass cases and shelves there was no continuity or connection. An electric contour map of Darden County was edged into a corner. Its circuits no longer worked. Beside it stood a mannequin in a colonial costume, which leaned against a display of pioneer farming artifacts. In another room, Gant found himself in a large photograph, scoring the winning touchdown in the Gator Bowl. In the old sun porch were portrait photographs of the winner of the Miss Darden County Beauty Pageant between 1940 and 1984. Martha was in the fourth row, Miss Darden County for 1962. Next to the beauty contest winners was a five-foot long model of the U.S.S. *Darden County*, an LST launched toward the end of World War II.

As he wandered through the silent rooms, Gant tried to remember his old life—before the house became a museum. It had been his once and promised home. There had been polite, half-drunken parties, visits from Episcopal clergymen, and blue-haired aunts in white gloves. There had been evenings in the library. His parents had been great readers. His father, when the spirit moved him, recited Shakespeare and Milton. I read a bit myself, he thought. Wolfe and Hemingway and *The Naked and the Dead* in my room at night. He saw his parents, gray and elegant, and charming. He was born after his mother was forty, after his parents had been rendered obsolete and terminally genteel.

He left the library and entered a long hall that led to the back of the house. In the office, which had once been a large pantry off the kitchen, he found an elderly woman seated behind a desk. Surprised, she started when she saw Gant in the doorway. She had been reading Ronald Reagan's book on the evils of abortion.

"My Lord! Trip Gant! Don't surprise me that way!"

She was plump and round, with an empty, good-natured face, and a hearty voice. She had been Gant's high school history teacher, and he had gotten her the museum job after she retired. She laid the book aside. The president's face smiled up from the dust jacket.

"What brings you here?" she said.

"Out for a run. How's business?"

"It's so quiet. Too quiet for me. I like a little excitement now and then. Last week was real slow. Fifteen came in. And five of them were from one family. From Ohio. They were lost and I told them how to get back to the interstate. They signed the visitor's book, though. Things will pick up when the elementary schools have their tours in April. This week has been the worst, though. One visitor! Since Monday! And he was a mental case. Let me tell you. I thought that I would never get him out of here. . ."

Gant was half-listening. My next project, after the trial, might be getting this place fixed up. Do some public work. Good for the soul. I could get a real curator to come in, someone who would give the place a theme. Or I could move back in myself. Help re-vitalize the city center. Could leave Martha in Buckingham Hills.

". . . he was wearing *rags* like one of those awful people you see down at the courthouse. I heard this sobbing and I couldn't tell where it was coming from. . ."

No, thought Gant, I couldn't live here. It's dead. It may as well be a museum.

". . . finally I realized that it was coming from upstairs, which, as you know, is not open to the public. Well, there he was. This old man. Rubbing the walls like they weren't real. Crying the whole time. . ."

"You don't mind if *I* go upstairs do you?" asked Gant.

The woman laughed.

"Why, Lord no! After all, this is the Noble Robert Gant the Third Museum!"

They laughed together. It sure is, Gant thought.

His old room was on the left at the top of the stairs. There were five other bedrooms, a sleeping porch, and his father's study. He tried his bedroom door but it was locked. He thought of asking for the key, then decided not to. The room would tell him nothing.

He tried the door to his father's old study and it swung open easily. The room smelled of stale air, dense and constricting. Cardboard boxes were scattered about. The panes in the bay window that faced Beaumont Street were curtainless and streaked. He closed his eyes and saw himself as he watched his father, like a photograph taken in a hall of mirrors. Slowly, he paced the perimeter of the room.

Downstairs, he said goodbye to his old teacher and started his run back to the office. He quickly covered the downhill part of his route. As he ran, he did not think of the museum or the study. Briefly, he had wondered why he stopped in the first place. There were other things to think of: the trial, the Swedish toilet, and the new tape from Akins which was in his desk.

XVII

The picture was cleverly done. There was the courthouse. Superimposed over the front of the building was the figure of Christ, which was at least ten stories taller than the Confederate monument. Christ's right hand pointed downward to the face of T. Thurston Cope. The face in the snapshot was a younger Cope. The eyebrows were bushy, the hair combed into a perfect flattop. The young Cope wore a suit with wide lapels and a snap-on bow tie. There was a signature across the bottom of the picture. Bunch, sitting ten feet or so across the room, could not tell whether the name was that of Christ or the judge. Copies of the picture, printed on calendars that advertised liver-mush, auto parts stores, and funeral homes, hung in the sheriff's office, the register of deeds, and in all of the official rooms of Darden County.

Besides Bunch and Cope, there was also Gant and Rollins, a director from public television. They had gathered in Cope's chambers for the pre-trial conference.

"We'll hear from Mr. Bunch first," Cope said.

Bunch turned away from the picture. The signature is probably Cope's, he thought. The judge does not want to be upstaged.

"Your Honor, I'll need four days to present this case. You can see from the list of witnesses and exhibits that I want to run straight through the evidence. I'm not out to confuse anyone. As for my clients, well, the less time spent in court, the better for them. . ."

"I'm sure of that," said Cope. Bunch saw that the judge's smile was forced. His teeth might crumble, he thought.

". . . yes, Your Honor. Anyway, I'll begin with Loomis' driver. Then the highway patrolman, the ambulance attendant, the doctor from the ER at County General. The wreck reports and pictures of the car. . ."

"They're not at all like you said they were, are they?" said Cope. "Like you wanted me to believe?"

The smile was still there. Bunch could not think of an answer. He had tried to avoid the judge for a long time. You don't get away from the judge, he thought.

Gant cleared his throat.

"It's entirely possible that Roy wasn't trying to deceive you. He might've told the truth as he saw it."

"Many things are possible," said Cope. "Even that Mr. Bunch was deceived by his clients."

"How often does a lawyer come upon the unexpected?" said Gant.

"Hourly," said Bunch.

Rollins laughed. He was in his early thirties. He wore a well-trimmed beard, corduroy jacket, jeans, and expensive running shoes. Sourly, he reminded Bunch of Pffippert and the fourteen hundred. Cope had not laughed.

"Very well, Mr. Bunch. What other evidence do you intend to present?" For the moment, Cope seemed to have given up on the question of Bunch's deception.

"Mrs. Fite will testify to corroborate the wreck report and to describe her own injuries. She will also describe the nature of her relationship with Mr. Fite and how the accident changed it. . ."

Bunch went on to discuss the expert witnesses and the points he hoped to prove through their testimony.

"And we'll end up our side of the case by putting Charles Fite on the stand."

"Sounds like good television to me," said Rollins. "You build to a grand climax."

Cope and Gant glanced at each other. Yessir, Bunch thought. They love it. They're thinking about how fine they'll look on camera. State-wide. There will probably be clips on the national networks. Bunch turned to Rollins.

"So you're experienced in televising trials?"

"Sure. Last month in Raleigh I did the Master's case. State legislator dismembers prostitute in bathtub? I did the vote-buying trial in Gaston County. Not particularly exciting. Last year I produced the Swayney mass murder in Asheville. Those were the big ones."

"Do you have instant re-play capabilities?" Bunch asked.

"Do we have. . ."

Gant chuckled, turning from Cope to Rollins to indicate that they should join in. Rollins gave a couple of puzzled chortles. Reluctantly, Cope followed.

In another hour the business of the conference was finished. Gant described the experts, from Duke Medical and Harvard Divinity, that he would put on the stand. He wanted extra time for cross-examination. Bunch felt Cope's eyes on him the whole time. Rollins had the last word, which seemed appropriate to Bunch.

"Now I want you gentlemen to understand how my production crew will operate. We're going to have three cameras in the courtroom. We always make sure, however, that our productions in no way interfere with the course of justice. Our aim is for the proceedings to continue as naturally as is humanly possible."

Or as unnaturally, Bunch thought.

The mob was thick that day. Raymer had told Bunch that Cope had rescinded his order about keeping the steps cleared. It wasn't like Cope, he thought, as he weaved his way through the squatting bodies. If he could get away with it, he would use fire hoses and machine guns.

The people on the steps glanced up as he passed. Sometimes they lingered over him, with a mixture of curiosity and vague hatred. None of them moved to make way for him. They were all shabby, stranded in the sun in their K-Mart clothes with no idea of going anywhere. As Bunch reached the bottom of the steps he saw Goforth climb out of a bottle-green, 1980 Trans-Am and cross Broad Street, heading for the courthouse. At first, Bunch was not sure that it was Goforth. He was dressed in a black western suit and wore a very tall, red cowboy hat with a silver, feathered sunburst on the front. A mass of gold chains hung around his neck. The long, curly hair was the same, though, and Bunch would never forget his loping, redneck walk and canine face. Cursing, Bunch popped from the mob and hurried away, glancing over his shoulder as he went, seeing Goforth disappear into the crowd. He crouched behind a pick-up truck. His breath came hard. He lit a cigarette anyway, his hands shaking. From his position, he could see the top of the steps. Goforth emerged from the mob and entered the building.

There were all sorts of reasons why Goforth should be at the courthouse, he thought. And all of them have to do with me. He tossed the cigarette away and began to run, his briefcase banging against his leg.

He reached the intersection with Hodges Boulevard. Someone behind him called his name. He put his head down and resumed his half run, the best that he could manage. At Hodges and Fourth, the light was green and a long line of traffic blocked his path. The caller caught up to him, and they stood side-by-side waiting for the light to change.

"Roy?"

Furtively, Bunch turned to him. The man wore a long, Indian-cotton shirt, faded jeans and shower clogs. Gray hair hung to his shoulders. The face was thinner and more lined, but Bunch recognized Ed Snavely. The light changed and they started to cross the street.

". . . sold the Winnebago. . . that was in Tucson. My daughter's friend had a friend. Dixie Anne. You remember my wife Dixie Anne? She liked this friend. Said he provided. . . an essential mystery that I don't have. I tried to be closer to the essential mystery. I tried. What do you think?"

Bunch did not answer. The only thing to do was to beat him to the elevator and hide in his office. He was not surprised that Snavely had turned up. He fit in with everything else. Snavely went on talking.

"I tried to find the essential mystery. I could never understand what it was supposed to be. I guess that's why it's a mystery. I ate brown rice and raw fish. I got in hot tubs. I listened to this person who said that he was a holy man. He talked a lot about the essential mystery. One day at breakfast we had this big bowl of something that was blue and mashed up. It smelled bad. I excused myself and went outside and got in the Winnebago and started driving. Was it Tucson where I sold it? I don't know. Everywhere started to run together."

Bunch ran into the lawyer's building. The elevator doors closed before Snavely had a chance to finish telling him about the essential mystery.

When the conference ended, and after Bunch and Rollins had left, Cope leaped up and ran about his chambers, waving his hands, his robe swirling about him. His words poured out in a single sentence without beginning or end. Gant watched impassively. Such fits might occur an infinite number of times during the trial, he thought.

Gradually, the fury blew out of the judge. He stopped waving his arms. The robe ceased its swirling. The words came more slowly. Words that Gant had already heard too many times. Cope sat down.

"I ought to write up a contempt citation right now," Cope said. He smoothed his hair back in place. "Roy Bunch is on dangerous ground. How could such a man have been permitted to practice law. . ."

"He won't be practicing for long," Gant said. He did not like revealing even a hint of what was to come, but it seemed like a good idea in this situation.

Cope's smile returned.

"What do you mean?"

Gant turned gravely professional.

"As president of the Darden County Bar Association, I've been looking into some of Roy's past indiscretions. I can assure you that the proof is available and will be acted upon—when the trial is over."

"Indiscretions?" Cope sounded like a teenager about to hear a dirty joke. "Does it involve drugs? Money?"

"Ted, I'm not at liberty to say. An investigation is still underway. I can tell you this: Roy Bunch will no longer be a practicing attorney once these charges have been completely substantiated."

"Come on, Trip. We're friends. You can tell me."

"I'm sorry, Ted. The details are highly sensitive. I'm bound to secrecy. What if there was a leak and Bunch found a way to escape what is coming to him?"

"Yes. Certainly. I'm sure that it's important to keep these things secret until the proper time. But, Trip, I'm the judge here. Why can't you tell me? Just a little bit. Just give me a couple of hints. Is he a communist? Is he homosexual. . ."

"You need to trust me for the time being. Trust is very important if we are to see justice done."

"Come *on*, Trip. . ."

Gant flashed a firm, no-nonsense smile. He wanted to reach out and slap Cope, but the urge died quickly.

"Beside my special investigator, you're the only person that knows about this. You must forget that we ever had this conversation."

"Of course, but not even one little hint?"

"None. And we must stick to the trial strategy."

"I'll do my best, but. . ."

"I know you will. . ."

". . . but I want so much to win a victory here for goodness. Do you remember what the President said about the Shining City on the Hill? I keep thinking about those words. That Shining City."

Cope's eyes turned misty and Gant was afraid that he might cry.

"By the way. How is Martha?" Cope asked quietly.

"She's fine. She's taking up tennis again. Yesterday she brought home about five hundred dollars worth of outfits."

Cope seemed to forget about Bunch and the Shining City. He chuckled, trying to sound like an understanding, fellow husband. Gant could hear the child-like longing beneath his words, however.

"Martha sounds about as bad about tennis as Bitsy is about appliances. She came home last week with another microwave. That's the third one she's bought since we moved to Helmsville. She can't get enough of them, I guess. The reason I ask about Martha is that both Bitsy and I have found her to be a little distant lately. We wondered, and I don't want to be too personal here, if everything is okay with you two. Perhaps she's a little depressed?"

"No. I've never know Martha to be depressed. She

seems to me to be happier than at any time since before Christmas."

"I'm certainly glad to hear that," Cope said, his voice flat and without conviction.

"I appreciate you concern," Gant said. Martha was incapable of depression, he thought. She lacks the necessary development.

Cope excused himself for his mid-day Bible class. He had organized the class for the clerks and court reporters. None of them had much enthusiasm for Cope's interpretation of Holy Writ, but they liked working. As Gant walked down the hall, he tried to decide whether he should go back to the office or take the rest of the day off so that he would be fresh for the jury selection the next morning. As he passed by the county offices in the nearly empty lunch-time building, he convinced himself that telling Cope about Bunch was only a minor hitch. Besides, there would be little sport if the plans went too smoothly. The main thing was to keep Cope in line until the showing of *Gone With The Wind*. As he started down the main staircase outside the Superior Court, he heard his name called. A skinny young man in a western suit and cowboy hat came down the stairs to meet him.

"Mr. Gant?"

"Yes?"

"I'm Bobby Goforth."

"Come with me," Gant said.

"Sure, Mr. Gant. Whatever you say."

He lead Goforth into the county law library. Goforth kept up a steady stream of conversation to his back; about how Mr. Akins said he wasn't supposed to see Mr. Gant. And how he and Charlene just had to thank him on account of how he was gonna take care of that no good son-of-a-bitch, Roy Bunch.

The library was empty. Gant checked the room out before he allowed Goforth to come in. Once Goforth was inside, Gant locked the door. Goforth sat down, tilted his chair back and propped his feet, shod in red cowboy boots embossed with golden snakes, on the conference table. He grinned at Gant, showing brown teeth.

"Hell, me and you are partners. We got the same aim and all. Get ridda Roy Bunch. . ."

With a quick, fluid motion, Gant reached down and jerked Goforth's chair from under him. With a thud, Goforth tipped onto the floor, one boot still resting on the table's surface.

"What. . . What. . ."

"Shut up," Gant said. "Listen. You don't know me. You've never seen me. If you try to contact me again, it will be the worst day of your life."

Goforth did not try to get up. Gant could tell that he knew better.

"I wanted to thank you," Goforth said in an injured tone. "Face-to-face. Man-to-man."

"So you have. Now get out of here and don't come back."

Gant backed off a couple of feet and allowed Goforth to stand. Goforth brushed himself off and re-arranged his hat.

"There's another reason, besides trying to thank you, that I came here. Akins said that he would take care of it, but I wanted to see you personally. See, we need some more money. Charlene don't like that trailer we're staying in. It's got roaches bad. We want to move to the Atlantis Apartments, only we gotta pay a deposit. And my Trans-Am needs a valve job and I want to get me a Doberman Pinscher. . ."

"That's enough," Gant said. "I might have guessed it was money. I'll give you a thousand."

". . . the dog costs four hundred itself. . ."

"Shut up. I said a thousand. That's all for now. Akins will get it to you. There might even be a little more after the trial. Now get out of here."

Gant unlocked the door and Goforth slouched past him into the hall. He paused.

"All I got to say is that me and you is partners whether you like it or not."

Gant took a step toward him and Goforth disappeared around a corner. Gant sat down. His hands shook. If Goforth had returned to the room, he would have strangled him. Someone could have seen them together and everything would be ruined. I might have gotten away with telling Cope a couple of things about the Plan, but not this, he thought. I'll call Akins today. He's supposed to keep an eye on Goforth. And I'll get his money, too. It'll be worth every dime. As he thought about Goforth and Cope and the Plan, his lower tract clenched and unclenched. After fifteen minutes it subsided enough for him to walk back to his office.

"Ladies and gentlemen," Bunch began. "During the course of this trial you will meet several people, citizens, like yourselves, of our community. You will hear their stories. These stories are unusual, and yet the events in them are true. They involve real people, and these stories must be understood. . ."

The television lights were painfully bright, and the jurors winced and strained their eyes. To Charles they seemed a power-giving sun. But the show was not as it was meant to be. It had been spoiled, and he knew that this show was not the one promised to him.

Charles had walked into the courtroom for the jury selection two days earlier, and had seen the little judge sitting behind the big desk and glaring down at him with his narrow, mean eyes. As soon as the family came in, the judge made Marcelline and Luther take the two precious spirits out. As usual, Bunch did not do a thing to help. He just sat there and did not protest or anything. After that, the judge told Charles to stand up, and asked him where he got that robe. Before Charles

could even start to tell him, the judge told him to take
the robe off. Charles said that he was the Daddy and the
Daddy wore the robes and that the judge should take his
robes off. The judge came out with a whole string of
words that did not make any sense. Troy and Darren
stood up and yelled at the judge and there was a big
commotion when the bailiffs took them out. Bunch got
up and said that he wanted the trial moved to another
town and that he wanted another judge. The judge got
real mad then and called Bunch a lot of names. Charles
had to give Bunch a little credit because he did not back
down. After that, the judge said he was going to have
Bunch taken to jail. Before that could happen, though,
the beautiful lawyer went up and talked to the judge.
Charles could not hear what the beautiful lawyer was
saying, but after that the judge kept his mouth shut
about the robe and even let Darren and Troy come back,
if they promised not to cause a disturbance. Charles
winked at the beautiful lawyer, but he made like he
didn't see it.

"You will meet Tinka Arndt Fite, a woman who has
spent her entire life in our city, who has worked in our
textile industry, and who has taken part in the spiritual
life of our community. Tinka Arndt Fite is a woman,
who, in many ways, is perhaps not unlike many of
you. . ."

Tinka, clad in a yellow mini-skirt, red tube top and
red wig, tried to rise to acknowledge the introduction.
Gently, Bunch pushed her down into the chair.

The judge was still mad, Charles thought, even after
the beautiful lawyer told him how to act. When Charles
heard the judge talk, the hum was strong within him,
and he thought of the swimming pool. He sensed that
the family thought about the pool too. Ever since they
put Cumby down there, the complaining had stopped.
New dances had been created. Heavy stamping and
growling. Knives and two-by-fours were waved in the

air. Charles made them leave their weapons at home, though. He had seen enough T.V. shows to know that the police did not want anybody but themselves to show weapons in public. He would stick with that—for now. He even left the .22 at home, hidden so that when he did bring it out again it would be a sign to the whole world.

During the first two days, Bunch and the beautiful lawyer asked a whole crowd of people a lot of stupid questions, like what they did for a living and what church they went to, and if they had ever heard of him and Tinka. Charles did not like any of those people. They were like the people out at the Darden Grove Mall who would not follow him, or like the quiz show contestants who should not have gotten trips to Las Vegas and Bermuda, but did anyway. Once Bunch told the judge that he doubted whether any of these jurors were enough like Charles and Tinka to have a fair trial. The judge said that the only place people like Charles and Tinka could be found was in communist Russia or a lunatic asylum. Bunch got mad again and said that the judge was trying to prejudice the jurors. The beautiful lawyer ran up to the desk again, and that kept the judge quiet for awhile. Later on, when Charles had gotten bored and was thinking about the way Cumby looked now, down at the bottom of the pool, Bunch asked him if he had any questions for the jurors. Charles asked one of them, a blonde woman who looked a little like Wanda, if she had ever fellowshipped. The judge asked Charles what he meant. When Charles told him, he got excited, and the blonde woman said that she had never been spoken to like that in her life. Bunch told her that she could leave if she wanted to, and that the meaning of fellowshipping would have come out sooner or later anyway. After that, Bunch did not ask if Charles had any more questions.

"You will also meet Charles Junior Fite. . ."

Charles followed the camera, grinning, scowling,

mugging. He forgot about the people in the jury box. He hoped that the ones on the steps out front could see him. Since the first day, he had toyed with the idea of going to them, giving them the word one more time to see if they would follow. The judge would not like that, but Charles felt that he might not be able to do anything about it this time.

". . . he's also a life-long resident of our city. A man who, until August, 1987, led a quiet, uneventful life; a man who was content to mind his own business, and who as a result of the defendants' negligence, had his life completely and utterly changed."

Bunch went on talking, while Charles twisted his head around to catch the camera.

". . . the most important question, ladies and gentlemen, is not whether the plaintiff, Charles Fite, has suffered physical injuries or emotional distress. The most important question is what he deserves."

Gant glided back and forth in front of the jury box, pausing occasionally to look into a juror's face. Charles stopped following the camera to watch him.

"Charles Fite believes that he is God. We take that, in our society, to be a measure of a person's mental state. And yet, has it not been said by great leaders of all faiths that there is a bit of the Almighty in each of us? Is this bit of God a mark of insanity? Has not this element of our souls been manipulated time and again by unscrupulous men for their own advantage?"

Gant walked over to the plaintiff's table and smiled at Bunch. Bunch pretended to read his notes. Gant returned to the jury box.

"Do any of us deserve money for having that bit of God within us? Do we deserve anything more than simple grace? These questions will be determined here, by you, as representatives of this community. Each trial, each human conflict, has at its heart an essential truth.

We accept, both legally and spiritually, the idea that truth is at the center of our lives. When this trial reaches its conclusion, we will know the truth about ourselves and what Charles Fite deserves. . ."

To Charles, the beautiful lawyer seemed a kind of Earth God himself and he debated with himself whether or not it might be possible for two Gods to exist.

". . . you will hear from experts in psychiatry and theology. You will be asked to weigh questions which have been important for men and women since our ancestors first began to think, and feel, and gaze towards the heavens. . ."

Charles wallowed in the beautiful lawyer's voice, though he did not understand the words. The sound was enough.

". . . you might ask yourselves this: Are all of us, as human beings, entitled to extra rewards for that little bit of God within us? My opponent has depicted his clients as simple, common people. And yet, are not all of us part of the same world, even those who feel that bit of God in ways different from their neighbors? Is Faith of Our Fathers Insurance Company, is Loomis Trucking and Freight not composed of individuals who deserve a fair hearing?"

Gant ended his opening statement and Cope recessed for lunch. Charles bounded out of the courtroom, the family trotting behind him. Flashbulbs popped, and the camera followed him up the aisle.

After the room emptied, Bunch packed his briefcase and left by the back stairs, peering around each corner to make sure that Goforth was not there. When he reached his office, he found that Alda had gone to lunch. A copy of the morning paper lay on her desk. The headline read:

GOD TRIAL STARTS TODAY IN SUPERIOR COURT

Below the headline was a picture of Charles and another of Cope, both in their robes. Without reading the story, Bunch went into the back room and had two quick shots of bourbon. A little of the morning's tension dropped away and he felt better. He tried to think about the strategy for the trial. Strategy would not have much to do with it, he thought. He had wanted to howl a couple of times, at Cope, at Charles, at the camera. Rollins and the public would be happy then, howling being part of their expectations for the trial. They would have the show that they wanted. Another show would eventually come along to replace it-wars, a hostage crisis, an election.

He gave up on the trial strategy. At best, whatever he was to do would be a reflex conditioned by being a lawyer, a performance addict.

The telephone rang. Bunch jumped when he heard the bell, and he let it ring six or seven times before he answered. The voice on the other end was ancient and cracked.

"I need to see you," said the voice.

"Who is this?"

"My name? It doesn't matter. I need to speak to you in person. In person. About Charles Fite."

"What about Charles?"

The line went dead. Bunch shrugged. Another voice. A religious nut probably.

Bunch forced himself to go over the points he wanted to cover with the first couple of witnesses, ate a bag of potato chips, brushed his teeth at the stained sink in the bathroom, and, at one-thirty, went back to the courthouse. As he entered the back door, he met Raymer.

"You seen what's going on out front?" Raymer asked.

"What's going on that I need to see? The usual crowd?"

"Them and more. Your boy Charles is preaching. He scares me."

"He must be pretty fucking bad to scare you. Why hasn't God's own judge sent you peace officers out there to blow him away?"

"Because we ain't been told to. It's weird, Roy. First, he tells us not to bother with the usual crowd out there, and now this. He must hear it. He'd have to be deaf not to."

Bunch had heard the booming noise from the front of the courthouse as he ducked through the sidestreets off Hodges Boulevard. He had thought that it might have something to do with Charles, but he had not wanted to find out.

"He's in his chambers now," said Raymer.

"Maybe he's so deep in prayer he can't hear. Maybe God is saying some serious things to him."

"God? It ain't God that's up there with him. It's Trip Gant."

Charles had gotten a bull horn from somewhere. His voice was deep and resonant, filling the street. Tinka, Thelma, Marcelline, and the others danced slowly at the base of the Confederate monument.

"POOOWWWEERRR!"

"LOOOVVV!"

"POOOWWWEERRR AND LOOOVVV!"

Rollins had placed two mini-camera crews across Broad Street to cover the action. Charles played to them, even as he longed for the soul of the mob at his feet. The power was strong. If he could only say the right word or do the right thing, they would follow him.

"THERE'S JOHNNY CARSON! THERE'S RONALD REAGAN! THERE'S THE PALOMINO MOTEL. HERE'S DADDY!"

He spread his arms wide as he danced, waiting for the moment. The crowd remained impassive, watching and ready for the gesture which he had yet to make.

Cope and Gant looked on from the judge's chambers

on the third floor. Cope sputtered and stammered, threatening to call the deputies. Gant did not listen. He was too interested in the crowd below. At the base of the monument, the fat women shuffled and preened. A man in a baseball cap did a kind of sexual clog dance, pausing in mid-step to thrust his pelvis toward the mob. Another, dressed like the first, but with only one leg, sat on the steps, and clapped his hands in rhythm. An old man leaned against the shaft of the monument. He was thin and white-haired, and if he had not been so shabby, he might have put on a distinguished appearance, like a professor emeritus or a retired executive. He had a certain apartness, Gant thought, as if he were an observer who had lost the vitality to even see. Gant considered going down to speak to him, to find out how he happened to be there. It would be a waste of time, he thought. The man was probably moronic.

Smith pressed his cheek against the coolness of the granite. He had been in this place before, only he could not remember when. There was a vague sadness there. Like the house that he found when he had grown restless and afraid of the others at the motel. He had wept and wept, weeping through the streets until he was back at the motel again. He had used up his small store of energy so that he could not longer even pretend to fellowship. No one in the family cared. They were too caught up in the trial, in television and the dance that they did with sticks and knives. He was an old, old man and it did not matter if he was gone or if he cried. He understood this, for he had been old for a long time.

Even if he was old, lately something had changed in him. It started after the others did what they did to that man. He had watched it from his blankets. He had seen such things before, but this was the first time in years that it had bothered him. He wondered why and also wondered why he had tried to call that lawyer and tell him about it. He got scared when he heard the lawyer's voice, and he hung up when Darren and Troy told him to get his mangy old ass outside to hear Daddy. Smith thought that he might try to see the lawyer again. Maybe one day soon. If it mattered. He tried to think of reasons why it might matter.

Charles was still bellowing at the crowd when someone said that court was about to start. The family half-danced behind him into the courthouse, Rollins and his mini-camera recording every foot of their progress. The mob did not move. Smith closed his eyes and nestled against the shaft.

XVIII

Bunch slowly chewed the Whopper and took another
sip of beer. The eleven o'clock anchorman described
Charles' daily sermon. Charles was followed by
courtroom sketches of a serious and judicial Cope. Then
there was a shot of Bunch as he questioned a witness.
Bunch winced. The fat hung over his belt. Next came an
interview with Gant. There would be startling revela-
tions before the end of the trial, he said. The reporters
begged and shouted for more, but Gant only gave them a
smile. Bunch swallowed the last chunk of the Whopper,
drained the beer, and switched off the set.

The first afternoon of the trial had been fairly routine; a disappointment to the assembled multitudes,
Bunch thought. He began by calling the truck driver, a
big swarthy man in a tight tan suit, who was obviously
uncomfortable on the witness stand. After a dozen questions, Bunch established that the driver, Leon Smyre,
had outrun his headlights; that he was clearly exceed-
ing the speed limit; that he was screwing around on

those back roads to avoid the scales on the interstate. The bailiffs brought in an enlarged county map and Bunch asked Smyre to point out the route he had taken. Slowly, with much prodding, Bunch took Smyre through his journey. When Bunch had finished, Gant waved the witness from the stand.

Bunch decided that it was time for a motion. He asked Cope to grant a directed verdict, since the evidence made out a prima facie case of negligence. Cope denied the motion and accused Bunch of wasting the court's time with frivolities. Bunch asked Cope if a verdict would be contrary to the needs of the viewing public. Cope pounded the gavel even though the spectators, preachers, reporters, and other lawyers were silent. Bunch shrugged and called the next witness.

He introduced the wreck report through the highway patrolman. Next, the emergency room intern described the injuries which he had seen inflicted upon Charles and Tinka Fite, and noted that none of these injuries were of a crippling nature. Through the intern, Bunch got the hospital bills admitted into evidence; one thousand two hundred and nine dollars and sixty-two cents worth of non-crippling pain. Again, Gant asked no questions, and the afternoon ended. Most of the spectators did not even bother to go out front to watch Charles in action.

Bunch went to the refrigerator for another beer. They'll get their money's worth tomorrow, he thought. Tinka was scheduled to testify in the morning. He had considered prepping her first, but why bother? His brain hurt. It had hurt all day. It felt swollen, as if it had been injected with a toxic chemical. He rubbed his temple and sucked on the beer. It tasted cool, but metallic. The telephone rang.

"You'll burn in hell!" A woman's voice.

Bunch started to hang up. The calls had started to come during the jury selection. Male voices. Black voices. Red-neck. Educated. Ignorant. All those voices babbling at once. He decided to speak to this one.

"Where will you burn?" he asked.

"I ain't gonna burn. I'm saved."

"You're sure of that?"

"I was born again!"

"So was I."

"That's a lie. You and that man you work for is gonna burn."

"What's it like? To burn?"

"Even you know what it's like."

"How do you know that we're not burning right now?"

The line went dead. Bunch finished the beer and popped another. The conversation had provided a little satisfaction. But his head still hurt and he was restless.

As he pulled up, he saw Faye and a man get out of an old, black Cadillac. Bunch cut the engine and waited. The man walked her to the door of her apartment, his hand pressed into the small of her back. They kissed lightly and the man pulled her close. After a moment, they parted. The Cadillac slowly drove by, the light catching Bunch's face as he climbed out of his car. Bunch called her name. She waited for him, the apartment key in her hand. She was erect and silver beneath the parking lot light. Bunch liked the way she looked, but it only made him sad.

"What's his name?" Bunch asked.

"Buddy. He runs the Exxon over on Hodges Boulevard."

"Sounds like a great guy. Nice car."

She opened the door and wedged herself between Bunch and the interior of the apartment.

"He's a whole lot nicer than most of the men I been around. You want to come in, don't you?"

"Yes."

"There isn't going to be any messing around."

"Yes."

They sat on opposite ends of the couch.

"I've seen you on T.V. You're fatter there."

"Thanks. You're the same. You look good."

"I take care of myself. How long did you watch me?"

"Not long."

"I don't enjoy getting watched."

"Neither do I."

"I'll bet you enjoy being on T.V."

"Don't we all?"

She got up and began to tidy up the living room, putting away Billy Junior's school books, carrying an empty glass to the kitchen. She moved with the quick steps and efficient motions of an angry woman.

"Where's Billy Junior?" Bunch asked.

"At his daddy's," she said from the kitchen. "Visitation."

She slammed some cabinet doors and started the dishwasher. When she returned to the living room, she seemed just as angry.

"Bill wants to see more of him. Now that he's married again, he wants to play daddy. This morning Billy Junior tells me about how he's gonna get to go to Carowinds every weekend this summer. How his daddy's gonna get him a new bike. It'll be custody next. I can feel it coming."

"Sorry. Can I help?"

"No. Forget it. I'll make out. You gonna win your case?"

Bunch laughed.

"Who the hell knows? It's up to the good citizens."

"I think it's wrong."

"What's wrong with it?"

"Speaking up for a man like that."

"Charles?"

"Yeah. And to make people decide such a thing. If he's God."

"If he's God, he loses." As he spoke, he remembered that this was Gant's idea.

"Everybody's talking about it."

"Who's everybody?"

"People all over. The women that come to my shop. The neighbors. The T.V."

"I've gotten a few phone calls myself."

"It suits you fine. You get to show off, parade around. You believe everybody is a fool. You and that Gant. The only difference between the two of you is that he's got more money and a better haircut. . ."

She stopped, as if surprised by her words. Bunch went to the door. His head was not any better, but at least he was no longer restless. He could go home and sleep with an expectation of bad dreams. Faye stayed on the couch.

"Why'd you come here?" she asked.

"My head hurt."

"That isn't a reason. I haven't heard from you since that banquet, and you say you came here because your head hurts."

"It's the best reason I have."

"I never understood nothing you said. Ever. What're you going to do if you lose?"

"Keep on going. The same as before."

"Are you sure?"

"The plaintiff would like to call Tinka Arndt Fite."

Tinka shuffled to the stand. Her ass, Bunch thought, waves around like it isn't attached to her body. She wore a faded pair of star-spangled hot pants and a tube top with the Harley-Davidson logo embossed on it. She perched on the edge of the chair, folded her hands, and smiled for the camera. A crowd-pleaser, Bunch thought.

Slowly, Bunch guided her through her account of the wreck, and she got it all right. Gant objected a couple of times on leading questions, purely for the sake of harassment. Bunch saw that he was not after anything substantive—yet. "How long have you been married to Charles Fite?" Bunch asked.

"About twenty years."

"How old are you?"

"Thirty-seven."

"And Charles led a quiet life before the wreck?"

"I guess."

"And he spent most of his time at home, tending to his own business?"

"Except for when I'd take him out in the car. He couldn't walk none then."

"Did he ever act. . . unusual in any way?"

Bunch was on dangerous grounds. It was difficult to determine what Tinka might consider unusual. She rubbed her hands together. Sweat cut small ravines through her thick makeup. She was trying to remember.

"Well. . . I don't know. He'd get mad. I couldn't tell why. He talked back to the T.V."

Bunch took a deep breath. It was time to ask the big one.

"Did he think he was God before the wreck?"

Tinka's confusion disappeared.

"That was before he became God. Leastways, before I found out he was God."

She was strong and loud. The spectators were satisfied.

"And he thinks that he's God now?"

"I done told you. He *is* God. He fixed me up. I used to be plugged up with Jesus. . ."

Cope pounded the gavel.

"I don't want any such slighting references to our savior in my courtroom. Do you understand?"

Tinka craned around Bunch.

"What's he mean, Daddy?" she asked Charles.

Bunch jumped back into her line of sight before Charles could answer.

"He means that you shouldn't mention the name of Jesus. We want to understand Charles," Bunch said.

"Oh. That's fine. Daddy don't like to talk about Jesus no way."

Then it was Gant's turn.

"May I call you Tinka?" Gant asked.

"If you want to," she said coyly.

"I want to go back to what you said earlier about your husband's condition before the wreck. He couldn't walk. Isn't that right?"

"Crippled since he was a little boy."

"And some weeks after the accident, he could walk."

"He sure could. That's how he went out and got the Precious Spirits, and Luther and Marcelline. . ."

"Of course. Would you say that he's better off now than before the wreck?"

"Objection," Bunch said. "Mr. Gant is asking for conclusions that are beyond the knowledge of this witness."

"Overruled," Cope smacked with satisfaction. "Proceed."

"He's God," Tinka said.

"Is there anything better than being God?" Gant asked.

"I can't think of nothing."

"So you'd have to say that Charles Fite is better off now than before the wreck."

"That's right."

Bunch objected again, though he could see then there was little point in it. Gant had her describe a typical fellowshipping session. She discussed Charles' love of television. She told of his drinking habits and drug use. Bunch saw that the spectators, the preachers, the media jocks, the experts, and the lawyers were having a good time now. At his back, he could feel the keenness of their concentration, protected, as it was, by their immunity to the show before them.

Bunch tried a few more objections, gave up, joined the spectators, and watched Gant work. He could see that Trip was enjoying himself, just like he said he would.

"So Charles, or Daddy, or God, made a choice about

fellowshipping and winning other people to his point of view, about showing all of us the best way to live. Is that right?"

Tinka had warmed to Gant.

"That's right! I used to worry and worry! My nerves was so bad back then! I was waiting for the end of the world! Thought about that old rapture all the time. I'd get scared. Worried about dying. Then, when Charles changed, it got to be so nice. Of course, sometimes ain't as nice as others. Like when I do a wrong thing and he makes me stay down in the swimming pool. It stinks so bad. . ."

Before Tinka could finish describing what was in the pool, Charles leaped from his chair. He bounded high into the air and landed on the other side of the table, in front of the judge's bench.

"THE BLOOD. THE PRECIOUS SPIRITS," he howled.

Tinka stood, moaning and praising the name of Charles. The cameras followed him around the room. The spectators shouted in wonder. He danced for a good three minutes before the bailiffs could subdue him and drag him away.

Cope called for a recess.

"Mr. Bunch, I'm going to keep your client out of the courtroom unless you can control him. And that goes for his wife, too," Cope said.

Bunch, Cope and Gant were in chambers. Bunch shifted his eyes to the Jesus picture. No help there, he thought.

"Perhaps," Bunch said, "if you spoke to him it might make a difference. I've tried, but nothing seems to work. After all, he's unbalanced. Maybe it's the cameras. Mr. Gant was informed of Charles' reaction to television long before we came to trial."

"This has upset everyone," Gant said. "I think Judge Cope has shown a great deal of patience with these provocative, orchestrated. . ."

"Orchestrated?" Bunch said. "This is normal for Charles. What the layman might call insanity. You've seen him out front. I didn't send him out there. In fact, wasn't he prohibited from preaching? Until the trial started, that is?"

Neither Gant nor Cope answered. There's something here I don't know about, Bunch thought. He took a guess.

"I suppose the sermons and dancing are part of the show."

"This isn't a show," Gant said. "It is a trial with serious ramifications."

Bunch barked out a laugh.

"You bet. With the cameras, the press. Hell, *60 Minutes* might cover this one. Maybe *Entertainment Tonight* would be more appropriate."

"I don't believe that the cameras should be removed," Gant said, as if he were making a declaration of principle.

"Nor do I," Cope said quickly. "The public has a right to see and hear this case. . ."

". . . and the privilege of seeing us in action," Bunch said.

Cope's face twisted as he tried to think of a reply. Gant spoke before any words came out.

"Can we work out a compromise?"

"That man, that jackal, cannot come back into my courtroom," Cope finally managed to say.

"I've got no objections to Charles watching the proceedings. Give him a television and he'll be fine. He's got a right to hear what's being said about him, though. And he does have the right to testify, if it comes to that," Bunch said.

"Ted," Gant said. "Roy has an excellent idea. But in

the spirit of fair play, I think it might be best if you spoke to Charles alone. Just one more small chance? Perhaps you can make him behave."

"Sure," Bunch said. "As one judge to another. Maybe he'll listen to you. Respect for the judiciary and all that." Bunch wanted to laugh again, but did not.

"But, Trip. . . I can't. . . I don't want to be any nearer to him than I have to be. Contact with jackals can lead. . ."

Gant whirled on him, leaning across the desk. Cope drew back, startled. Gant's voice was smooth and polite.

"But you will, won't you, Ted?"

"I suppose. . ."

"Good. It's settled. We can get on with this," Gant said.

"It doesn't look too hot for Loomis Trucking to have Daddy Charles removed for acting nuts, does it, Gant?" Bunch asked.

Gant smiled serenely.

The bailiffs tugged and shoved Charles down the narrow circular stairs that led to the bottom of the county jail. They thrust him into a small room with a concrete floor and pale green walls. The door clanged shut. The room contained two folding chairs and a bolted down steel table. He slowly danced up and down the narrow space.

He hummed. I won't stay in this room forever, he thought. When I get out of here, they're going to be some changes made. As he shimmied around the table, he thanked the voice for telling him to move. The swimming pool would have to stay a secret for awhile longer. One day the whole world would know of it, and see what a right thing it was. There could be swimming pools all over; places where people could learn how to act. He danced for awhile, slowing down, picking up the beat as the hum rose and fell. He did not hear the footsteps in the corridor and the opening of the locks. He only stopped dancing when the door swung open. There was the judge, with the two bailiffs standing behind him.

"Don't close the door," the judge said. "And you two men stay right where you are."

The judge sat down and asked Charles if he needed anything. The judge tried to sound friendly, but Charles was not fooled. He kept dancing.

"What you want from me?" Charles asked.

The judge's jaw was hard, but his eyes blinked like a rabbit's behind his glasses.

"We want you to behave so that we can get on with the trial."

Charles sat down. He could see that the judge was uncomfortable being so close to him.

"You like being on T.V.?" Charles asked.

The judge did not answer.

"Makes you feel real, don't it?"

"And do you want to get back on T.V.?" the judge asked.

Charles did not like his tone. It was like he was talking to an idiot or something.

"I'm gonna be on T.V. no matter what. You run me off the steps one time too. And now I'm back," he sneered.

The judge quit trying to be nice.

"Don't use that tone with me. I'm the judge here. I understand. . ."

"You don't understand. You ain't the real judge, because I'm the Daddy."

"If it weren't for me, you wouldn't even be able to spew out that filth of yours in front of the courthouse. You're a jackal. The worst. . ."

"I'm God. . . ."

"You won't get back in my courtroom. I can promise you that."

The judge left the door closed behind him. Charles resumed his dancing. The hum was louder than ever.

Martha yawned and stretched.

"Maybe we shouldn't go to Hilton Head this year. Europe. Spain. Daddy sent me there. One of my high school graduation presents. Remember the pictures I showed you? Probably not. It was only a tour, though. Lots of ugly girls from Atlanta and Charleston. Educational. We saw lots of churches and paintings. I remember the sun. It's wonderful there. Burned clear down to my soul. . ."

Gant did not listen to her. She was a minor nuisance this evening, following him into the study, clicking ice cubes in her glass. It was her third drink since dinner. As he studied his trial notes, he decided that there might even be something on her mind. Probably not, he thought.

". . . Bitsy called today. She wanted me to go to Heritage Village this Friday. I can't say I'm interested in the world's largest Christian shopping mall. Besides, all she wants to do is compare prices. A couple of weeks ago we went to Darden Grove and she priced six different food processors. If it isn't the prices, it's how the Goddamned things work. The last time we went to their house, she heated up six different casseroles in the microwaves. She timed them. Ted bought her a stop watch. Can you believe it?"

"Interesting," he answered. By her inflection, Gant could tell that she had asked a question. He could not concentrate on the notes. Besides Martha's presence, there were other problems.

". . . And angel food cake. If I have to eat another slice of her cake, I'll puke all over her tree-of-life rug."

I should have expected these problems, Gant thought. I can't stop Cope from keeping Fite out of the courtroom. Not after their little conference this afternoon. Still, I'll get him back when he testifies. By then, I'll have finished off Bunch's experts, such as they are. That goddamned Cope. A glimpse of the tapes would budge him. But I must not get ahead of myself.

"I start tennis lessons next Tuesday. The instructor's named Jerry. A cute boy. Just out of Carolina. . ."

Then there was the old man. He sat with Fite's family every day. He watches me. He tries to catch my eye when we recess, like he has a question. But what? Nothing, probably. He did not notice that Martha had disappeared until he heard her padding down the grand staircase. When she returned to the study, she posed naked in the doorway, like a shy young model on her first all-nude assignment.

"What about it, Trip? Is it O.K.? Do you like it?"

Slowly, she massaged her nipples.

"I like it," she said. "Charles Fite would, too. Fellowshipping, he calls it. I'll bet you thought that I wasn't paying attention to your trial. Your big deal of a trial. I watch it every day. You're taping it, aren't you?"

"Yes." There would be a day when he could watch his performance at leisure. A perfect day.

She rubbed against the edge of the door, like a stripper hunching in a carnival tent.

"You haven't answered my first question, though. Do you like it? Would Charles?"

A sudden pressure grabbed Gant's bowels.

"Maybe," he said, "you should join Charles for the rest of the evening. They're out on Charlie Justice Boulevard. Spiritually, it's your part of town anyway."

He threw the car keys to her. They landed at her feet. She did not pick them up.

"Take the Mercedes. The tank's full."

"I thought I would check to see if there was anything left. Inside of you, I mean."

She laughed. Except for the tapes, Gant had not seen her naked more than a dozen times in the last ten years.

"There's nothing that you could begin to understand," he said.

"I'm sure of that."

She turned, leaving the keys on the rug.

"I'm going downstairs. *Dynasty* is coming on."

He wanted to say that he had some other tapes that she should see, but he checked himself.

"Put your clothes on, Martha."

"Yes, dear," she called over her shoulder. "I wouldn't want to embarrass you."

The next morning, Bunch parked behind the courthouse. As he locked the car, he heard the shouts and chants of the crowd out front. The morning news had carried two reports from the courthouse steps. The first was an interview with the Dean of the School of Fundamentalism at the East Coast Bible College. He was a youngish, blond man with a strong resemblance to Pat Boone. He spoke of the necessity of all Christians standing up and being counted. He described, in his even, pleasant voice, how the entire student body of his college had been bussed in the night before for a candlelight vigil. The screen showed dim pictures of clean-cut young men and women bearing their candles in the darkness as they sang, "Onward Christian Soldiers." The dean concluded by brightly noting that his "boy and girls were there to do battle, if necessary, with the forces of evil." Meaning me, Bunch had thought, as he sipped his coffee and smoked his first cigarette of the day.

The next interview was with a woman named Debbie. Bunch had seen her, or someone just like her, many times at the courthouse. She was short and skinny, shrunken, with a frizzy permanent and popped-out eyes.

"Why are you here?" the interviewer asked.

"See what's gonna happen."

"What do you think will happen?"

"Something, but I'm going to see it."

Bunch had switched off the set before the cameras could finish with Debbie.

As he reached the back entrance to the courthouse, he

ran into the family. They looked worse than usual. Their faces were creased with dirt and their hair hung in greasy strands. Their eyes were wide, tense, and restless. Luther clutched the huge pickle jar containing the dead monkey. Bunch remembered that he had given him the money for the alcohol.

"What can I do for you fine people?" Bunch said. It was a good idea to come on friendly. Even without Charles, there was no way of knowing what they were capable of.

"Is there anything wrong with your monkeys? I mean Precious Spirits?"

The family stared at him.

"No sir," Luther finally said. "The spirits is fine. We need Daddy. Things ain't right without him."

"We love him," said a fat woman who held the two living monkeys on belts that had been made to serve as leashes.

"That's right," Tinka said. "I got to have him back."

The others made noises of agreement.

"I'll talk to Judge Cope and see what I can do," Bunch said.

"You better," Tinka said.

They marched away, singing, half-dancing. As Bunch watched them go, an old man stayed behind, calling to him.

"The swimming pool. Go there."

One of the punks grabbed the old man's arm. Bunch suddenly remembered the old man from the last visit he made to the Palomino.

Ms. Williams, the social worker, was Bunch's first witness that morning. She wore the same tight pants suit she had on the day he met her, and she answered his questions in that same, untouched child's voice. Through her, Bunch introduced parts of her reports on Charles' condition before the wreck. No, she said,

Charles Fite had not been unbalanced when he was her client. Yes, he had certain emotional problems. No, he was not different from other handicapped individuals living on the edge of poverty.

When Bunch had finished his direct, Gant swept to the edge of the witness stand. He's going after her hard, Bunch thought.

"Now, Ms. Williams," Gant began, "Did Charles Fite take part in any of the programs for the handicapped?"

"No. He did not."

"He wasn't enrolled in any of Darden County's job-training programs?"

"He was not. I did not think that Mr. Fite, at that stage of his development, was suited for these classes. You see. . ."

"So you didn't try to place him in any of these programs which might have helped make him a productive member of society?"

"That's not exactly how it was. . ."

"You mentioned in your report for January, 1985, that Charles Fite would bang his crutches together when asked questions about his home life. That statement, by the way, is contained in the same report which Mr. Bunch had admitted as plaintiff's exhibit P-14. Mr. Bunch did not ask you to refer to this material, so I want to cover it now."

A metallic sludge flooded Bunch's mouth. I've left her naked up there, he thought. He had not taken time to go through every report. Instead, Ms. Williams had given him the passages that showed that Charles was only a pathetic, misunderstood victim of the social order. He began to scribble notes for re-direct, trying to keep an eye on Gant at the same time.

"Getting back to my question: Did you consider the banging of the crutches to be unusual behavior?"

"No. You must understand. . ."

Gant turned to the spectators.

"Of course not. Unusual behavior in the Department of Social Services only includes the belief that you are God."

The audience laughed long and loud. The trial had been dull that morning, and with Charles in jail, it promised to stay that way.

"Objection," Bunch said. "Mr. Gant has no right to badger this witness. He can confine his witty asides to his evening interviews."

"Reluctantly," Cope said. "I'll sustain. However, the testimony of the witness does produce a certain amount of mirth in me."

"And I'll take exception to that statement, Your Honor," Bunch said. His mouth tasted worse than ever, and he could feel his anger rising, too.

"Exception noted. Proceed, Mr. Gant."

Cope smiled for the camera. Another Goddamned comedian, Bunch thought.

"Charles Fite had, or I should say has, a drinking problem. Isn't that right?" Gant asked.

Ms. Williams was flustered. Automatically, she smoothed the dark brown hair from her face.

"He drank. Many poor people drink. It eases the. . ."

"So you recommend vodka as an antidote to poverty?"

"That's not what I'm saying. . ."

"Are most of your clients heavy drinkers?"

"Some. However, you must understand. . ."

"Do you urge them to drink?"

Bunch was on his feet again.

"Your Honor, I want that last question stricken from the record. It is prejudicial and of no probative value. . ."

"Very well," Cope said wearily. "I hope, Mr. Bunch, that you won't take up the whole morning with a series of petty objections. Mr. Gant?"

"Just a minute, Your Honor," Bunch said. "All of these objections I've offered go to an important matter. That is, will Mr. Gant be permitted to use this courtroom as a stage, as an exhibition ground for his ego? I'm tired of it. Charles Fite wants his own T.V. program. Perhaps Mr. Gant considers himself a candidate for a similar position. Maybe they could work out an agreement, sort of like Johnny Carson and Ed McMahon. I don't know who would end up as the straight man, though."

The spectators laughed again. This time Cope pounded his gavel and glared at Bunch.

"You will refrain from any more characterizations of defense counsel."

"Don't be too hard on Mr. Bunch," Gant said. "After all, he is in an unenviable position; advocating, as he does, the blasphemous and the destructive."

The preachers in the front two rows clapped and cheered. Bunch sat down.

"Didn't Charles Fite beat his wife?" Gant asked Ms. Williams.

"On occasion. This is fairly common among the disadvantaged. And also among those who aren't disadvantaged, I might add."

There was a quaver in her voice and Bunch hoped that it was from anger rather than panic. Gant, genial and smooth as ever, pressed on.

"It can be shown, Ms. Williams, that in the years before the traffic accident, that Charles Fite beat his wife, drank heavily, and did not participate in any of the programs specifically set up to help people like him. This can be determined from your reports and testimony. Isn't that right?"

"There can be differing interpretations of the same material."

Gant handed one of the reports to Ms. Williams.

"Do you recognize this?" Gant asked.

"It's a report I wrote on Charles Fite."

"And this is not one of the reports that Mr. Bunch asked you to read from, is it?"

"No."

"Will you read from this report, dated February 19, 1987? Which, I may add, is more than six months before the wreck. I've marked it at page six, paragraph three."

Weakly and softly she began.

"Mr. Fite shows a marked tendency toward a sociopathic, if not psychotic disposition. He is subject to violent day-dreams. While it is difficult to get him to discuss his home life, he willingly describes these dreams. He refused to consider that they may be harmful to his well-being. Therapy is a possible alternative."

She was nearly inaudible as she reached the end of the passage.

"Your Honor," Gant said. "I submit this passage into evidence as defendant's exhibit D-5."

"So admitted," Cope said. "Mr. Bunch, you surely must have some questions for your witness."

Bunch did not want to look at her.

"Ms. Williams, you mentioned therapy as being only a possible alternative. You obviously considered other alternatives?"

"I tried very hard to help Mr. Fite. I thought that perhaps with understanding and empathy, on my part, he would not have to undergo psychological treatment. You see. . ."

"Go ahead," Bunch said. "Take your time."

"You see. I thought at the time that a psychiatrist might recommend commitment—to a state hospital."

Bunch felt Gant's smile at his back. He had asked the one question that he should have left alone.

"Why. . . ah. . . did you not want to see Mr. Fite hospitalized?"

Her voice was a bit stronger now.

"Those hospitals are terrible places. Patients are left unsupervised, unattended. They are given drugs to keep them docile. There is not real treatment. I thought. . . I thought. . ."

"That you could help him?"

"Yes. That I could heal him."

"Is it your considered opinion as a professional that Charles Fite was unbalanced at the time of the automobile accident of August, 1987?"

"I. . . I don't know. I wrote those reports. . . I don't know."

There was nothing left to ask. Bunch excused her. She hurried past him. His heart was a mass of gristle.

"Yes. Belief of this sort can be brought on by a traumatic experience. For example, the plains Indians believed that they could become shamen, holy men, by passing through painful rituals of purification."

Babbington seems plausible, Bunch thought, just as an expert on God and the devil should.

"Now Father Babbington, you've had a chance to see and hear Charles Fite. How would you describe his condition?"

Babbington, who had been precise and scholarly so far, became more excited.

"Troubled. Deeply. Certainly not normal."

"Could his beliefs have been brought about by the accident?"

"Certainly. There have been similar incidents in the past. Take a situation that I recorded in my latest book. You find it between pages 238 and 242. In 1956, a Mister Cormac O'Malley, a respected layman in the diocese of Boston, was in a wreck. He was returning from a Knights of Columbus banquet. His injuries seemed slight. His doctor recommended aspirin, bed rest, that sort of thing. Within three or four days, however, he was acting strangely. Refused to eat. Slept little. As time went on, he neglected his job and family. One morning, before mass, he visited his priest and told him that the devil had come in the night. The devil wanted poor Mr. O'Malley to kill Ted Williams. Mr. O'Malley, who was a devoted Red Sox fan, went into a kind of trance after he made this revelation. He was in psychiatric care for over a year. The devil appeared to him often during that time, still demanding the death of Ted Williams. I must add here that Mr. O'Malley was only saved by the efforts of the church. An exorcism was necessary."

"Yes. . . well. . . getting back to Charles Fite. . ."

"Just a minute. I'm not finished. Many of the delusions which afflict people in all walks of life may be ascribed to the devil. That's what's wrong with Mr. Fite."

Bunch tried again.

"What we're concerned with, Father Babbington, is Mr. Fite's delusion. The important thing is. . ."

Babbington spoke sharply.

"The *Devil* is what I'm talking about here! The prince of the air. Your Mr. Fite is one of his minions. Oh, I've been sitting here listening to your fine arguments, and I've read up on Mr. Fite. What's important is that the devil is in our midst."

"Thank you, Father Babbington. No more questions."

The coming disaster was palpable to Bunch. Gant would not have to try very hard on this one.

Gant circled the dead space near the witness stand.

"Father Babbington," Gant said. "Can you elaborate a little more on that last point you raised—about the devil?"

Babbington leaned forward, gesturing with his small, pudgy hands. Bunch saw that he was taking to Gant.

"Certainly! The devil can take hold of you at any time. My research has shown that the devil has often appeared in children who are, as we know, pure and without blemish. Then, too, famous people have fought the devil face to face. Pope Innocent once threw a demon from the balcony of St. Peter's. That particular demon had taken the shape of a Dutch heretic. Elvis Presley encountered satan many times during his life. And President Calvin Coolidge is thought to have banished satan from the White House following a state visit by the British ambassador in 1926. . ."

Bunch massaged his temples as Babbington went on. Yes, the slippage is major, he thought. First, Ms. Williams. Now this one. A joke is a joke, but. . . I've still got Pffippert—and Charles.

Babbington slowed down for breath and Gant asked him a question.

"Do you feel that Mr. Fite is the devil?"

"If not the devil himself, he is at least under the power of hell. My considered opinion is that no amount of therapy can help. An exorcism is needed. And the quicker the better."

Babbington turned to Cope, who had listened to the priest without comment. A bad sign, Bunch thought. Signs are getting worse all of the time.

"Your Honor," Babbington said, "if you would allow it, I could perform this exorcism right now. I have my vestments and oils here with me. If you would only bring Mr. Fite in, we could heal him once and for all. This trial would not have to continue, and we would have a powerful victory for Mother Church. Do I have your permission?"

Gant was at the bench before Cope could give an answer. Bunch was right behind him.

"I don't hold with the Catholics," Cope said, "but he might be on to something."

"Sure," Bunch said. "Let's bring Charles in. I don't have any objections. I'm sure Charles will be just fine after he gets a good washing in holy water."

"I would object most strongly," Gant said. "Think of how it will look, Your Honor. Do we want to turn this trial into a circus?"

Bunch laughed.

"The only thing we don't have is a clown car full of midgets."

"I'm going to side with Mr. Gant on this one," Cope said.

"Then I'll take exception to that. Besides, an exorcism would make an interesting reading up at the Court of Appeals."

Gant and Bunch resumed their seats. It would have been worth seeing, Bunch thought. Anyway, whatever was inside of Charles was there on a permanent basis. No exorcism could begin to help.

"Father Babbington," Cope said. "I'll take your offer under advisement. However, at this point in the proceedings, an exorcism isn't possible."

"Not possible! But, Your Honor. . ."

"No further questions," Gant said.

"Mr. Bunch?" Cope asked.

"No questions."

"Recess until two-thirty," Cope said, banging the gavel.

As the disappointed spectators left for lunch, Babbington rushed up to Bunch.

"You could've done more!"

"You did enough, Father," said Bunch as he closed his briefcase. "Don't blame yourself, though. I picked you as the expert, relying on my unfailing good judgment."

"The devil is real," Babbington said.

"Of that, I haven't the slightest doubt."

Anthus Board wires ran all over the courtroom, intermingling with the television cables and hook-ups. Pffippert, clad in designer jeans and a T-shirt which proclaimed that he had run in the San Diego Marathon, described how the board worked.

"Using the Anthus Board, you've conducted tests on Charles Fite?" Bunch asked.

"I have."

"And what do these tests reveal?"

"The evidence clearly shows. . ."

"Objection," Gant smiled.

Cope, who like the jurors and spectators was enthralled by the Anthus Board, was startled by Gant's voice.

Gant turned his smile on Bunch.

"This test is not recognized in North Carolina, nor in any other jurisdiction."

Gant produced an official-looking journal and passed it to Cope.

"This is the May, 1986, issue of the *Journal of the American Association of Psychologists*. Please take note of the table of contents. You'll notice that the lead article is entitled, 'Quacks and Unreliable Informational Analysis.' It deals specifically with the work of Doctor Amadeus Anthus."

Cope read for a few minutes, nodding. He handed the journal back to Gant, who held it out to Bunch. Bunch shook his head. I should've known, he thought. I should know much more than I do.

"Are you sure you wouldn't like to examine it?" Gant asked. "It makes for fascinating reading. It's probably new to you."

Again, Bunch shook his head. His mouth was dry with failure and anger.

"Perhaps Mr. Bunch will learn a few new things before the trial is over," Gant chuckled. "Briefly, the article compares the Anthus Board to the notorious Orgone Box of Wilhelm Reich. There are, I believe, several law suits pending against Doctor Anthus."

Pffippert ran his hands through his beautifully styled hair. Bunch managed to feel a little sorry for him, a little pity for all the people he had involved in the case. Pffippert had not looked so bad since that day he first brought Charles into his office. After this, he wouldn't be the greatest shrink in Helmsville.

Bunch rummaged through his briefcase until he found the advertising circular for the Anthus Board.

"Your Honor," Bunch said. "I have here direct testimonials from well-respected members of the psychiatric profession which prove the worth and validity of the Anthus Board."

"Let me see those things," Cope said.

Bunch watched as Cope's lips curled in a sneer at the smiling couple on the cover of the circular, the same circular that Bunch had not bothered to read. Cope turned his sneer on Pffippert, who seemed to Bunch to look less and less like an expert witness.

"What in the world is the Productive Living Institute?" Cope asked.

"The PLI is one of the most well-respected therapeutic communities in the world," Pffippert answered.

"Well respected for what?"

"For helping troubled individuals to grow and learn and to reach their full potential as human beings. I've been there myself. . ."

Someone in the audience laughed.

"I don't doubt that you've been there," Cope said. 'This smells of jackaldom to me. I'm going to rule this. . . thing inadmissible."

"Judge Cope," Pffippert said. "Dr. Anthus is one of the most enlightened men you'll ever meet. Why, he's a good friend of Mortimer Adler. . ."

Bunch was on his feet.

"Excuse me, Doctor Pffippert. Your Honor, there are two reasons why you should allow this test into evidence. First, you can show how far-sighted you are. Accept the Anthus Board and you will set a precedent. You will blaze a trail for enlightened jurisprudence. Secondly, Mr. Gant has known of Doctor Pffippert's evaluations for months, as those evaluations are part of the record of the deposition we took in January. He raised no objections then, and he has no grounds now."

"Your Honor," Gant said in his most reasonable tone, "I would leave the question of ground-breaking to your fine judicial sense. As for the references to this device during the deposition, any second-year law student learns that such evidence during the deposition may be admitted for purposes of discovery, but not as substantive evidence at trial. Mr. Bunch should familiarize himself with the rules of evidence. It may be of some future value to him."

"Mr. Gant's arguments are convincing," Cope said. "Mr. Bunch, you may question the witness as to the issues of this case without reference to this machine which you have brought into our midst."

Well, I still have Pffippert, Bunch thought. And he's seen enough of Charles with or without the Goddamned Anthus Board to know that he's crazy.

"Dr. Pffippert," Bunch began in a steady voice. "You have examined Charles Fite on two occasions, I believe."

"Yes." Bunch did not like his tone. It was petulant, full of self-pity.

"And do you have an opinion as to the state of his mind?"

"No. I did until the Anthus Board was ruled inadmissible. I don't anymore. Years of research went into that system, and to have some obscure legality. . ."

Bunch was sweating, shining in the television lights. He tried again.

"You did interview Charles Fite before he was given the Anthus tests?"

Pffippert dismissed the question with a wave of his hand.

"Preliminary interviews are of no importance. They might be interesting, but they don't prove much."

"In your report, which was cited in the deposition, you described a malady called Von Bey's syndrome. Would you say that Charles Fite is suffering from the effects of this disease?"

Pffippert, who had been slumping lower and lower in the witness chair, raised himself straight up.

"Without reference to the Anthus Board, I am not qualified to discuss any of the symptoms or circumstances surrounding Mr. Fite's condition. I make this statement as a matter of principle. If this court refuses to recognize the latest revolution in mental health evaluation, I refuse to recognize this court."

Bunch slowly rubbed his hands over his face. He had never been so aware of the cameras until now. It was a dream, like being naked on a stage before a huge audience.

"Dr. Pffippert, I will ask you once more. You have interviewed Charles Fite. You did prepare a report based on those interviews. I want an answer from you right now. What is Charles Fite's mental condition at the present time?"

Pffippert jutted his chin out, haughty and offended.

"I have no opinion. None. It was taken from me by this court."

"Your Honor," Bunch managed to say. "Will you instruct the witness to answer the question?"

Cope smiled.

"Mr. Bunch, I can't put words in the mouth of your witness. You called him in as an expert. It seems to me that he is doing the best job he can."

"Then I want the jury to see a copy of the report which was admitted during the deposition. All references to the Anthus Board may be stricken," Bunch said.

The fucking report, Bunch thought. It was almost nothing, but at least it said that Charles was crazy. Before Cope could give an answer, Pffippert broke in.

"I refuse to stand behind any portion of that report. I repudiate it."

"You *what*?" Bunch asked Pffippert.

"Repudiate it. I stand on my principles."

Excess flooded Bunch's brain.

"You don't have any principles, you sneaking little chicken shit. . ."

The spectators were laughing. The gavel was pounding. Pffippert assumed his most pained, benevolent expression. Bunch went quietly when the bailiff took his arm.

Gant lowered his rock-hard buttocks onto the toilet and gave a couple of preliminary grunts. He was tighter than usual, but who could tell when there might be a flow? Everything else was going so well. The next day Charles would be on the stand and he would complete this phase of the triumph. After he had polished off Bunch's experts, it had been easy to convince Cope to let Charles go home, just to show how fair the proceedings were. It had taken a little more convincing to keep Bunch out of jail, but Gant got him off with an apology and a fine. Bunch did not show even a hint of gratitude, but what could be expected? Even Bunch could see that the trial was over. It was easier than I imagined, Gant thought. Bunch had taken care of that. That's why he's Bunch.

Bunch felt tired, old. The weight of the earth was greater than it had ever been, pulling him down. His suit hung in long, heavy wrinkles, like the skin of an aged lizard. When the deputy opened the door to the viewing room, Charles leaped up.

"Those people up there say I'm crazy," Charles said.

Bunch sat down and lit a cigarette.

"Only nobody believes them. The whole thing has turned to shit. I fucked up. The experts fucked up."

"I got the truth. Not a one of them said I got the truth."

"Yeah. That's terrible. Tomorrow, you're going on the stand. It won't matter about Tinka or Babbington or that Goddamned Pffippert. Or even Gant. It's your show."

"Are the cameras gonna be on me?"

"Count on it. If you can't count on another Goddamned thing, you can count on the cameras."

"And that little judge is gonna be there?"

"Count on that, too. Somebody like Cope is always
there."

"He blocking me up."

"That's his job. Forget him. Be yourself. It's the best,
the only fucking shot we got left."

"Are them people still out front?"

"They hardly ever leave."

"They want me bad. Want what I got. . ."

"Charles, they've been watching you for awhile. None
of them care. Admit it. Even if you are God, it's not
working. Some people will watch you. Hell, they'll
watch anything."

"Them's. . . them's only words."

"Yeah. Nothing but words."

Bunch's eyes hurt, and he had not stopped sweating.

"Anyway," Bunch said, "your pal Gant fixed it up so
you can go home tonight. Be here tomorrow if you ever
want to get on television again."

Charles bolted through the door. Bunch finished his
cigarette and tried not to think about anything.

It was nearly six when Bunch left the jail and went
back to his office. He had no real reason to go there, but
he did not want to go home. I'm glad it's nearly over, he
thought, as he waited for the elevator. I said the words
"chicken shit" on television. It came out of my mouth,
like almost everything else that ever got me in trouble.
Charles will be on the stand tomorrow and that means
more trouble. Gant will have his witnesses and I'll have
my cross-examination. I may even make some dents in
their testimony. Who knows? I can smell this jury,
though. They're thinking about jackals.

He got off the elevator and turned the corner that led
to his office, still thinking about what was left of the

case. After Charles and Gant's experts would come the paying of the bills. Pffippert's fourteen hundred. That bastard, Bunch thought. Catching me outside of Cope's chambers, after Cope had finished with me. The money, he says. Says that he's going to sue me for ruining him professionally. I should've given him a shot to his perfect teeth right there. Tells me that our professional relationship is at an end. After this, I don't want to hear any more about professional relationships.

As he unlocked the door, he heard something move behind him. He whirled, swinging his briefcase in a wide arc. Goforth, he thought. Goforth with a .45. Whoever made the noise tottered away. Bunch stopped swinging. It was the old man who muttered about swimming pools.

"I need to speak to you," Smith said.

Bunch locked the front door and motioned Smith into his office. He pulled the bottle from the desk and poured a stiff one.

"Sorry about swinging on you. I'm nervous. The trial. Drink?"

Smith shook his head.

"I thought you'd be out at the Palomino. Fellowshipping and dancing."

"I've left the family. They didn't notice—now that Charles is back. That's one of the advantages of being invisible much of the time. You come and go as you please."

"An advantage I've never had."

Invisible. Sure, Bunch thought. Why shouldn't I be talking to a guy who thinks he's invisible. It fits. Perfectly.

"You seem to be a busy man, so I won't waste your time," Smith said.

"I'd say that time is about all I have these days. And most of it's wasted. So you got something to tell me?"

"Yes. There's a dead man in the swimming pool."

"Are you sure you don't want a drink?"

"Positive. Charles Fite killed him. I saw it. The others helped. Charles finished him off. Shot him. In the head. Do you believe me?"

"No."

"I thought you wouldn't. You must go see for yourself."

"What's the man's name?"

"I don't know."

"Why did Charles kill him?"

"I don't know that either."

"Why are you telling me?"

"Sometimes you can't stand things anymore. That's when you tell. Or run. Or disappear. I don't know why I picked you."

"You could tell the cops."

"I don't like to deal with the police."

"O.K. If there is a body out there, what do you think I should do about it?"

"That's up to you. Will you go there?"

"I'll think about it."

As Bunch unlocked the door, Smith paused.

"I've been here before," he said.

Then he was gone.

Bunch poured another drink. Why did I go through with that one, he thought. Must be the trial. Lowers my resistance. The mysterious messenger. But the swimming pool. The coughing and voices on the day I wanted to start running and never stop. He sipped the drink slowly. Charles and the family would be gone by eight in the morning. An hour before the trial starts up. An hour to go and see.

XIX

The morning traffic slackened as Bunch turned off the interstate and onto Charlie Justice Boulevard. As he passed the Palomino, a smoking old Ford pulled out. Quickly, Bunch whipped into the parking lot at the Third World Lounge. From there, he could watch them as they left.

A pick-up truck followed the Ford. It was driven by one of the feral boys. Charles sat beside him. Bunch made out Tinka, the fat women, and the two guys in the baseball caps; all were hunched down in the truck bed. He waited five more minutes before he slipped into the Palomino.

He parked as close to the pool as he could and checked his watch. Nearly ten after. He wondered if the old man was watching and laughing; whether Charles might have set him up—as a test. Fuck it. I'm going to have a look.

He turned the corner of the building, making for the pool. There's nothing there, he thought. No murdered

corpse. I took the word of an ancient man who lived with
Charles Fite. Would I believe Charles if he said there
was a body in the swimming pool? Tinka? Luther? The
Precious Spirits? But Righter has been here; and he
came out blue all over. He reached the edge, but did not
look down. He checked his watch again. Almost eight-
fifteen.

The shallow end was filled with trash, three or four
feet deep in places—garbage that had built up over the
months, food containers, paper, clothing, a wing-tip
shoe. The smell was there, too, the same smell from the
day he first saw the family. Tinka had opened the door
and it had punched him in the face.

His eyes traveled from the shallows to the diving
board, and down. More trash, car parts, greasy and
black, cardboard boxes with rags hanging out of them.
The shadow of the diving board stretched over most of
it. Streaks of human excrement stained the white concrete, like a painting, in drips and drabs that pointed
toward the drain. And there was a thing wrapped in a
blanket. And out of the blanket a white hand grabbing
the air.

Bunch turned away from the hand, then made himself look at it. Slowly, he went around to the diving
board, following the hand. If I look long enough, he
thought, it will clench and unclench. He walked out
onto the board. Yes, he said to himself, there's more to
see. There's always more to see.

The blanket had fallen away on one side. He was a
big, naked man. He used to have eyes. Black streaks
criss-crossed his white body. Black and white; a terrible
white, Bunch thought, like the whiteness of all the
bones in the world. The man's knees were drawn up into
his chest. He had passed through rigor mortis long before and was beginning the transformation into his
component parts: liquid, gristle, bone.

Bunch squatted for a closer look. He had no doubt

that Charles had done it. How would the court put it, he thought. "Caused the death of blank or caused others to induce the death of blank." I'm not sick, he suddenly realized. I don't want to run. He took one more long look at the naked man. If I could, he thought, I would pray for you, whoever you are. He stood, balancing his weight on the edge of the board.

"Congratulations," he said. "You've seen the worst thing in the world."

Dimly, he heard the rotten, wet crack of the board. He was halfway down, scrambling, kicking the air, trying to find a grip. He closed his eyes as he hit, rolling off soggy boxes, screaming and turning to keep away from the big, naked man.

The fellowshipping session the night before had been a good one. In the middle of the dancing, with the motel office turning different colors, the voice came to him, stronger than ever. It was not just that he and the voice were the same. He, the voice, the family, all the people in the world were the same, too. And they were all part of him. And he saw what he had to do.

Charles and the family got to the courthouse to find the preacher and his students ready to shout him down. They waved their signs and called him names. He did not pay attention to them. Even they were part of him now. He did not start out with a shout. Instead, he spoke in a low, soft voice, like the voice that came to him after the wreck. Soon the crowd calmed down and waited solemnly for his next word.

". . . there's things you need to see, want to see. I can bring us all together. If you wait, today you will see. When I do what I'm going to do, you'll be O.K. You'll be free."

It was the shortest speech that he had ever made, but he knew that it was the best. Quickly, he left the steps, the family following, slowly humming the jingle. As he took his seat in the courtroom, he patted the waist of his robe. The .22 was ready. It would take one more sign, a soft murmur, before he would be shown when to use it.

At ten minutes before nine, Trip Gant concluded his morning interview with Rollins. It was going well, he told the cameras; better than he expected. Not exactly true, he thought, but it sounds right for television. He was smooth and clean, inside and out. He nearly smacked his lips at the sweetness of it all.

At the top of the stairs, just before he entered the courtroom, he ran into Goforth. Goforth looked bad, like he had been on a drunk. Gant took his arm and jerked him into a restroom.

"I guess you don't remember our last conversation," Gant said.

"It's Charlene, Mr. Gant. I tried to call you, tried to call Akins. She left last night. Got me drunk. Took the car, all the money, the T.V. She even took Waylon. He's my new Doberman pup. I was getting him trained real good. He can bite through a four-inch stick. The best dog I ever had. . ."

Tears started down Goforth's dirty cheeks. Gant released his arm. He tried to ignore a kick that ran from his stomach and barrelled into his lower tract.

"I thought she loved me," Goforth whined. "Bunch, he ruined her. She was a good woman. . ."

Gant weighed his alternatives. He had the affidavits. Bunch might sign anyway, especially after the jury came back. Akins might even catch her. A woman in a Trans-Am with a color television and a Doberman would be easy to find.

"What am I gonna do, Mr. Gant? Charlene's gone. Say, could you loan me fifty?"

Goforth's tears had stopped and he managed a cringing smile.

"Not a dime," Gant said. "Our relationship, our partnership as you called it, is at an end."

"I. . . I don't. . ."

"You broke your part of the bargain."

Gant left the restroom. His bowels still twitched, but he could work this out. He would call Akins as soon as the morning's testimony was over. Goforth trailed along in his wake.

"How 'bout ten? I had to thumb down here. At least a little for bus fare and something to eat?"

"And enough for a pint of liquor? Who are you? If you come near me again, I'll have your redneck ass pinned under the slammer."

"I'm. . . I'm. . ."

"You're gone," Gant said, disappearing into the courtroom. The last of the spectators, hurrying for a seat, came behind him, shoving Goforth out of their way.

Bunch slid toward the drain, the diving board clattering behind him, barely missing his head. He scrambled away from the dead man, arms and legs flailing, no longer aware of the smell or what he was sliding in. He came to rest against a mushy mattress. I'm not here, he thought. I'm anywhere but here. He felt himself for broken bones and found none. He stood and checked himself out further. It was bad enough. He had scraped both cheeks and blood ran down over his shirt and jacket. A sleeve had pulled away from his jacket and hung from the shoulder. His pants had burst, the seat and crotch ripped open, and hung like a kilt. His left shoe was missing and it took a couple of minutes for him to find it, as he gingerly picked his way through the debris. As he moved, he discovered new places where he hurt; the arms, the legs, his back.

He swayed, trying to keep his footing, trying to think. He tried, too, not to look at the dead man, a mummy left from a lost civilization that offered no clues as to its origin. It could be worse, he thought. That's what we're supposed to think when the diving board collapses beneath us, when we fall into the vat of boiling gravy.

Laugh, he told himself. Go on. Another joke. Laugh at that poor bastard over there. You don't even know who he is.

Finally, he started to move. He slowly edged his way around the body. There was no ladder, so he would have to work his way up the slick bank to the shallow end. He could see that the climb would be a slow one. The hand-holds were few, but Bunch knew that he had to make it.

He slipped backwards several times, besmirching himself further, opening up new scrapes and holes. Several times he imagined what would happen if Charles came back, and he found a new burst of energy. Eventually, he flung himself over the edge. He stayed on all fours for awhile, heaving and retching, not bothering about where his vomit spattered. He rested before he could stand again.

On his way downtown, he checked his watch. It had been shattered in the fall. I'm late, he thought, but when I get there that won't matter.

By nine forty-five, the spectators were in a mood of righteous impatience. They complained loudly about the delays inherent in the American legal system; about the selfishness of lawyers; about the general unsoundness of Roy A. Bunch. The preachers spoke of scripture and barbecues and budgets. The reporters groaned about deadlines. Rollins ordered his cameraman to stop taping. If all had listened, they would have heard the singing of the Bible students, and the low, but strong voice of the mob.

Cope called Gant to the bench and whispered.

"Can I find him in contempt again? He knows that he should never be late, especially on today of all days."

Gant shook his head. They, he thought, can't do anything right. Goforth, Bunch, and this idiot. The pull on his bowels was strong again.

"Come on, Trip," Cope begged. "Just one more time. I've had to hold back for almost the whole trial."

Gant wanted to strike him, but checked the impulse. "No," he said. "You've been told how this will turn out, and I want it to be perfect."

It took Bunch a long time to get to the courthouse. Twice he had to pull over and vomit, once in a gas station where he tried to drink a Coke. The first couple of swallows came straight up, and the station manager told him to clean up his mess or he would call the law. Bunch ignored him and kept driving. As he drew closer to the courthouse, the naked dead man kept coming back to him, like a brother who had vanished years before. One of my brothers, he said over and over.

His head was fairly clear when he got downtown. He parked in a loading zone on Broad Street, left his briefcase behind, the mass of useless notes and pleadings, and started for the courthouse in a gimpy, half-run.

Two blocks away, he saw the mob. It was bigger than it had ever been: the next of kin to the naked dead man; the permanently defeated; the forever crushed; the always revengeful. There were the mini-cameras and the students with their placards. None of it mattered. Neither did Cope nor Gant nor Charles. The only thing that was important was what he had to say.

He dove into the crowd, shoving ahead.

"Look at him now!" a voice shouted. Laughter followed.

They gave way slowly, sullenly. Hands grabbed at him, and the loose sleeve was pulled completely away from his jacket. He shook free and kept moving. Halfway up the steps, a face pressed close to him. It was Snavely.

"The essential mystery," Snavely shouted above the hymn-singing students. "I've thought and thought. I believe that it's a broken insect, turning on its back, trying to stop the pain."

Bunch did not stop to answer. It was difficult to hear anyway, for the students from the East Coast Bible College had broken into an earsplitting version of "How Great Thou Art." The mob babbled in fury and anticipation. Bunch pressed beyond Snavely to the foot of the monument. He thought he saw Smith there, and wanted to tell him what he had seen and what he was to say, but the man he thought was Smith was quickly swallowed up in the swarm of bodies.

The crowd was packed tightly against the doors. Bunch lunged and butted against it without any effect. I should have gone to the back, he suddenly realized. But it's right that I'm here, with my brothers and sisters. The mob had one voice now, high and wild. He lowered his shoulder and wedged his way in, crawling past shirtless, long-haired boys, unemployed mill workers, bleached blonds in tight jeans and halter tops. Suddenly, one of the doors opened, a hand took his, and he was jerked inside.

Raymer stood with ten other bailiffs in a line on the other side of the door.

"I could see you, but I couldn't do anything until you got closer. Goddamn. What happened?"

The other bailiffs remained in line. They hefted their night sticks and tried to appear tough and confident; but their eyes were nervous and afraid.

"A lot," Bunch gasped.

"You stink real bad. What happened? Get in some trouble out at Brenda's?"

"Listen. Call the city cops and tell them to get out to the Palomino Motel. Charlie Justice Boulevard. They'll find him in the swimming pool."

"Find who?"

"Him. Never mind. Call them."

"I'll go when I can. Something happened this morning. Charles said something to them. It's getting bigger all the time. The sheriff's calling in all the boys so that it don't get out of hand. . ."

"Out of hand."

"Yeah. If you ask me. . ."

Bunch did not wait for him to finish.

A long "Ahhhhh" went up from the spectators when Bunch burst into the courtroom. Rollins turned all of the cameras on him as he came down the aisle. Derisive cheers followed him, and Cope pounded his gavel for order.

"How dare you come into this court in that condition," Cope said. "Look at yourself."

"He's been out fellowshipping!" yelled someone from the back of the room. The laughter was general, but Cope paid no attention to it. He was intent upon Bunch.

"Your Honor," Bunch said, "I'm resigning from this case. . ."

"That's not possible," Gant said, rising quickly. "Mr. Bunch is the attorney of record and the trial is at a critical stage. The code of ethics prohibits a resignation under these circumstances. It's contrary to the profession, to public policy, to. . ."

The cameras turned back and forth between Bunch and Gant. Rollins directed his crews as if they were gunners.

"I've got something to say that's much more important than my resignation," Bunch said, his voice rising above Gant's. "There's a. . ."

"And I've got this to say," Cope interrupted. "This court has had enough of your insults and your jackalish ways. I'm going to find you in contempt again. That'll be three hundred dollars and a night in jail. And I expect a public apology for all that you've said and done since the beginning of these proceedings. And as for your disgusting and outlandish appearance. . ."

"Your Honor," Gant said. "That won't be necessary. As President of the Darden County Bar Association, I can assure you. . ."

"O.K. Fine," Bunch said, ignoring Gant. "Your Honor,

you can take everything I have. Only out at the Palomino Motel, there's a dead man in the swimming pool.
If you think this trial is more important than him. . ."

A woman screamed as Charles jumped onto the table
and began to wave the gun around.

The .22 gave off a bright, popping noise, like a fire-
cracker. The round caught Cope in the mouth. He shook
his head brokenly from side to side.

"Jackals," he coughed. Any other words that were
meant to follow were lost in blood. It was bright red
when it started, but quickly turned to deep purple, running over his robe, the deposition, the complaint, the
answer, and the pleadings. He pressed his hands to his
mouth, but nothing could stop the flow. He fell out of
sight behind the bench.

Bunch saw Charles pull the trigger before he heard
the pop. He ducked beneath a table and flattened himself out as best he could. He heard Charles fire again
and the sound of the spectators pounding their way toward the doors. The table shook. The spectators fell,
pummeling each other. A large blonde woman rolled up
next to Bunch. Her dress was ripped and she tried to
cover her expansive red panties by pulling the torn
edges together. She jibbered; sometimes a shout, then a
whisper. Bunch tried to pull her close to him in order to
calm her, and himself. She recoiled at his touch, and
rolled back into the stamping, dancing feet.

The table flipped over and the spectators danced on
Bunch, kicking and slashing. He managed to pull himself to his feet by grasping the railing behind where the
table once stood. The press of bodies lifted him from the
floor and moved him first in one direction, then another.
Then he found his feet, driving away from the pops that
continued to come from Charles' direction.

He wedged himself into a small alcove, a bay in the
wall below another picture of Cope and Christ. He felt
reasonably out of the line of fire; with the wall at his

back he could kick away anyone who tried to press too closely upon him. From somewhere outside the courtroom, even above the din and shrieks of the preachers, reporters, and lawyers, he heard whoops, cracks, and shattering glass. The main doors to the courtroom gave way and the people from the steps, the mob, poured in. They struck out with bottles and sticks as they came, driving the spectators back toward Charles. A chair was hurled through one of the big courtroom windows. In a moment the other windows were shattered. Bunch turned his face to the wall to keep flying glass from his eyes. Finally, when the glass stopped falling, he turned and looked.

The family stood on the only upright seats, singing, dancing, thrusting forward with their hips. Tinka, her blouse gone, danced frantically, her large, white breasts vibrating. The others tore at their clothes as they danced. The two boys lashed out with knives at the people below them. One of the fat women, finally naked, held a squirming monkey aloft for all to see. Luther hoisted the jar high, but someone below caught his arm and the jar dropped into the mass of struggling heads, arms, and faces. To Bunch, they seemed to dance for a long time. But the mob finally rolled against them. They went down as one, still dancing.

Rollins and his last camera crew went over next. Rollins rose and fell, his mouth opened in a scream. The noise was unbearable, a full, sustained oceanic roar. Ed Snavely's head floated by. It seemed to be detached from his body, a perfect television head. And then Bunch saw Charles.

He danced atop Cope's bench, the robe flying about him, the pistol held high. He seemed to be laughing. From near where the court reporter's desk had been, a big, tattered bailiff drew down on him and fired. The impact lifted him high and pitched him backwards.

Bunch did not have a chance to ponder what might

have happened to Charles. Pain leaped upward and hands pulled him down. Goforth had bitten deeply into his left leg. Together they disappeared among the dancing feet.

When Cope gurgled and died, Gant quickly turned and sprinted up the aisle, one step ahead of the thrashing spectators, two steps ahead of the yearning mob. As he ran, dodging like an all-star halfback, he realized that the plan, or what had been the plan, was gone.

Outside the courtroom, he heard the mob break through. He turned down a long corridor, racing past county offices and startled secretaries. He took several more turns in the labyrinth of halls and doorways, the sound of the riot growing behind him.

He slammed the door of the law library and locked it behind him. He slumped against the door and tried to think of a way to save the plan. Nothing came to him. Cope was gone. The tapes were useless. Bunch had ruined himself. Everything was for nothing. There would not be a jury to hear his experts and his summation. His lower tract throbbed so hard that he grew dizzy. His mouth was dry and he longed for a drink of water. The mob was near, tearing and ripping.

Gradually, the mob sounds grew fainter. He slowly edged into the hall. Thick, oily smoke filled the offices and corridors. He realized that he had better keep moving.

The courthouse steps were covered with clothes, placards, shoes, food, and broken glass. A young girl sat on the sidewalk, quietly weeping. People, mild and curious, lined the opposite side of the street. Reinforcements from the city police arrived and bulled their way into the building. The roar from inside was punctuated by more shots. Gant felt a terrible weariness. He sat down at the base of the monument.

This was a place that he had always known, yet it had turned distant and strange. He felt as if he had been transported to a far distant country where he understood nothing of the language and customs. He knew that he should get away, go to the office, even his home; that there was still some danger in staying where he was. He did not move. Instead, he watched as an old man slowly climbed the steps. The throbbing in his lower tract was stronger. He could nearly hear it, as if the particles were detaching themselves from a larger mass. He stood when the old man reached him. His heart bubbled now, almost in time with his lower tract. It was huge and wet inside his chest.

"I know you," the old man said. "From long ago. . ."

Gant's heart was a bomb. His lower tract burned and heaved. The old man smiled.

"You're. . . You're my son! That's who you are!"

"NO!" Gant shouted.

The courthouse and street spun about him. Sweat, not the pure, clean sweat of a run, but a thick, grimy, gravy poured from him. The old man came closer, arms reaching.

"My own son! A dear boy! How straight and handsome you were! How I feared you!"

Gant pressed his back against the monument. His heart was in his ears and eyes. He tried to stand, but his legs gave way. The halfback was gone. The lawyer was gone. Only a tight, dry hole was left.

The old man bent down, embraced him, and kissed his cheek.

It gave way all at once, his lower tract dissolving into a flowing, steaming river. With the last of his strength, he jerked away, stumbling, falling down the steps. His bowels flowed in earnest, pouring black and brown and green, a river without beginning or end, a river which could find no home in the sea. He dropped into a black, stinking night.

XX

It was full summer, mid-July. The air-conditioning in Bunch's office was out of order most of the time. Alda complained, but the heat did not bother Bunch. He opened the window, put his feet up on the sill, and reared back in his chair. There was the city below him. And here I am, he thought.

He had healed quickly. The doctors were surprised that there was no permanent damage. The newspapers and television called it a miracle. The bite had, however, been fairly serious. He had to take a series of shots for the infection. The human mouth, he was solemnly told, is the most bacteria-infested orifice in the body. And Goforth's mouth at that, he thought.

The courthouse was scheduled to re-open in another couple of months, all bright and new—complete with a plaque honoring the memory of Judge T. Thurston (Ted) Cope. There would be a special dedication, with speeches by his widow, the governor, and maybe even Senator Helms. All in memory of a Christian patriot who did his duty to the end. Bunch wondered if Gant would be there. Probably not, he thought. Such events were no longer Gant's kind of show.

Bunch had seen Gant only once since the riot: in the Emergency Room at County General. Bunch had been sitting on the examination table while an intern stitched up his leg. Bunch kept watching the parade of wounded in the corridor so that he would not have to think about what was being done to his leg. Gant had been quickly wheeled by, covered with a sheet, only his face and his blond helmet of hair visible. A team of doctors and nurses trotted along beside him.

Now, among the lawyers, Gant was rarely spoken of. There were rumors about seclusion in a private hospital in Asheville, and that his wife was living in Hilton Head with the tennis pro from the Country Club. His firm had handed his cases over to his partners. Officially, he had taken a leave of absence.

That's what we all need, Bunch thought: a good long leave of absence. Bunch had not seen Goforth, although he knew he could reappear at any time. And then there was Smith. Bunch told the sheriff's boys, the State Bureau agents, and the reporters all about Smith. They searched through all the missions and flophouses in Helmsville. There was no sign of him. Not even the family could remember him very well.

Bunch wanted a cigarette and a drink. Then he remembered that he no longer kept either in the office. Other doctors, not the Emergency Room interns, had warned him: his heart, his blood pressure, all that internal, ticking doom waiting for him. He sighed. The window will have to be enough, I guess.

Charles' trial was supposed to start in the fall, but no one would lay odds on it reaching a jury. He could cop to insanity. He has a strong case now, Bunch thought. But so does the D.A. And me; I'm the star witness. At least on the naked man in the swimming pool. Cumby was his name. No one knew much about him. Tinka made the identification. Bunch wondered if Charles would hold it against her. Then, again, the D.A. had cut an attractive deal with Tinka and the rest of the family in exchange for their testimony against Daddy. Immunity is a wonderful thing, Bunch thought.

He had seen Charles once more. Charles' new lawyer, a kid from the public defender's office, asked Bunch to meet him on the psychiatric ward at County General, and Bunch agreed. Even as a witness for the state, Bunch figured that he still owed a little responsibility to his old client.

Charles had a room to himself, like the other "dangerous cases," as the big, tough-looking nurse had put it. There was a guard and window in the door so that he could be watched at all times. Two surveillance cameras hung high on the wall facing the bed.

The public defender had been nervous.

"I don't know how he'll react when he sees you. Most of the time he's completely unresponsive. I've got to try every angle though. . ."

"Charles," the nurse said. "You have visitors."

Clad in a hospital gown, Charles was propped up in the bed. An arm was handcuffed to the night stand. He did not move or speak.

"Charles," the public defender said. "Do you remember Mr. Bunch?"

He did not answer. The public defender tried a few more questions and gave up. He motioned Bunch to the door.

"It's useless. He won't even walk any more. The doctors can't figure it out. No permanent damage. Hell, the bullet got him in the shoulder. They think it's his nerves. Whatever it is, the muscles have started to deteriorate."

"Am I on T.V.?"

Bunch jumped when he heard Charles' voice.

"Yes, Charles. You're on right now," the nurse said.
"That's real good. I wanta be sure."

He arranged his face into a grin and batted his eyes at
the cameras.

From the office window, Bunch could make out the
top of the Confederate monument. The mob had started
to drift back in twos and threes. Bunch guessed that by
the time the courthouse re-opened they would be back in
full force, and in plenty of time for Charles' trial. The
sun was high over Helmsville. This isn't bad, Bunch
thought, sitting here with a good chair under my ass
and my feet propped up. I could stay like this all day.
Just what I want. Each of us, whether we know it or not,
sometimes gets just what we really want.